Cop

or

Killer?

Cop or Killer?

A Luca Mystery Book 6

Dan Petrosini

Other Books by Dan

Luca Mystery Series

Am I the Killer—Book 1

Vanished—Book 2

The Serenity Murder—Book 3

Third Chances—Book 4

A Cold, Hard Case—Book 5

Cop or Killer?—Book 6

Silencing Salter—Book 7

A Killer Missteps—Book 8

Uncertain Stakes—Book 9

The Grandpa Killer—Book 10

Dangerous Revenge—Book 11

Where Are They—Book 12

Burried at the Lake—Book 13

The Preserve Killer—Book 14

Suspenseful Secrets

Cory's Dilemma—Book 1

Cory's Flight—Book 2

Cory's Shift—Book 3

Other works by Dan Petrosini

The Final Enemy

Complicit Witness

Push Back

Ambition Cliff

Acknowledgements

Special thanks to Julie, Stephanie and Jennifer for their love and support, and thanks to Squad Sergeant Craig Perrilli for his counsel on the real world of law enforcement. He helps me keep it real.

Chapter 1

Driving home, I couldn't force the image of the body out of my mind. I could still taste the bile that sprayed the back of my throat when I saw it. Curled in a fetal position, the decomposed corpse was the nastiest in the fifteen years I'd been hunting killers.

Though it was April Fools' Day, it was as real as it gets. The poor bastard must have been soaked in acid: though major parts of the body's skull were visible, facial recognition was a nonstarter. Forensics would have its hands full with this one.

Who did this? It smelled like retribution, and there was no question the killer wanted to conceal the victim's identity. The question was whether the motivation was either of the time-honored favorites: money or love. Was the dead man a Romeo to another man's Juliet? Or was he caught stealing from the wrong guy?

We'd get more information once an autopsy cleared up how he'd been murdered. Was it with a gun, a knife, a beating with a blunt instrument? I shuddered at the thought he could have been thrown alive into a vat of acid.

I considered whether it could be a professional mob hit or a smart-ass who had searched the thousands of whacko boards on the Internet for a way to get away with murder. I knew I should wait for more data, but since we didn't get many stiffs in Collier County, I needed the challenge.

The winter season was still in full swing, and that meant traffic and tourists. Usually, the backups would get to me, but with my mind consumed with the new case, I suddenly found myself pulling into our garage.

As soon as I stepped into the house, I could smell tomatoes roasting.

"Mary Ann, I'm home."

"In here, Frank."

I took a deep breath. "Smells amazing."

"How was your day?"

"I found a body."

"And you're smiling over it?"

"Uh, no, no. Just that I found it."

"Where?"

"Off Collier Boulevard, down by Rookery Bay."

"Where's that?"

"All the way down, by Eagle Creek Golf Course, right before you get to Henderson Creek."

"Who's the victim?"

"No clue. So badly decomposed you can't even tell if it's male or female."

"Yuk."

"Whoever did it must have used an accelerator; the head was eaten away and—"

"Okay, Frank. We're about to eat. Can you shut it down?"

***

There was a cup of coffee on my desk. "Morning, Frank."

"Morning." I took a sip. Perfect. Derrick hadn't brought me an over-milked coffee in months.

"I just got back from the morgue. You never told me how you found that body."

"Just lucky, I guess. I was driving on Collier, going to check out that attempted break-in at Eagle Creek. It felt like I was getting a flat on the front passenger side. I pulled over but couldn't see anything wrong with the tire. But I caught a little whiff of something. It smelled like a decaying body."

"Mr. Bloodhound strikes again."

"I know. So, I looked around and thought I saw something on the other side of the canal, and sure enough, there it was."

"And boy, is it tough to look at."

"It made me gag when I saw it."

"Me too, so disfigured I didn't know what I was looking at."

"Borge said it was a male."

"I couldn't tell either way."

"No doubt whoever did it wants to hide the victim's identity."

"Looks like he went a little too far."

"Between forensics and pathology, we'll find out who it is. Do we have a time of death yet?"

"At this point, a couple of weeks. Borge said four to eight weeks or so."

"He's doing the autopsy today. We'll know more soon."

"You think he was from around here?"

"Tough to say. He could've been moved."

"But that's dangerous for the killer, right, Frank?"

"Usually. But who knows; this could have been something not planned. A fight that spiraled out of control and, *bam*, a guy is killed. Wherever it happened wasn't a good place to keep the body. The killer contemplates what to do, where to dump the corpse He starts thinking like a TV show and uses an accelerator to speed up the decomposition before moving the body."

"He'd leave a trail."

"If, if it was moved. We'll see."

"Did you inform the sheriff?"

"Chester is up to speed. I asked him to hold off alerting the press until the autopsy is complete, and he was fine with it."

"I'm surprised."

"He likes to play it by the book, but he knows the risks when it goes public, so he gave in to me."

"It'd be nice if he had our backs a little better."

I wanted to say, hell yes, but said, "We need to check into all missing persons. Look back two months, and I'll check the archives."

"We don't have an age range, so all males?"

"Twenty to seventy."

"Just Collier?"

"No, Lee and Charlotte as well. And let's see what Dade has. It could be a gang out of Miami that dumped it out here."

"Good idea. I'm on it."

Derrick picked up the phone. Pulling up the Southwest Florida missing persons archives, I began to wonder if this guy was missed by anybody. Did he have a wife? Were kids waiting somewhere for their daddy to come home?

What a mess if the victim had children. I'd seen all kinds of tragic situations: a mother out grabbing milk and killed by a drunk driver, a father with four kids under ten years of age murdered over a parking spot, but the worst was the parents shot dead during a home invasion in Newark witnessed by their three children.

Was this some intergalactic message to end the exploration of having a kid with Mary Ann? A warning because I was leaning toward saying yes? Maybe it was because of my skewed reasoning: one third my desire, and two thirds an effort to give her what she wanted.

Realizing I was looking at the screen but not seeing it, I shoved fatherhood aside and went down the line. Not having a narrow age range was like trying to tie a bow tie with one hand.

My eyes settled on the sixth line: Allesandro Roma. Was it the stylish name that grabbed me? I opened the file. Thirty-seven years old and from East Naples. Just a couple of miles from where the body was found. Plus, this guy had a record. I jotted down his wife's contact info.

Chapter 2

It felt colder than normal in the autopsy suite. Hoping the sweater in my locker was going to be enough, I said hello to Dr. Borge, who performed the autopsy. I got along as good as anyone with the pathologist, but he still wouldn't volunteer information.

"What can you tell me about John Doe? We have a cause of death?"

"Strangulation."

"Can you speculate on what was used?"

Borge peered over his glasses. "I don't do speculation."

"What is your professional opinion on what was used?"

"The severed trachea suggests a thin metal wire."

That was bad news. The killer probably wore gloves to prevent getting cuts on his hands. "What age is the victim?"

"Once the bone analysis is done, we'll know."

"I'd really like a range, Doc."

"Thirty to forty."

"What was used as an accelerator?"

"Hydrochloric acid."

It wasn't the cold that made me shiver. "Was it used uniformly? Like he was in a vat or something?"

"The victim's feet were spared."

I thought of a bathtub immediately. It looked like Mary Ann was right; getting more exercise would help my memory. Or could it be the vitamin D pills I was choking down?

"How tall is John Doe?"

"Six foot."

"I assume the fingerprints are gone?"

Borge nodded.

"Hair color?"

"Black or brown."

"How about some help with the time of death, Doc?"

"You'll have to wait for the pathology reports."

"Give me something to work with. Please."

"Five to ten weeks."

***

Derrick was staring at his screen when I got back.

"John Doe was strangled to death, likely with a wire. He has brown or black hair and is somewhere between thirty and forty years of age. Borge thinks it went down anywhere between five to ten weeks ago. Here's the interesting thing, the victim's feet were the only things not eaten up. What does that tell you?"

Derrick looked like I'd asked for the meaning of life, but he recovered quickly.

"Uh, he was submerged, headfirst. Maybe in a barrel."

"Not bad, but I think the killer used a bathtub. Doe was six foot."

"That's useful data."

"Did you get anywhere with missing persons?"

"There's a couple of interesting guys, but let me slim it down with his height and the new age range."

I logged into the portal. Allesandro Roma was thirty-seven. Clicking open the report his wife filed, I scrolled to the description. Roma was six feet, one inch with black hair.

"I've got a possibility."

"Who's that?"

"A guy whose wife reported him missing ten weeks ago. He was thirty-seven and lived close to where the body was found. Black hair and six feet one."

"Whoa, sounds like a match. We going to pay a visit to his wife?"

"Not yet. Let me see what she has to say."

Punching in Mrs. Roma's telephone number, Derrick came over and sat on the corner of my desk. Glaring at him as the call was answered, I spoke with Roma's wife and hung up.

"Too good to be true."

"What'd she say?"

"Her husband took off with a waitress. The woman said she was sorry that she'd forgotten to report she knew where he was."

***

My sunglasses fogged as soon as I walked into the station. In the mood for an iced coffee, I was headed to the cafeteria when Derrick yelled down the corridor.

"Frank, come here."

I turned on my heels. "What's up?"

"We have an ID on the body you found."

"Who is it?"

"Jimmy Garrison. I just started looking into him. He's from Lee County. Are you okay, Frank?"

"Yeah, just a bad headache."

"You take something?"

"Not yet. I'm going to grab a coffee, it usually helps. I'll be right back."

Jimmy Garrison? What a frigging punk. As I pulled open the freezer door, I wondered if Mary Ann knew the piece of shit was dead. No damn ice. Who were these people who emptied the trays of ice cubes and didn't bother to refill them? I poured the coffee into the sink and went back to my office.

"Frank, this Garrison has a record. A couple of priors, drug offenses for possession, but he was just arrested for trafficking and distribution."

"We're not going to waste time tracking down his killer. Whoever it was, we should send him a Christmas card."

"What?"

"Just saying, whoever did it did us a favor taking him off the streets."

"There's a note in the record about cooperating with the cybersex unit. That's where Detective Vargas works, right?"

"Really? What's the name again?"

"Jimmy Garrison."

"Give me his social. I'll check with Vargas."

I sent a text to Mary Ann, grabbed Garrison's info from Derrick and left.

***

The Cherokee had barely cooled down when Mary Ann opened the passenger door.

"What's the matter, Frank?"

"The stiff I found was none other than Jimmy Garrison."

"I heard. What's the problem?"

"Well, you know I said some things when he called you, remember?"

"How could I forget? But that's nothing, he was harassing me. What do you think; they're going to think you killed him?"

I shrugged.

She patted my thigh. "Don't worry, it's nothing."

"There's something else."

"What are you talking about?"

"Well, I. I took a ride by his place."

"You did what?"

"I just wanted to scare the bastard off, that's all."

"You're crazy! You know that? What happened when you went there?"

"Nothing really. I just told him he'd better lay off or there'd be a price to pay."

"You threatened him?"

"I was just trying to make sure you were safe, that's all."

She wagged her head. "I don't know, Frank; that's completely against the rules."

"I'm sorry. Really I am." I reached for her hand. "It was dumb of me, but I was afraid he'd do something stupid. He was really pissed when you pulled that deal from him."

She pulled her hand away. "Don't turn this around and blame me."

"No, no, I'm not. It's just that he thought he had a deal to kill the drug charges by snitching on that pervert."

"He would have if the parents of the victim would have let the kid testify. You know we can't drop a distribution charge for nothing."

"I'm not sure about how to play this."

"Play this?"

"I want to avoid the suspicion, that's all."

"Come on. You know you've got to be straight up with this."

Easy for her to say. I was the one whose reputation was going to get trampled on. "Well, just stick to your case with him. Nobody needs to know anything more than that."

"Frank, I reported that Garrison threatened me."

"Okay, do me a favor and just keep it at that."

"You're making a big mistake, Frank."

"Just do what I ask, okay? I'll handle it."

Chapter 3

Derrick got up. "I'm going up to talk to Detective Vargas about Garrison and the case she was involved in. She said she had a copy of the case file for me."

"I'll come with you."

"I don't think that's allowed, since you guys are, you know, together."

"It's okay. You ask all the questions. I'll just be there in case you miss something."

"I don't know if that's a good idea."

"Let's go."

Vargas handed Derrick a file. He said, "Thanks. I'll read through it later, but I'd appreciate if you could summarize your connection to Jimmy Garrison."

I said, "Connection? She was working a case, that's all."

Derrick shook his head, and Mary Ann threw up a palm.

"Connelly, in Narcotics, was running surveillance on Garrison. He's a decent-sized dealer, and they picked him up after filming him receive several shipments. Connelly leaned on him to give up his supplier, but Garrison claimed he'd be killed in retribution."

I said, "Looks like he was."

"Please, Frank, let Derrick handle this."

"Thank you. Go on."

"Garrison said he had information on a sexual predator, and Connelly asked me to talk with him."

"What did he have?"

"Garrison said he knew that a Seymour Gilmore was a pedophile."

"And how did he know this?"

"The pervert regularly bought cocaine from him, and one time he delivered drugs to Gilmore's house. When he was there, he saw a kid he knew in the house."

"How did he know that abuse was taking place?"

"The eleven-year-old was in his underwear."

Mary Ann had related the story when it happened, but hearing it a second time was still jarring. I wanted to find this Gilmore and make him look like Garrison. I made a mental note but kept quiet.

"So, you offered a deal to Garrison in exchange for his information?"

"We'd known about Gilmore but couldn't put together a strong enough case. I went to the DA, and he was good with accepting a plea, reducing it to possession."

"What happened with the arrangement?"

"You have to proceed with these cases delicately. We went to see the kid's parents, but they were adamant about not allowing their son to testify. Without the kid on the stand, we had nothing but Garrison's witnessing of a child in underpants in another man's house. Disgusting imagery but not prosecutable."

"So, you informed Garrison the deal was off?"

"Yes, and he went nuts. He claimed that I'd gone back on my word, which was totally untrue, as I had told him it was conditional. We had to have something solid to put Gilmore behind bars, otherwise criminals would be conspiring with each other."

"And that was it?"

"No. Garrison harassed me, even threatened me. It's in the report."

Derrick said, "What? I had no idea." Then he swiveled his head, looking at me as if I were an alien, before going back to Mary Ann, "How long did the harassing behavior last?"

"For a couple of weeks. It wasn't daily, just every couple of days he'd call."

"When did he stop bothering you?"

"About two months ago."

***

As soon as we entered the stairwell, Derrick said, "You had to know about this."

"About what?"

"You know what I'm talking about. Garrison was harassing your girlfriend."

"It ended."

"And now he's dead."

"Just what are you saying, Derrick? If you have to something to say, spit it out."

"Why didn't you say anything once we knew it was Garrison? You made like the name didn't mean anything."

"It didn't register at the time."

"What a coincidence. Now that she tells me, you remember?"

"It's not like that."

He stopped on the landing and looked me in the eye. "You know what bothers me most? The fact you never told me about it when it was happening."

"It had nothing to do with you."

"That's bullshit, and you know it. She's not only your girlfriend, she was your former partner. We're supposed to be close. Something like that you should have told me about."

"I'm not like that. What can I tell you?"

Derrick shook his head. As he took off down the stairs, I said, "I handle my personal affairs myself."

With the tension high, root canal was preferable to sitting in the office with Derrick. There were two hours to kill before I was due in court, so I continued down the stairs to the shooting range.

***

The TV was blaring a political ad as I entered our house.

"Mary Ann, I'm home."

No response. Something was off, and it wasn't my danger sensor talking to me. Mary Ann was sitting at the counter, drinking a glass of wine as she watched the news. A hunk of camembert cheese on the counter was throwing off a horrible smell. How could something that tasted so good smell so bad?

"Oh, having vino without me?"

"I needed it after today."

"What happened?"

She shook her head and took a sip of wine.

"What's the matter?"

"Are you really that oblivious?"

"I swear, I don't know what's going on."

"What was all that with Derrick? You never told him about Garrison?"

I shrugged.

"You think it wouldn't come out? I filed a damn report about it."

"I don't know why you and Derrick are making such a big deal about it."

"You really are oblivious, aren't you? It's about trust, Frank. Not to mention protocol."

"I guess I screwed up."

"Guess? There was no reason to withhold the information."

"But I was worried about how it would look if they knew about my visit to Garrison."

"You know damn well it would come out. If that's all there is to it, it'll fade away."

I shrugged. "I'll tell Derrick about it tomorrow."

Chapter 4

Because it involved my personal life, especially Mary Ann, I resented the thought of explaining myself to a junior detective. If I said I had my reasons, that should be enough.

I was up half the night thinking of how to tell him. A good opening is what I needed, an icebreaker. Maybe something in the case would provide an easy way to inform my partner. Whatever wisdom I had collected told me to march in and tell him straightaway. Problem was, pride had tied my ankles together.

In no hurry to get to the office, I drank a cup of coffee in Dunkin's parking lot before going in. I poked my head in the door, pleased that Derrick was on the phone. I scanned the top of my desk. No cup of coffee. No doubt Derrick was still pissed. I retreated to the cafeteria for another coffee.

Knowing what to do and doing it—why was the second part of that so difficult? Just do it, Luca. I splashed a bit of milk in my cup and reluctantly headed to talk to Derrick.

"Morning, Derrick."

"Morning."

"Look, before this gets any further, I'd like to clear the air between us about this Garrison business."

Derrick leaned back in his chair. "Okay, go ahead."

It was the first bout of cockiness I'd seen in him. "I should have told you about Vargas and Garrison. I just felt it was a personal thing. It was too close to home, if you know what I mean."

"Garrison threatened one of us, Frank. It doesn't matter what the two of you have going on. She's one of us."

"It was a mistake."

"The balls of this guy, threatening an officer. If he wasn't lying in the damn morgue, I'd put him there myself."

"You're not kidding. Say, instead of chasing whoever killed this cretin, we have anything else to chase down?"

"I don't understand. It's the only murder we've had in months. We have to find Garrison's killer."

"I know, just wishing we didn't have to waste the county's resources on such a bag of shit."

"We're better off with only one case to deal with. We can focus on it."

My cell vibrated. It was the sheriff.

I ended the call and banged my desk. "How the hell did that happen?"

"What?"

"Ethan Dwyer escaped from jail."

"Sounds familiar. Who's that?"

"A serial killer I put away before you got here. The nut killed five men. Said he was on a mission from God."

"He broke out of the Immokalee jail?"

"Not the prison. He was getting therapy in the adult stabilization unit at the David Lawrence Center."

"This guy killed five people! What the hell was he doing at Lawrence?"

"A couple of years ago a study showed that Florida was way down on the list of states caring for people with mental illnesses. It's a serious problem, and the legislature pressured for a fix."

"Some fix!"

"No shit. Dwyer's IQ is off the charts."

"What happened? How the hell did he get away?"

"Chester said he's looking into what went wrong, but it looks like he outsmarted the guard watching him."

"Really?"

"Dwyer is the most unusual killer you'll ever see. Smart as hell, but there's also another side to him. A dark side. This guy held grudges for decades before acting. He carried on normally and then, bingo, he starts killing."

"Did it take a long time to catch him?"

I exhaled. "Longer than I wanted. Chester was throwing conniptions left and right. He brought the FBI in."

"Is that how you got your contact?"

"Yeah, it was the only thing good to come out of it. Chester didn't think I was up to it." I didn't want to admit to my own doubts at the time. "But we bagged him."

"Detective Vargas was on it with you, right?"

"Yeah, it was a wild ride. Everyone was convinced it was another person of interest, but I stuck to my guns." Not exactly the truth. I had believed it was someone else, too, until I changed my mind. "I'll tell you about it sometime."

"Sounds unreal."

We needed to keep Dwyer in Florida. I issued a statewide alert, circulating photos of Dwyer. I asked for them to be on the lookout for cars with a single, white male, thirty to forty years old that matched Dwyer's description. That might help if he was driving out of the state. The problem was the endless possibilities to flee by water. Florida has thirteen hundred and fifty miles of coastline, the most in the nation.

I grabbed my jacket off a hook. "Come on. We're going down to David Lawrence."

"You go. I want to stay on this Garrison case."

I wanted to tell him to get his ass in the Cherokee, but said, "Make sure you read through the Dwyer case file. I just emailed it to you."

***

The David Lawrence Center was off Golden Gate Parkway, just east of Interstate 75. It is supposed to be a secure facility, handling its own security, even with convicts. They had failed miserably in this case.

The center had an inpatient program for people in a mental health crisis, but most of their activities seemed to focus on addiction treatment. I knew a patrolman who'd gone there to deal with his drinking and an ex-neighbor who'd gotten hooked on pain meds. I'd seen the demons haunting them and was thankful such a place existed.

The center's crisis unit operated in a twenty-eight-bed building with a separate wing containing four beds for children. I followed the signs to the stabilization unit. The glass front doors were locked. At least they got that part right. There were two cameras covering the entrance. I hit the call button and was buzzed in.

The place had a spa smell to it. I tried to identify the aromas as I waited for the administrator. Just as I realized the dominant smell was lavender, a woman approached.

"How may I assist you, Officer?"

She was wearing a gray business suit and some kind of Indian necklace. "It's Detective Luca, and you are?"

"Dr. Beatrice Acorn. I'm the administrator of the crisis unit."

"I'd like to ask questions regarding the escape of Ethan Dwyer."

"Certainly. My office will provide privacy."

I followed her down a bright corridor to an even brighter office overlooking a garden with a fountain. A woman, a patient, I assumed, sat on a bench in the sun, thumbing through a magazine.

Except for a solitary pen, Dr. Acorn's desk was empty.

"I must caution you, certain patient information is confidential; therefore, I'm limited in what I can reveal. And I am unable to discuss security. The sheriff is communicating with headquarters on that matter."

"I understand. What was Ethan Dwyer doing here?"

"The David Lawrence Center is the Baker Act receiving facility for Collier County. The act mandates that individuals in danger of harming themselves or others be admitted for care."

"Dwyer was suicidal?"

"I can't discuss particulars of his status."

"But you admitted him based upon what?"

"The prison psychiatrist made a diagnosis which we accepted. We're not in a position to judge a finding concerning a patient in crisis. These cases must be handled with care. The patients are in a fragile state and at high risk."

"I understand. After he was admitted, what happened?"

"Every patient undergoes a complete evaluation by our professionals. This is not to contest a finding but to safely identify the issues they face. For example, whether they have suicidal ideations or are a danger to others. Our goal is to stabilize the patient and recommend facilities that have the treatments required to work through a patient's challenges."

"How long was Dwyer here?"

"Three days."

"How long does a patient with similar issues normally stay?"

"Four days, five, maximum."

"Do you think he was faking his crisis?"

"Detective Luca, our staff is highly trained. The thought that someone would be able to effectively simulate, over a period of days, is simply unfathomable."

Really? That's because she'd never met Ethan Dwyer.

"I'm going to need the video from all the cameras on the property."

"There are privacy issues, Detective. I am not authorized to release recordings of the patients. You must understand, we have a robust outpatient program, and the participants don't want the privacy surrounding their attendance compromised."

"You check with whoever you need to, but I'm not leaving without at least the outdoor surveillance."

"I understand the nature of your request, but the outpatient entrance would pose a problem."

"I'll do without that at the moment. Turn over the balance of the footage, and if I can identify Dwyer leaving on the tape, we may not need it."

"That is fine. I appreciate your respecting our privacy issues. You can understand, if people knew their visits would be public, most wouldn't seek treatment."

"I'll need a schematic of the property. Something that shows all the exits and windows."

She opened a drawer on her desk. "This is a complete layout of the campus." She slid a piece of marketing material across the desk. "All the windows in the facility are hinged at the bottom and only open six inches."

I took the map and asked to see the room Dwyer had stayed in. A search of his room didn't turn up anything. I was given six DVDs of surveillance and left. It was time to visit the prison.

Chapter 5

I remembered, it was a couple of months ago; I was gassing up the Cherokee, and at the next pump a father was showing his young boy how the pump worked. The kid was excited, but it was the father's smile that caught my attention. He looked like he was going on a month-long vacation, igniting the mental tug-of-war I was having about becoming a father.

My concerns were giving me so much anxiety that I needed to talk to someone about it. I couldn't even decide whether it was easier to talk to a man or to a woman. I thought a woman was a better choice, but then a guy would at least understand where I was coming from.

I recalled how doubt had filled my head as I turned onto Dockside Court. It was stupid, but checking the East Naples location of the office had sealed my decision. Dockside Court was a long cul-de-sac that ended just short of Henderson Creek. No one would know I was there.

A tiny sign on the mailbox was the sole clue there was an office in the house. The driveway was empty, easing my anxiety. I parked in the driveway, behind a stand of coco plum bushes shielding a side entrance.

After a quick knock on the door, I walked in. It was not as I envisioned, but things rarely are. It may have been the white galley kitchen, but it felt like an apartment, not an office. There was a smell of something baking. The only thing that looked used in the kitchen was the coffeemaker. It was either a clever room freshener or came from the main part of the house.

Behind a half-opened door, someone was behind a desk, talking on the phone. To the right, a pair of gray club chairs were separated by a plexiglass cocktail table. There was a black Moleskine on the seat of one chair. Was this where it would take place?

I heard the phone call end, and a woman in a black pants suit emerged.

"Hello, Mr. Luca."

She didn't look anything like her picture. She was at least twenty years older. Practiced smile. Medium build. Short, wiry hair. A round, wrinkle-free face with just a hint of a turkey neck. Why didn't people update their photos?

"Hello, Dr. Bruno."

"You found it okay?"

"Doing what I do, I get around the county."

"You don't patrol, do you?"

"No. But between interviewing and chasing leads . . ."

"Shall we get started?" She swept her hands toward the chairs.

I nodded, sinking into a chair as Dr. Bruno moved the notebook to the table and sat. She crossed her legs.

"You're a homicide detective, correct?"

"Yes, ma'am."

"No need to be formal. It helps if you think of this as two friends having a chat."

Yeah, right. "Okay."

"When you made the appointment, you mentioned your fear of being a father."

"It's not that I'm afraid."

She smiled. "There's no need to get hung up on the word fear. There are varying degrees of apprehension that we all suffer from. It's what makes us human. How long have you been seriously thinking of fatherhood?"

"Less than a year."

"Was this the result of a new relationship?"

"Yes. Mary Ann definitely wants a baby. She's my girlfriend, but we'd get married if we have a kid."

"Are you feeling pressure from her about this decision?"

"No, no. She's been pretty good about it. She really wants to be a mother, but she doesn't pressure me about it."

"Good. Do you feel a need to please her? To give her what she wants?"

"She's a good woman, and I know it means a lot to her, but I can't really say that I'd do it to please her."

"That is good. Becoming a parent is an important obligation, and it would be a mistake to have one person in a relationship drive the decision. How long have you been in this new relationship?"

"It's a bit complicated. We used to be partners."

"Mary Ann is a homicide detective as well?"

"She was. Now she's assigned to the cybercrimes unit and at times narcotics detail."

Bruno jotted a note. "How long has the relationship been romantic?"

"We started dating when we still worked together, even moved in together. It's more than a year."

"May I ask how old the two of you are?"

"I'm forty-three and she's thirty-six."

"Is the biological clock issue important to you?"

"Well, it's not like it doesn't matter. If we're going to do this, we have to get moving."

"Do you feel pressure to act because of it?"

"No, not really."

"Good. Could you describe your concerns about becoming a father?"

I'd rehearsed what I was going to say, but it still sounded jumbled. "I don't want to sound selfish, but I like the way things are now. It's just me and Mary Ann, and I get to do the job I love. We have freedom. We go and come as we like. It's nice."

"You're afraid a baby will come between you and Mary Ann?"

"I guess so."

"That's a natural feeling. The fact is, it will to a degree. Both of your attentions will be directed toward the baby. It's not like the baby is in competition with you for Mary Ann's attention. Both of your worlds will likely revolve around your child."

I hadn't thought about how impossibly obsessed other fathers were with their children. Might that happen to me?

"That's a good point. You're probably right."

"It's really nothing to be concerned about. Relationships may change somewhat, but it all balances out."

"I could see that."

"You mentioned a concern with your job. Do you believe a baby will prevent you from doing your job?"

"No, not prevent me. Just that it'd take away my focus, you know what I mean?"

"That'd you have responsibilities as a father that would clash with work?"

"I guess, you know, sometimes, when I'm working a case, I can get obsessed. It's all I think about. I work crazy hours. It wouldn't be fair, to the baby and Mary Ann.

"You're worried you'd feel overwhelmed or possibly pulled in two directions?"

"Something has to give, doesn't it? Mary Ann is going to need me to help her, especially in the beginning, and if a case comes up, I can't be in two places at the same time. Right?"

"It's important to develop a healthy balance in life. We all have many demands on us. It's critical that we know when to say no to things like work."

"How can I say no when a murderer is on the loose?"

"You have an unusual job. I realize it is an important one and one that society depends on you to perform. That said, though, you're not the only one who can do it. None of us operate in a vacuum, and, as good as we believe we are at something, when we're gone, someone else will fill our shoes."

If she keeps talking, I'm gonna put a gun to my head. "But there's only two of us in the department, and I'm the one with experience—"

She put up a hand. "I understand there are circumstances; there always are. What I'm saying is not to make a mistake in ordering your priorities. You don't want to have any regrets that you didn't spend enough time with your family. When our lives draw to a close or a relationship fails, that is what will end up consuming you."

Rolling it around, I tried to process a response when Dr. Bruno tapped her wristwatch.

I can still hear her say, "We're out of time."

Chapter 6

Though it was months ago, I also remembered the second visit like it was yesterday. I had rapped on her door, reminding myself not to bring up the lack of sleep issue or the chance my kid would be colicky. Up in Jersey I had two disturbing cases where fathers had lost it over their babies crying, and they ended up behind bars.

Dr. Bruno appeared from behind a door leading to the main part of the house. Was she wearing the same pants suit she had on yesterday? There was that practiced smile again and the baking smell. Nobody baked two days in row, unless it was Christmastime. The fragrance was probably some psych tool to make patients comfortable. Patient? Is that what I was?

"Hello, Mr. Luca. How are you today?"

"All good. Thanks for seeing me so soon. I wanted to keep things moving."

"I understand. You want to get this behind you as quickly as possible."

"I hope so."

Settling into the same chairs as yesterday, she said, "It will. Don't try to force it, though."

"Okay."

"You mentioned other matters that were on your mind. Would you like to discuss them?"

"Sure. It's not like I won't try to be the best father I can, but kids become who they are from their parents."

"Parents are the richest source of education for their children, the ultimate teacher."

"That's right, but I'm not only talking about how to tie your shoes or ride a bike. More important is they learn how to treat people, if they curse or not, what kind of an attitude to have, things like that, from their parents."

"Absolutely. Don't you believe you'll set the proper examples?"

"I would hope so. I'm not perfect, but I think I'd really try to do my best."

"Then it should be fine."

"My dad told me something a long time ago. I told him I didn't want to have kids because I was afraid of the world we lived in. All the drugs and violence, and that was before I became a police officer. He said not to worry, just bring them up the way you know how. I was like, are you kidding me? It sounded so stupid. I remember shaking my head and walking away. But you know what? The more I thought about it, the more it made so much sense. He was trying to say, just be who you are, and it will turn out fine."

"It's a simple piece of advice that covers a lot of ground."

"I know. He was a basic guy, but he knew about life."

"Knowing what he said, what worries you about having children?"

"I can't be there twenty-four seven; no one can. And as they get older, they're exposed to other kids who can have a bad influence on them."

"You can't protect anyone. All you can do is instill a value system in them that will act as a deterrence. A child with a strong foundation is better prepared to navigate the pressures and pitfalls of the world around them."

"I know, but what if something happens to me?"

"Are you referring to the dangers of being a law enforcement officer?"

"Yes, but I'm a cancer survivor, or hope I am."

"Tell me about your experience."

"Out of nowhere, well, not exactly, there was blood in my urine. Anyway, one night I passed out in La Playa's bathroom, and the next thing I know, I'm lying in a hospital bed, and they tell me I have tumors in my bladder."

"How frightening."

"And it got worse. Originally, they said it hadn't breached the bladder's wall, but it had. They removed my bladder and made me one out of my intestines." I pointed to a device on my wrist. "Since I lost the nerve endings that give the sensation to go, this sounds an alarm to pee every couple of hours."

"The miracle of modern medicine."

"I'm grateful, but you never know, it can come back."

"I assume you're being monitored?"

"Oh yeah, I'm not taking chances."

"Good. You've had a terrifying experience, and it is completely natural to worry about a recurrence. That said, you cannot allow it to control your decisions in life. If you do, then, even though you have beat cancer, you have lost the larger battle."

"You're right. I guess the combination of the risks of both of us being police officers and the cancer scare is giving me the jitters."

"Does Mary Ann work in the field as well?"

"Yes, but we talked about this. She would take some time off and then would request a transfer to a desk job."

"That is an excellent solution."

My pee-pee alarm went off, and I ignored it. "I wouldn't have it any other way. It's tough enough on a kid, of any age, to have one police officer as a parent. Having two would be too scary."

"You both seem to have thought this through. The fact that you felt the need to speak with someone about it is further evidence you're taking the responsibilities of fatherhood seriously."

"I wish everyone did. We'd have a lot fewer problems in this world."

She nodded. "Is there anything else you'd like to talk about?"

"How much time you have?"

"As much as you require."

"Just kidding, Doc. You've been very helpful."

It wasn't anything Dr. Bruno had said in response to my concerns that made me feel better. It was her pointing out the fact that I was there that comforted me. She was right; I was approaching this like an adult. Most of the time. Things would change, for the better, according to her. She was confident, but I needed more time to process all of it. I pulled out of her driveway and parked in the cul-de-sac.

Walking toward Henderson Creek, I looked right toward Collier Boulevard. I'd run into Garrison's body on the other side of Collier Boulevard. It was closer than I thought to Dr. Bruno's office.

To the left, two boys were fishing in the creek. Just past the boys was Red Necken BBQ. I'd heard of it but had never eaten there. I headed over to check it out. The smoky smell of meat being grilled hung in the air as I reached the boys. I was glad to see the boys take steps toward each other as I approached. I climbed higher on the bank and waved to them as I followed the barbecue scent.

A tattooed man in a leather apron was flipping chunks of meat on a black, barreled grill that was hooked up to a pickup truck. Was this where they did all the cooking?

I climbed the stairs onto a deck where a handful of people in shorts and T-shirts were eating. A waiter carrying plastic baskets of food told me the hostess was up front. My pee alarm rang again. I grabbed a menu and ducked into the bathroom.

Chapter 7

Cutting to the head of the prison visitor line, I surrendered my pistol and went through the metal detector. Warden Franklin's office was on the inside of the first set of barred gates. Franklin had run the Immokalee Prison for a dozen years, and this was the first time he'd lost a prisoner.

Franklin shunned wearing the suit and tie most wardens did, opting for the brown uniform his prison guards wore. Sitting to his left was the prison psychologist wearing a white lab coat. Why would a head doctor need a lab coat?

Franklin made the introductions. The psychologist was a string bean named Dr. Benett.

"I'm as pissed off as you, Detective. This is the first one I've lost, but I have to tell you that if these damn lawmakers knew the consequences of what can happen when they're trying to do good—"

"Believe me, I know it's not your fault, Warden. The Lawrence Center is responsible. The sheriff is conducting an inquiry. We'll find out what went wrong. In the meantime, I want to get a handle on how Dwyer was doing here, what his state of mind was, and what contacts he'd had."

"Sure. Dwyer was doing damn well until this bullshit. He started a reading program for the inmates and was not only teaching the GED but doing a lot of one-on-one. But what was it, Doc? Two weeks ago, he suddenly stopped teaching and wouldn't come out into the yard."

Dr. Benett said, "It was closer to three weeks. Mr. Dwyer began complaining that he was feeling depressed."

"Well, he was just about given a life sentence; he should be depressed."

"I'm referring to a clinical depression. His condition worsened, and he totally withdrew. He even stopped eating regularly. Severe depression is not uncommon when a person is institutionalized, and I am obligated to refer an inmate for treatment when someone is experiencing a crisis like Mr. Dwyer was."

"Do you believe his condition was real?"

"I don't understand your question, Detective."

"Is there a possibility Dwyer was faking it?"

"I've been here for close to twenty years, and I've never experienced anything remotely resembling what you are suggesting."

"Maybe it's because you never had someone like Ethan Dwyer. Warden, were there any inmates that Dwyer was close to?"

"I grilled the guards in his block, but they all said he pretty much kept to himself unless he was teaching or tutoring. Most of the time he was reading in his cell or in the library."

"I'd like a list of anyone who has visited him."

"Sure, for the last sixty days?"

"Since day one. Dwyer plays a long game. I want to know anyone from the outside he had contact with."

"No problem. I'll have it sent over later today."

"Thanks. I'd like to examine his cell."

***

Accompanied by two guards, the warden and I passed through three sets of gates before entering the prison's bullpen area. This place always reminded me of the prison in *The Green Mile*.

A heavily tattooed inmate with a shaved head was mopping the area. Whatever the mixture was, it was heavy on the bleach. He stiffened when he saw Franklin and stopped swabbing the floor.

"Afternoon, Warden."

"Afternoon, Beasley."

"You can continue. We're going up to Block C."

The inmate got busy, and we clanged our way up the steel staircase. The second level was quiet.

"Most of the prisoners in the block are out in the yard."

We passed cell after cell whose barred doors were open. We stopped in front of a locked cell. As a guard opened it, I heard a low chant and peeked into the next cell. A bearded inmate was sitting on the floor in a full-lotus position. He looked so serene I wanted to figure out what he was repeating.

Dwyer's bed hung off the cinder block wall. It wasn't made. A stainless steel table with an attached stool was fastened to the floor. On the table were no less than thirty pencils, lined up and evenly spaced. A concrete shelf was overflowing with books.

A messy stack of papers was on floor at the foot of the bed. I picked the papers up and cycled through, looking for a clue. They appeared to be quizzes that Dwyer made for his students.

I studied the books on the shelf, heavily weighted toward history. There were plenty of mathematics, science, and Spanish instruction books as well. I picked up *Reality is Not What it Seems - The Journey to Quantum Gravity*, by Carlo Rovelli. I didn't have a clue what quantum gravity was, but the first part of the title fit my day.

Placing it back on the shelf, I noticed the corner of a book that was behind the others. The green book's title was *Depression: Causes and Treatments*. I waved the book at the warden.

"Tell Dr. Benett that Dwyer had this. See if he changes his mind about the sham Dwyer pulled."

Just before leaving the cell, I took another look and marched to the bed. I pulled off the sheet, revealing a pile of paper torn into tiny pieces, none larger than an M&M. I fingered a couple. There were pencil markings on them.

Was there a clue here? Dwyer was too smart to leave something behind. If it was important, he would have flushed it down the toilet. Unless. Unless he was interrupted right before being taken to the Lawrence Center.

I pulled out a plastic evidence bag and gently scooped the pieces into it. Putting this puzzle together would be a challenge and wouldn't win me any fans at the lab.

Chapter 8

The David Lawrence Center claimed to have reported Dwyer's disappearance once they realized he was missing. The question was, how long did it take for them to realize he'd escaped? Most institutions would circle the wagons for a while, see if they could clean up a mess before anyone found out.

But Dwyer was a dangerous man, and they knew it. Chances were they searched for him for an hour or so before calling the sheriff's office, who sent an officer and put out an all-points bulletin.

Roberto Cano, the guard on duty at the time, had been grilled, claiming Dwyer must have slipped out when he was in the bathroom. I didn't buy it. Two other guards said Dwyer had complained he hadn't had sex in over a year, also saying he'd pay for the chance to get laid.

If Cano did something wrong, the sheriff would find out. My job was to put Dwyer's ass back in jail. First up was figuring out what happened after Dwyer had left the Lawrence Center.

No one in the immediate area saw a car waiting or anyone resembling Dwyer get into a vehicle. He probably left on foot.

Even if Dwyer had help, chances were he was still in the county. Where was he hiding? He was as cunning and as patient as they get. He might be holed up right under our noses. We needed the entire department tuned into finding him. The press would know about this at any minute, making my job harder. Time to chat with the sheriff.

Chester slowly rose out of his chair as I walked in.
"Have a seat, Frank."

Frank? He needed me. "I realize the Dwyer escape is important to the department, and I wanted to keep you abreast of what I'm doing."

"We have to get him back behind bars before the press gets a hold of it. They'll scare the hell out of everyone."

"I understand. If it comes to it, we'll have to figure a way to assure people that Dwyer is not a random killer. He is very specific in his targets."

"Speaking of that, I'm concerned he may have you and Detective Vargas in his sights."

Mary Ann and me? Targets? The thought had crossed my mind, but I had dismissed it. "I've considered that, sir, and we'll take extra precautions."

"I'd like to organize coverage of your home."

"If you could hold off on that. It would spook the neighbors."

"That's your call, but make sure you inform Detective Vargas of the offer."

"Absolutely, sir."

"You know Dwyer better than anyone. Where do you think he is?"

"I have the feeling he's right here in Collier. For the moment anyway. He didn't have time to get far."

"You believe he had help?"

"Usually with a breakout there's help from the outside. But Dwyer is different. He'd know getting anyone involved would increase the risk. I'm going to go over the video from Lawrence, and the warden is giving me the names of anyone who visited Dwyer in prison."

"Good. You have enough manpower?"

"I would really appreciate an increase in patrols, maybe five extra cars on the street, specifically looking for Dwyer."

"I'll find the resources to get them on the road this evening. Anything else?"

"My partner is investigating the murder of James Garrison. I could really use him to hunt down Dwyer."

"We need that homicide solved. Taking him off would derail the investigation before it gained any momentum."

"I understand, sir, but keep in mind that Garrison wasn't an ordinary citizen. He was a drug dealer."

"I'll think about it. Is that all?"

"Sir, I know it's a touchy subject, but I'd like to have Detective Vargas on the Dwyer case with me. She knows almost as much about Dwyer as I do."

"I'll give it consideration, but it would require a waiver from the inspector general."

"Thank you, sir. One thing that I want to be sure of is that everybody has a picture of Dwyer and is actively searching for him. The more eyeballs the better."

"Consider it done."

"I'd also like to have the portrait artist make up a several sketches of Dwyer, with glasses, facial hair, hat, different hair colors."

"I'll get that happening immediately."

"Thanks."

***

Between Garrison and Dwyer, my mind was skittering like a hockey puck. Remembering a conversation I needed to have, I picked up the phone.

"Robert DiBlasi?"

"Yes. Who is this?"

"Detective Luca, Collier County Sheriff's Department."

"Detective Luca? Is Ethan all right?"

"You don't know anything?"

"I have no idea what you're talking about. What's going on with him?"

"He's on the run."

"On the run? He escaped from jail?"

"Not quite. He was sent to a mental health facility and walked out."

"What was he doing there?"

"I think he was faking severe depression to get out."

"Oh my God."

"He hasn't called you?"

"No."

"When was the last time you saw him?"

"I took a flight down about a month after he went in. He seemed to be doing okay."

"You're still up in New Jersey?"

"No, we finally made the move down. We're living in Mangrove Bay."

"Good for you; it's a nice spot."

"We're happy. But hearing this is very upsetting."

"How is your wife doing? I remember she wasn't feeling too good."

"She's a hundred percent. She volunteers at the library five days a week now."

"Are you retired?"

"I wish. I'm working at the firm's Fort Myers office."

I'd need to set up surveillance on his house, to be sure he wasn't harboring Dwyer. With both of them out of the house every day, we'd find out quickly if anyone else was living there.

"He may reach out to you. Ask for help, money, that sort of thing. If he does, I need to know about it immediately, okay?"

"Yeah, sure."

"Just so you know, if you assist him, in any way, you'd be committing a crime."

"I understand. I don't want to get into trouble. What should we do if he contacts us?"

"I know it's difficult to betray your brother, uh, half brother, but it's for the best. We don't want to see him get hurt, or worse, killed. If he contacts you for help, agree to help but call me. We'll find a way to bring him back into custody so no one gets hurt."

"I can't believe this. It's surreal."

That made two of us. "I understand. This your cell, right?"

"Yes."

"Save my number, and call me immediately if Ethan contacts you."

Dwyer didn't have any friends or other family that I knew of. Was there someone in prison that he befriended and who was recently released? I should have asked the warden about that. I jotted a note to myself to check that out as I cycled through the prison breaks I had read about. Not one of them was a solo act.

But, then again, none of them was Dwyer. He needed a place to stay out of sight, and food, and money. He could work off the books in the back of some kitchen, deal drugs, or engage in some type of criminal activity, but he'd need connections. No dealer would trust a guy off the street, and if they knew who he was, they wouldn't want the heat.

Did Dwyer have another lockbox? Could he have put money away and hidden the key somewhere? It seemed like a stretch, but Dwyer was a long-range planner. Anything was possible with him.

Chapter 9

There was no one else in the media room. Not sure why they gave the room such a fancy title. It was nothing more than three monitors hooked up to DVD players. In the corner was a pile of tape players stacked up.

I set my coffee down and slid the first disc in. It was from April 4th, the day Ethan Dwyer slipped out of the David Lawrence Center. The center had reported him missing just before 11 a.m. I figured it took them time to realize he was gone and then an hour searching, hoping he'd show up. Still missing, they probably had a meeting about what to do before calling their corporate masters for instructions.

Dwyer was too smart to leave much earlier, when the place was just coming alive. My bet was he took off around breakfast, during the peak of the morning rush. There were five exits: the main entrance, inpatient egress, one for employees, another for the kitchen, and a dock area for freight.

I went straight to a time stamp of 8 a.m. on the video surveillance of the dock area. The clarity was higher than I expected but still herky-jerky. The dock was empty, and I sped forward until a young man came out and lit a cigarette. He left after five minutes. There was nothing until a truck from Avante Restaurant Supplies began to back into the dock.

Two men came into view as the driver came around, opening the back doors. One had a hand truck and the other, who was tall and thin like Dwyer, was wearing a baseball cap tucked low. I froze the frame and zoomed in. His back to the camera, he was wearing a jacket. It had been in the seventies that morning. Was he hiding his clothing?

I let it roll in slow motion. He walked gingerly, like Dwyer did because of his bad back, and slipped out of sight. Jotting down the time, I hit fast-forward, waiting for him to reappear, as my heart pounded.

He came back into view with an armful of vegetable crates. The truck had a side door. I continued watching the video until the time stamp hit 10 a.m.

Debating between looking at the kitchen or the inpatient egress, I opted for the inpatient video. There was no activity until 8:15, when a woman unlocked the doors from the inside. At 8:25 the first patient, a male, entered, followed by two women and another man at 8:27. A beefy male left the building at 8:29, returning four minutes later, followed by a young woman at 8:30.

At 8:36 a.m., the young woman left through the door held open by a male entering. As soon as she disappeared, a thin man, with his head down, slipped out of the building. I couldn't see his face, but his movements confirmed it was Dwyer. I hit rewind and watched in slow motion.

Dwyer was wearing beige pants, sneakers, and a white shirt. He turned to the left, out of the camera's view. I pulled out the campus map. He was headed toward the rear of the building where the tennis courts were. Just beyond the courts was a wall for privacy, not to prevent runners.

I watched it again. Was the woman with Dwyer? She was inside for just six minutes. Did she create the diversion Dwyer needed? How would he get her to do something like that? We needed to know who she was, and fast. I'd have the lab blow up shots of her, but I was hoping that the center had her on the footage inside.

***

Dr. Acorn came into the lobby wearing a green pants suit and a sneer. She wasn't happy to see me, but her sneer was a professional one. She said hello through gritted teeth, and I followed her to her office.

"I'm willing to assist the sheriff's office, but this clearly seems to be a matter for law enforcement professionals."

"This is an active investigation. If you refuse to help, we'll charge you with obstruction."

The color drained from her face. "I—I understand. I wasn't attempting to be uncooperative."

"I don't have to remind you that your facility had custody of Mr. Dwyer and failed miserably."

"We have armed guards—"

"Save it, ma'am. At eight thirty, on the morning of April fourth, a woman entered the inpatient section from outside. She stayed briefly, leaving at eight thirty-six. I need to know who that woman was."

"Patients are protected by privacy laws. You can't expect me to violate—"

"Look, Ethan Dwyer is a convicted mass murderer. Now, you can either do what I ask, or I'll call a press conference. We can do it right outside your building. I'll explain to the public how you allowed a serial killer to escape."

"I have limits on my authority, Detective. What exactly would you like me to do?"

"We need to speak with whoever covered reception that morning. Additionally, I want to review whatever CCTV you have of the lobby. We need to know who she is and whether she helped Dwyer."

"Would it be possible for you to limit your review of the lobby to the period of time in question?"

I'd get the entire DVD sooner or later. "Yes. I'm going to need a copy of that. I may need to have photos of her made if she proves to be a person of interest."

Acorn picked up the phone, and minutes later a woman in her late sixties knocked on the door.

"Mrs. Acorn? You needed me?"

"Come on in, Alice. This is Detective Luca, with the sheriff's office."

People always got spooked when we showed up. It was true that most cops considered everyone a suspect, but in reality, if you did nothing wrong, you had no reason to be nervous.

"Nice to meet you, ma'am. I'd like to ask you about a woman who came in the building on April fourth."

"Uh, April fourth?"

"Yes. Two days ago. Early in the morning, around eight thirty, a woman came in—"

"But there are a lot of patients who come in for their treatments."

"I understand, but what was unusual about this woman was she left just six minutes later. If I'm not mistaken, there aren't any treatments that short."

"True. I don't remember anything, though."

"It was just two days ago. Think it over, it's important."

She looked at Dr. Acorn. "I'm sorry, I—I don't remember."

"Okay. Take it easy, Alice. You're not in trouble. Relax. Dr. Acorn is getting the video feed of that morning, and we'll take a look at it together. How does that sound?"

Chapter 10

We decamped to what passed as a security office for the center, a coat-closet-sized room manned by, with all due respect to the security guys at the defunct chain, a Kmart cop. I thought a place like this needed a robust security presence. Apparently, they opted to quell disturbances that arose with a needle rather than force.

There was no room for all of us to sit. The Kmart cop loaded the disc and sidestepped out. I gave the seat to Alice and hit play, fast-forwarding to the time in question.

My eyes were glued to the glass entrance doors. I slowed it down as the time stamp hit 8:29.

"Okay, this should be her."

A white female, thirty to maybe forty years old, pushed through the second set of doors. Wearing a long-sleeved, cream-colored blouse and tan pants, the woman looked at the floor as she came in.

"Do you recognize her now?"

"Uhm, not really."

This woman needed memory supplements more than I did. "Did she stop at the front desk?"

"I don't recall. You know, most of the patients are regulars. They know where they are going, and, you know, they just wave or say hello, and go on their way."

If she was a damn regular, you'd know her, wouldn't you? "I understand, but since you don't recognize her, I'd assume she wasn't a patient who came frequently, right?"

She smiled. "Yes, that makes sense."

"Good, so if someone is new, anyone, not particularly this woman, comes in, they stop at your desk and sign in?"

"We don't have a sign-in sheet, but people usually ask where this and that are."

"You didn't know this woman?"

"No."

"Take a close look at her."

Alice leaned in, studying the woman. "I'm sorry. I really don't know who she is. Am I supposed to know her?"

Dr. Acorn said, "It's okay, Alice."

"Let me see if I understand this. A woman you don't know walks into your facility, and no one challenges her?"

Dr. Acorn said, "Alice is a volunteer, who graciously gives her time to help people."

"And that makes it okay?"

"Detective, you may be unaware, but there is still a stigma associated with mental illness. As unfortunate as that is, we must encourage people to seek treatment, offering them complete anonymity as they do. If we couldn't guarantee them absolute anonymity, most would not receive the help they so desperately need."

"I understand that completely."

I really did. We needed people to feel comfortable as they addressed their needs. What I couldn't understand was a place like this using a volunteer in a frontline position. I didn't know for sure, but I was ready to bet the fees they charged in their addiction programs were more than I made in a year.

Hopeful that pictures we'd make from the video footage of her entering would jar someone's memory, I left.

***

The office was empty. Before taking off my jacket, I sent a text to Derrick to see where he was. There was an envelope on the corner of my desk from the prison. I tore it open. It was the visitor log for Dwyer. I scanned the short list. Two names popped off the page.

Minister Booth and Jeremy Stokes had each visited Dwyer twice. My pee-pee alarm sounded, and I went to the toilet to coax my makeshift bladder to empty. Sitting on the bowl, I thought about the people from the Spirit of Fellowship Church.

Could it be that after everything they'd been through, they still wanted to help Dwyer? These people truly believed in their mission. But would they take it too far? It was a stretch I discounted, but tickling my abdomen to increase the flow from a trickle to a stream, I knew it had to be checked out.

DiBlasi, Dwyer's half brother, had been there once, as he said, but there was a woman named Anita Forester who had been there eight times in the past year. Who was this woman? Was she the same woman seen at the Lawrence Center? I cut short my leak, washed up, and called the prison while walking back to my office.

The warden's secretary was going to scan over the identity documents Forester had presented. While popping the woman's name into our system, a text came in. It was Derrick. He was on his way back. I'd have to push Chester harder, push him to take Derrick off the Garrison case.

Our database had nothing on Anita Forrester. But the DMV came through. There were two Anita Foresters, one in Lee County, and the other in Naples Park. It could be either one of them, as they were both in their thirties. I checked Facebook; there were eight women with the same name. Paging through, looking for those who lived in Florida, Derrick came in.

He stood in front of my desk. "We have to talk, Frank."

"Sure. What's on your mind?"

"You and Jimmy Garrison."

"Get to the point, Derrick."

"You never said anything about going to Garrison's house."

"I didn't?"

"You know damn well you didn't. What's going on here?"

"What's going on is you showing disrespect to your partner."

"It's tough to respect someone who withholds information in a homicide case."

I stood. "Are you accusing me of something? If you are, you damn well better have proof."

"Why didn't you tell me you went to see him?"

"You're making a big deal out of nothing. I went to warn the lowlife about making threats, that's all."

"It's not right, Frank. It's like you've been hiding things from day one on Garrison."

"That's not true. I may have forgotten to tell you something, but that's all it is."

Derrick's cell phone rang. "It's the sheriff." He answered it.

"Chester wants me to put the Garrison case on hold and focus on Dwyer."

"Good. I can use the help."

"Did you have anything to do with him pulling me off Garrison?"

"No. Chester's concerned about catching Dwyer. He's a serial killer, for Chrissakes."

"You're right. I'm sorry."

"You're making me paranoid."

"What's the status on Dwyer?"

"He slipped out the inpatient entrance at the David Lawrence Center on April fourth at around eight thirty a.m. There was an unidentified woman who went in and out about the same time. No one at the facility knows who she was. We have to assume she might have been helping Dwyer. I have the lab printing pictures of her from the video."

"What do you think she did?"

"I don't know, maybe nothing more than creating a diversion so Dwyer could slip out undetected."

"I can't believe the place didn't have more security. They deal with criminals all the time."

"Don't get me started. After this is over, we'll have to make recommendations to ensure that those who need help get it, but also make sure someone like Dwyer is properly guarded."

"Just like at a hospital with police."

"Exactly. I bet Dwyer had a damn good laugh after he got out. Anyway, the list of Dwyer's prison visitors includes a woman, Anita Forester, who visited eight times."

"No relation?"

"Not that I know of. You read the file; did you see any connection?"

"Uh, I didn't get through it yet."

An email pinged. The preview was Forester's driver's license. She lived on 99th Avenue. I said, "Read through it now. I'm going to see Forester."

Chapter 11

Naples Park was a community squeezed in between Route 41 and the bay and ran from Immokalee to Vanderbilt Beach Road. It was a premier location, and houses had begun to be renovated or torn down, but then the housing market crashed. The market came back but not enough for risk-takers to dip in, and it remained a hodgepodge of homes.

Anita Forester lived on 99th Street in a white cement home. Her block was a perfect example of the neighborhood's duality. There was a car covered with a tarp in her gravel driveway, and two others parked on the lawn. Across the street was a newly built, two-story home with a paver driveway and perfect landscaping. I'm sure they didn't appreciate the view Forester provided.

Her screen door was screenless. I hit the bell, and a minute later Forester came to the door. Dressed plainly in a blue dress that covered her knees, she reminded me of a nun. She looked to be in her late fifties—kind of late to participate in a breakout.

I introduced myself.

"Oh, would you like to come in?"

"Thank you. I have a couple of questions I'd like to ask."

The small house was neat but the furnishings worn. We sat at a half-moon table in the galley kitchen. A wooden crucifix and a painting of the Immaculate Heart of Mother Mary hung side by side.

"I have to say, Detective, you really look like George Clooney."

"I'll take that as a compliment."

"He's one of my favorites. Would you like something to drink?"

"No, thank you. This shouldn't take long."

"Good, I've got to pick up my granddaughter."

"You visited a prisoner named Ethan Dwyer at the Immokalee jail. What can you tell me about those visits?"

"He is an intelligent young man. It's a shame he's incarcerated, but he's doing a lot of good helping to educate other inmates."

Incarcerate. The term always bothered me. Just a fancy word to try and soften the reality of crime. "How do you know Mr. Dwyer?"

"I met him at the prison."

"How did you meet him at the prison?"

"I visit correctional facilities at least once a week. These men need human connections. We all do. I put requests in to visit newcomers, as they're the most vulnerable. I let them know they aren't forgotten and bring them things they need. It really has an impact."

"Do you visit prisoners at Immokalee regularly?"

"Yes. As I said, I go at least once a week; most times twice a week."

"What did Ethan Dwyer discuss during your visits?"

"Nothing special, just normal chitchat. He was a big reader, though, always asked me to bring him books and cigarettes."

"Cigarettes?"

"Yes. Every time I visited him I brought a couple of packs, with a book or two."

Dwyer had started smoking? He wasn't a smoker when we chased him down the first time.

"Did you ever see Mr. Dwyer smoke?"

"No. The visiting room is nonsmoking."

"The records state that you visited him eight times. Is that right?"

"I couldn't be sure about that. But it sounds right."

"And you brought him cigarettes each time, say two to three packs each time?"

"Not the first time I met him. But yes, two to three packs, but one time I gave him a carton that Mr. Gerey had given me. You see, Mr. Gerey had quit, and he knew I delivered cigarettes to the boys in Immokalee, so he gave me his last two cartons."

"Has Ethan Dwyer contacted you in the last couple of days?"

"No."

"Are you sure?"

"Yes, of course."

"Okay. You should know that he escaped from the David Lawrence Center on April fourth and is at large. I have to caution you, ma'am; Mr. Dwyer is a very dangerous man."

She put her hand over her mouth. "Oh my God. Please don't hurt him."

I gave her my card. "If he contacts you, please call me immediately."

Driving back, I thought about this woman and how she chose to spend her life. Was it crazy or admirable? She was living a selfless existence; was that the path to happiness? This woman was not only helping total strangers but the type of people I worked my ass off to put behind bars. I knew there was virtue in what we were both doing, but I'd have to leave it to the man or woman upstairs to decide who was righteous.

My mind shifted to the cigarettes. Forester had given him about forty packs of smokes. If he was using them as currency and selling them to other inmates at the bargain price of five dollars a pack, he'd have two hundred dollars in cash. It wouldn't go far, but it went somewhere.

As I rolled to a stop for a red light, a text came in. It was the lab. They had finished assembling the scraps of paper I took out of Dwyer's cell. They wanted to show me what they had.

Chapter 12

The paper-scrap puzzle would be as good a draw I'd have to help get Derrick fixated on Dwyer. I sent a text to tell him I was minutes away and that he was to meet me in the foyer of the forensics unit.

Derrick was glued to his phone when I breezed in. "It's showtime." I knocked on the window with my left hand as I signed the logbook. Through the door's window I saw Miller talking to a tech as Derrick and I slipped on protective clothing.

The whirl of the lock sounded, and we entered. Miller looked over his shoulder and came over. First thing out of his mouth was, "Where did you get this from?"

"Ethan Dwyer's prison cell. Why?"

"Oh. There were actually two drawings mixed up. They came from the same sheet of paper, though, and were made with the same pencil. Let me show you."

Below a piece of plexiglass were two pencil drawings.

I stared at the bottom image. A stick figure was waving with one hand. In the other was a gun. In the dialogue balloon coming from the figure was a greeting: "Hi, Detective Luca. I regret being unable to deliver a proper greeting, in person, when you visited. However, you must have known it was impossible for me to remain here the balance of my natural life. Don't despair, I'll see you, though you will not see me."

The top sketch was of an old building in a Mediterranean style. It had a curved entrance and five small windows. What the hell was it?

"He's poking his finger in your eye, Frank."

I stared at the gun in the stick figure's hand. "He wanted us to find this. What does he think this is, some sort of damn game?"

***

Dwyer was taunting me. Chester was right; I needed to be careful. If Mary Ann became spooked by all this, I'd have Chester get a patrol car to sit at our house. Needing to think and to relieve myself, I headed into a bathroom stall and sat.

The only upside to getting bladder cancer was the time I was forced to sit and coax my pee out. I was past the frustration of feeling like I was wasting fifteen minutes instead of the minute it took when I had a bladder. Mary Ann convinced me to use the time to let my mind roll things around without interruption. It worked.

The clock was ticking. If Dwyer was able to find his way out of Florida, there was no telling what he had planned next to become invisible. We'd never catch him. Where would he go? Dwyer had a rod in his spine. He was often in pain and couldn't sit still for long periods. That part about him was true. I had seen the medical records.

Dwyer needed a warm climate to help manage his pain. Would he trek out to Southern California? Maybe Arizona or Texas? I couldn't picture him in Louisiana or Mississippi, but who knew? Mexico seemed far-fetched for someone like Dwyer.

We needed help. I would go to see the sheriff and ask him to release pictures of Dwyer to the public. Dwyer was smart, but he was not the invisible man. Who knew what leads would come in? We also needed to release a picture and plead with the public for help in identifying the mysterious woman seen at David Lawrence the morning Dwyer fled. I preferred to wait a day or so after asking for help with finding Dwyer. That way we'd keep the focus on him before hitting the public with another face.

They were appropriate steps to take, but the picture of the building Dwyer had drawn nagged at me as I stepped up to the sink. What was it, and where was it? I wish I could show the image to people competing on *Jeopardy*. I bet they'd know what it was.

Drying my hands, it hit me that the history professors at Gulf State University might have an idea. I left a message with the history department before going to see the sheriff.

Even though my concern was growing, I played down the note from Dwyer when I spoke to Chester; I would decide whether to appear frightened. Chester said he'd have the pictures on the news that night. He could be indecisive at times, but when he finally made a decision, things moved quickly.

He also said he was waiting for an exception from Internal Affairs for Mary Ann to join the Dwyer investigation.

Heading back to my office, I was hopeful we'd get some help from the public and was ecstatic about Mary Ann. In spite of the troubling drawings, it was a good day. I swung into the office. Derrick was holding his head in his hands.

"What's the matter? You have a headache?"

"Headache? No, I'll tell you what's the matter." Derrick got up and closed the door.

"What's going on?"

"I received a call today from a friend of Garrison's."

"And what did the upstanding citizen have to say?"

"That you went to Garrison's house and had words with him."

"So? I told you about it. It was a one-time thing, that's all."

"You sure about that?"

"Absolutely."

"Yeah? Well, this guy, he was there when you came. Both times. He said you went twice, not once."

"Once, twice, what does it matter?"

"A lot. Your last visit was only a week or so before he was killed."

I pointed a finger in his face. "You better watch what you say."

"Or what? I'll end up like Garrison?"

"You got to be fucking kidding me!"

Derrick stormed out as I tried to calm down. My heart was pounding. I took a couple of deep breaths, visualizing a shimmering Gulf as I exhaled. My cell rang. I hoped it was Mary Ann. It wasn't. It was Gulf Coast University.

Chapter 13

Professor McCall was certain the image that Dwyer had drawn was of the Alamo. What was the significance of Dwyer drawing the site where a pivotal battle in the Texas Revolution took place?

The Mexicans killed all the Texans during the fight, but the brutality the Mexicans displayed inspired Texans and others to join the Texian Army. The bolstered force defeated the Mexicans, ending the revolution just six weeks after the slaughter at the Alamo.

The losing battle spawned the phrase, Remember the Alamo, which was used to promise revenge. Dwyer was a master at retaliation, sitting quietly for years before springing into action to even scores. Was he coming after *me* this time?

Or was the drawing a geographic decoy, leading me to believe he was headed to Texas when he was either staying in Florida or going elsewhere? Texas did have the heat his back needed. It was also a huge state. The Alamo was located in San Antonio, a three-plus-hour drive to the nearest beach. I Googled Alamo and got a a hit for a Texas city just an hour's drive to the beaches. It was typical Dwyer, even the geographic hint contained a twist. We had to keep an eye on two places.

Did the drawing represent a stake in the ground that he wouldn't give up? The symbolism was impossible to decipher. Something like this needed to be bounced around. I needed my ideas seasoned or discarded. Normally, I'd chew it over with Derrick, but I'd had enough hostility for the day. Besides, Mary Ann knew more about Dwyer than my official partner did.

As soon as Mary Ann arrived at Dolce and Saluto, we took an outside table. I really enjoyed their sandwiches and Italian vibe. I ordered a smoked turkey sandwich for the two of us to split.

Mary Ann pointed left. "Look, a rainbow."

A colored band of magic arched from the coast. "Nice. Let's hope it's a good omen."

"It's how you look at things, Frank."

"I know, I know. I appreciate being here with you. It's nice."

"That's fine, Frank, but you might as well tell me what's going on."

"I need to bounce something off you about what Dwyer drew."

"Isn't that something you should be discussing with Derrick?"

"Yeah, but you know Dwyer. He doesn't."

"Okay. Unofficially, then."

I showed her the photos on my phone before realizing she didn't know about the implied threat.

"I don't like this one bit. He's mocking you. He's an extremely dangerous man, Frank. You have to be careful. He could come after us."

"Trust me, I know. I spoke to Chester about it already. He's ready to plant a patrol car in front of our house. You just say the word."

"I don't want the neighbors getting scared. Let's hold off for now. What's this?"

"The Alamo."

"The Alamo in Texas?"

"Yep. The one and only. I can't figure out what it means."

"It's a revenge thing, Frank. After the Texans got wiped out there, they regrouped. Then they went out and won."

"But what is he going to win?"

"His freedom."

"Okay, but if that's the extent of his revenge plans, I'm okay with that. What do you think about it being a geographical marker, real, or maybe he's using it as a decoy?"

"If he really intended for you to find it and put it together, then I'd say he was trying to throw you off on where he is headed. But remember, this guy is crazy smart but not infallible. He could have been doodling as he dreamed about escaping to Texas and thought ripping it up would keep it from you."

"Nah, I don't buy it. Unless he really is goading me, telling me where he is, challenging me to come and get him."

"He's got to know about jurisdiction."

"He does, but he also knows I'd be a part of any effort to catch him. And he's right about that."

"It'd be too risky for him to stay in Florida."

"For most guys, I'd agree, but Dwyer, he really thinks everyone is a fool. And that's how we're gonna get him."

"What do you mean?"

"His ego. He really believes he can outsmart us, and that's going to lead him into making an assumption, a decision of some sort, that'll be the mistake we need to put him back in prison, where he belongs."

It seemed to take forever, but the waiter finally brought our sandwich. They had a special toasting process for the sandwich bread, so it took time. It was worth it; the sandwich was a work of art. I grabbed my half and started eating.

"Chester is waiting for Internal Affairs to approve you working with me on this, so get ready."

"I'll have to see you during the day as well?"

"You know you can't get enough of me."

She rolled her eyes.

Lowering my voice, I said, "I could really use your help. I feel like I don't even know where to start with Dwyer."

"Just do what you know how to do, Frank, and everything will be fine."

What kind of advice was that? Just do what you know how to do? I took another bite and thought. I rolled it around; she was right. When I followed my instincts and training, it always worked out. Then the handbag caper crossed my mind. That didn't work out, but that was because I hadn't followed my training.

This was different. Dwyer's intelligence and patience made him a real challenge. Was I up to it? Could something bad happen to me or Mary Ann?

***

My lunch high came crashing down before I had a chance to digest it. Chester called me and told me to put together a time line covering my whereabouts during the period Garrison went missing. I tried to read into his tone, but he was as neutral as Switzerland.

Chapter 14

Chester's desk was the clearest I'd ever seen. There was only one document in the center of his desk. I didn't have to guess what it was.

"Have a seat, Frank."

Frank? That was a good start. "Thank you, sir."

"I have to be honest with you, Frank. I was expecting more detail, especially from someone like you."

I have to be honest? Chester was even using that crap saying?

"I'm sorry you feel that way, sir. I thought it fully accounted for the time period in question."

Chester picked up the paper. "February sixteenth, a Friday, eight a.m. to six p.m., at work. Seven p.m. till one a.m., at a friend's home for a barbecue." He put the paper down. "Maybe you believe it's enough, but I have to be conscious of the way something like this looks. Members of this department have to abide by higher standards than the public. You wouldn't accept something like this from a suspect, would you?"

"What, now I'm a suspect?"

"It was just a reference, Frank. Take it easy. I'm trying to help here. We need more detail to put an end to suspicions you had anything to do with Garrison's death. I hope I don't have to remind you that if you had followed protocol and let the department handle the threats, we wouldn't be talking about this."

"I understand I made a mistake, sir."

"Good. Now don't compound it with something like this. I don't think I have to hold your hand, Frank. Provide detail, the whos and whats you were doing. Saturday is probably good enough. You were with

Detective Vargas the entire day, but add some color to that as well. And then Sunday and Monday, you just can't say you were home alone. Put some effort into this, Frank. I don't want Internal Affairs to elevate this."

Chester handed me the statement, and I said, "I'll get right on it, sir."

***

Derrick didn't know it, but he helped me fill in what Friday, February 16 looked like. I had nothing on my calendar for the day and searched the database for reports filed around that day. My hope that a report would provide cover for most of the day hit the jackpot. As a newbie, Derrick had filed a meticulous report on a suspicious death.

Derrick had taken a call that morning from a Dr. Brown from NCH Downtown Hospital. The doctor claimed that a husband had killed his wife while she was hospitalized. We hopped in the Cherokee to investigate.

As soon as the elevator door opened to the third floor, a man in a lab coat rushed over.

"Are you the police?"

"Yes. Detective Luca, and this is Detective Dickson, homicide."

He stuck out a hand. "Dr. Vincent Brown."

I wanted to avoid shaking a hand that could give me something and dug out my notebook as Derrick shook the doctor's hand.

Derrick said, "Tell us what happened, Doctor."

"He killed her. That's what he did."

I said, "Hold on, Doc. Is there someplace we can talk privately?"

"Yes, the physicians' lounge is right over here."

He led us to a windowless room with two couches and a muted television. Derrick closed the door behind us, and I said, "Okay, Dr. Brown, tell us what happened, but start at the beginning."

"Charlotte Binger, an eighty-two-year-old woman, has been a patient of mine for over ten years. Outside of diabetes, she was in reasonably good health until she was diagnosed with Parkinson's disease. That was about five years ago. Using a combination of drugs, I was able to stabilize the progression of the disease. She began having trouble swallowing about a year ago. I recommended that she chop her food into fine pieces. It was better than puree. But she resisted."

Derrick said, "What happened?"

"She had several choking episodes and had to be resuscitated at least once that I know of. At that point, I insisted she puree her food, but again she was stubborn, promising to finely chop her food and eat slowly. But whether she did as she claimed or not, she was aspirating and repeatedly contracted aspiration pneumonia. It was frustrating for me. Charlotte was in good health otherwise."

I wanted to shake this doctor. Frustrating to you? The woman was in good health? "Tell us what happened that led to you calling us."

"I thought it was time to discuss a feeding tube with her. It's a shock when patients hear it for the first time, but, the fact is, they can adjust. They receive much higher nutritional values, and their health actually increases in the period right after insertion."

Derrick said, "It sounds like she didn't want it."

"No. Charlotte was against it, but that husband of hers, instead of supporting her and reasoning with her, he hardened her resolve. She had another case of pneumonia and was admitted Tuesday in a weakened condition. Why he waited so long to bring her to the hospital is a crime right there."

Derrick asked, "So you feel the husband was negligent by waiting too long?"

"Absolutely, but that's not what killed her. She wasn't responding as quickly to the treatment as we would have liked, and the fact was, she was depressed. But Charlotte Binger went into a diabetic shock from an overdose of insulin."

I said, "And you think it was the husband who did it?"

"Who else would have administered such a deadly dose?"

"Did anyone witness the husband give her the dose?"

"Not that I am aware."

"How do you know it was the insulin that caused her death?"

"Her blood levels. We take readings every four hours, and there is no way, based upon the input of nutrients she was receiving, that the levels could have spiked on their own. It was a massive dose of insulin."

"What leads you to believe it was the husband?"

"First off, he had access to Charlotte's insulin. Secondly, he was at her bedside when she went into shock. He didn't even alert the staff when she went comatose. It took a nurse on her rounds to notice it, and by then it was too late."

"How quickly would a dose, the size you believe she received, cause her to fall into a coma?"

"It's difficult to say. My professional opinion is thirty to sixty minutes."

"Is there anything else you can tell me about her husband?"

The doctor snorted. "He made several remarks about the inhumanity of her condition and the lack of her quality of life. Who does he think he is, God?"

I wanted to ask the doctor the same question, but said, "Are there any puncture wounds that you could identify as being made by the husband?"

"A patient in her condition is being administered fluids and medicines intravenously. It would be virtually impossible to identify one puncture wound as the delivery location. Additionally, he could have introduced the insulin into one of her IV lines."

"Where is the body?"

"Come on. I'll take you to her."

An attractive female doctor came out of a room and walked ahead of us down the corridor. I watched Derrick's eyes light up and follow her bottom. I knew he was wishing she didn't have a lab coat on.

Dr. Brown pulled the sheet down. Charlotte Binger was rail thin— two or three days away from emaciation. Her hands were clenched and bent at the wrist. The poor woman had scores of deep purple bruises covering both arms.

What would an autopsy prove? Why put the family through it? I took the husband's contact information and told the doctor we would have the body taken to the coroner.

As soon as the elevator doors closed, Derrick said, "I can't believe this guy killed his wife. The bastard thought he'd get away with it."

"Don't be so quick to judge here."

"What do you mean? Dr. Brown said he did it."

"This is a nasty situation."

"What are we going to do?"

"You're going to take a copy of her medical records to the county medical examiner. I want him to review the case."

"You don't trust Brown?"

"It has nothing to do with trust. I'll see you back at the office. I'm going to see the husband."

***

The Bingers lived in a second-story coach home in Kensington. It was an older community in a convenient North Naples location. There were two cars in the driveway and several others parked at the curb.

A brunette, whose mascara had run down her face, answered the door. I introduced myself. She was Karen, Charlotte's older daughter. I offered my condolences and asked to speak with her father.

John Binger was a tall man with slumped shoulders. Was he uncomfortable with his height or was it the grief? His eyes were bloodshot, and his voice cracked when he thanked me for my sympathies. I said, "I know this is not the best time, but I have to ask you a couple of questions regarding your wife's passing."

"Who sent you? That damn Brown?"

"The law requires that we investigate all unnatural deaths."

"Society thinks it's better to starve to death? To live in pain? To have no quality of life, to be attached to—"

"I understand what you're saying, and I'm with you, but the law is the law, and Dr. Brown is claiming that you gave a lethal dose of insulin to your wife."

"Look, my wife was on death's door. She had been a vibrant woman." He grabbed a photo off the refrigerator of the two of them hiking. "See this? That's Charlotte. Not the bag of bones laying in NCH. That Brown, he wanted her to continue to suffer, to wilt away until she died."

"Your wife was near death?"

"She died months ago." He turned his head. "Karen? Karen, can you come in here?"

His daughter came in and wrapped her arm around her father. "Are you okay, Dad?"

"Yeah. Please tell this detective how bad your mother was these last days."

I swallowed hard a couple of times as she told me how her mother had withdrawn, speaking only to express her desire to end it all.

"Dr. Brown believed she could have lived for a long time."

John said, "Lived? More like survived. Neither of us wanted to live in the state she was in. We made a pact together and even told the kids. We didn't want to suffer, hanging on, hooked up to a bunch of machines like some damn science experiment."

Apologizing for interrupting them, I made my exit without asking if he had given her the deadly dose.

Chapter 15

Elbows on his desk and hands clasped, Derrick shook his head when I came back from lunch. He got up and closed the door. Not a good sign.

He said, "You going to level with me, or not?"

"About what?"

"Garrison."

"There's nothing to level about."

"You're going to play that game with me?"

"Look, you have something to say, I suggest you spit it out."

"How come you never said you called Garrison?"

"I really wish you'd stop with the Garrison bullshit."

"I'll bet you would."

"Look, let it go. Chester put you on the Dwyer case."

"You think you're pretty damn clever, don't you? But you can't fool me."

"Is that right?"

"You called Garrison, didn't you?"

"Yeah, I did. So what? I was just scaring him."

"Is that what you call it?"

"Yeah, that's right."

"That's not what was on his voice mail."

Holy shit. He got the voice mail? "It's nothing."

"Nothing? You call threatening to kill him just two days before he went missing, nothing?"

"He wouldn't leave Mary Ann alone."

"So, you killed him?"

"No, I didn't."

"You have to tell me, Frank. This is dead-ass serious."

"You know I wouldn't do something like that. I'm a damn homicide detective, for Chrissakes."

"I have to inform the sheriff."

"Oh, come on, Derrick! Don't start that bullshit."

"I'm sorry, Frank. I have to report this."

"No, you don't."

"You have something to hide? You better tell me. It will be easier that way."

"Look, we're partners. I was just blowing off steam. That's all. Garrison wouldn't leave her alone. What the fuck was I supposed to do. Let him continue? The guy's a badass drug dealer, the type of piece of shit who'd do something stupid to my girl."

"If that's all it was, you have nothing to worry about. But it's out of my hands. I have to let Chester know."

As he walked out the door I mumbled, "That's bullshit."

***

It took all of five minutes for the sheriff to summon me. This was tricky. I didn't have enough time to figure out how to play it. I took the elevator to the second floor to avoid running into Derrick.

Waiting outside the sheriff's office, I tried chitchatting with his secretary. She was polite, but there was a distance to her. Was word getting around already? Had Derrick opened his mouth?

Sheriff Chester was wearing a blue suit and a frown. He didn't get up to greet me.

"How are you, sir?"

"How am I? With a serial killer on the loose, a mutilated corpse, and a cloud over my lead homicide detective; you tell me. How should I be doing?"

"Sorry, sir."

"What the hell is going on, Luca?"

He never called me Luca. When he was pissed it was always Detective Luca."

"With the Garrison case?"

"Don't get cagey with me, Luca."

"I'm not, sir. I just wanted to be sure and—"

"Get on with it!"

"I know it doesn't sound good, but Garrison was threatening Detective Vargas, and I wanted to scare him off. That's all it was."

Chester leaned over and tapped a forefinger on his desk. "Not only does that not sound good, it's a violation of department code. You think the rules don't apply to you?"

"No, sir. Absolutely not."

"Then why the hell do you keep acting like a damn cowboy?"

"Sorry, sir."

"This is a serious infraction, but what really concerns me is the thought you had anything to do with the murder of James Garrison."

"I didn't, sir."

"You're the one who found the body."

"Yes, sir."

"From what I understand, it was hidden, so how was it that you found it?"

"I had a feeling. I don't know if it was the smell, but something was off."

"You realize whoever killed Garrison was the only person who knew where his body was, don't you?"

"I know it doesn't look good, but I've relied on my instincts my entire career. They've never failed me."

"I don't have to mention the handbag fiasco, do I?"

"No, sir."

"You found the body; that by itself can be explained away. But visiting the victim two times, threatening him in the company of others, is troubling. When you combine that with a phone call threatening to kill him just two days before he went missing—that is evidence. Do you know how devastating playing that voice mail to a jury would be?"

Jury? "But, sir, you know I would never do something like that."

"What you need to do now, Detective Luca, is truly account for your whereabouts for the time period between Garrison's last appearance and his disappearance. Every damn minute, not the summary you gave me."

"But, sir, if I may, I realize the call I made to him sounds bad, but it went to his voice mail. You know why? He was dead."

"We don't know that, but I don't have to remind you that making a call to someone who has been killed is a typical tactic to throw investigators off."

"Are you saying that's the reason I called him, sir?"

"What I'm saying is that you, by accounting for your whereabouts, will put any innuendos to rest."

"I will get that together, sir. Shall I present it to you?"

"No, Detective Dickson is handling the Garrison investigation."

"I thought you assigned him to the Dwyer case?"

"He's back on Garrison."

"Oh."

"You do understand that given these developments that there is no way I can recommend that Detective Vargas assist you on the Dwyer case."

Chapter 16

It wasn't past the two hours the doctors said not to exceed before relieving myself, but I made a beeline to the bathroom. The mirror reflected my red face. The only good takeaway from the meeting with Chester was that I didn't lose my cool. Mary Ann said remaining calm at times like that made things better. In this case, that was debatable. I covered the toilet seat and replayed what Chester said.

It really wasn't what he said, but what he didn't. Everything I'd accomplished since I'd been here meant nothing. Catching five murderers, one a serial killer, in three years was Sherlock Holmes good. Did I get any respect? No. Chester had to throw the frigging handbag thing in my face—again. I was entitled to a pass, and now I had to defend myself like some punk on the street.

I tried to estimate the time period I was now on the hook to vouch for as my pee trickled out. The sheriff was looking for the time between the days they believed Garrison was killed and his last sighting. If I wasn't mistaken, they thought the homicide occurred on February 19, and Garrison was last seen February 15th.

Four days, ninety-six hours to account for. Tough to recall in any circumstance, but nearly impossible, given that almost two months had passed. Mary Ann could help me cover for the times I couldn't. I finished up and headed to check what needed to be covered.

Derrick was out. I was glad, or was I? He was working the Garrison case. The message light was pulsing on my desk phone. A call had come in to the hotline. Someone claimed to have given Dwyer a ride. I jotted down the man's contact information and left.

Jack Peterson worked for Imperial Homes and was on a jobsite in Treviso Bay. I smelled glue as I approached the home. The front doors were open, and two men on their knees were laying wood flooring.

As soon as a pause in nailing opened up, I announced myself. A thirtyish male in jeans stood up. He waved and shimmied his kneepads off. I wondered how these guys were going to feel when they hit fifty. His coworker picked up his nail gun, and Peterson suggested we step outside.

"We appreciate you making the call on Ethan Dwyer. I have a couple of questions for you."

"No problem. Soon as I saw the picture on the news at lunch, I knew it was him."

"He's very dangerous."

"He seemed pretty normal to me. In fact, he moved kinda slow getting in and out of the truck."

"Tell me how you ran into him."

"We—"

"Who is we?"

"Me and Mikey Roberts. We were coming back from getting coffee, and we saw this guy hitchhiking."

"You pick up hitchhikers?"

"Not all the time, but it was me and Mikey, and we wanted to give him a ride. We asked him where he was going, and he said the Greyhound stop at the intersection of Collier and Davis."

"Is that where you brought him?"

"Yeah, we dropped him off there."

"Did he have anything with him?"

"You mean like a bag?"

"Exactly."

"No. He had a light jacket on. I think it was gray, and pants that kinda looked like the ones they wear in hospitals, and sneakers. He looked kinda down and out, if you know what I mean, like he could use a ride."

"How did he act? Did he say anything about where he was going?"

"He was quiet but very polite. He thanked us about ten times when he got in and the same when he got out."

"Did he say where he was traveling?"

"After he got in, I asked him, just to make conversation, where he was going, and he said to visit his mother in Atlanta."

Dwyer's mother had been murdered when he was a young boy.

"Without any bags?"

"Hey, what can I tell you? He said he was headed to Atlanta."

***

I put the Cherokee's siren and lights on and sped to the Greyhound stop. Did Dwyer have enough cash to buy a ticket for out of state? Or would he go north or to the panhandle and lie low? We could trace where he was heading. Unless he had a credit card under an alias, he had to use cash.

He may think he was safe paying with cash, but he wasn't. We could deduce how much cash the location took in and what tickets were bought with it. That would give us a couple of locations and buses to focus on. Almost every Greyhound bus was outfitted with cameras, and we could tap into them.

We'd know where Dwyer went in a couple of hours, max. I turned onto Collier and was at the Davis intersection in two minutes. I scanned the corners. I saw the Greyhound logo in the window of a Shell gas station.

I pulled into the station and slammed the steering wheel with my hand. There was a big sign that read: *Tickets Not Sold at This Location - Purchase Online or at a Full-Service Terminal.*

An attendant came over. "You want gas?"

"No. I see you can't buy a ticket here. Where is the nearest place you can get one?"

"I'm pretty sure it's up in Fort Myers. But you don't have to go there, you can get 'em online."

"Can you buy a ticket on board, from the driver?"

"Nah, they don't carry cash."

"You sure?"

"Yep. I've seen a ton of people try it."

The million-dollar question was whether Dwyer knew that?

"Do you have video surveillance?"

"Just of the pumps."

Chapter 17

"You're home so late. Is it because of what happened today?"

"What do you mean?"

"Right before I left, Chester's office called to say I wasn't going to be assigned to the Dwyer case. That's why I called you twice. Why didn't you pick up?"

I pecked her cheek and headed to the bedroom. "Frigging aggravating day, that's why."

"Get changed. I'll heat up some pasta piselli and pour you a glass of wine."

Stepping into a pair of shorts, I was comforted knowing Mary Ann would stick up for me. I was hoping it would be enough to put an end to the suspicion. Dwyer was what I needed to focus on.

Mary Ann handed me a glass of Dolcetto, a little-known Northern Italian grape. That meant it wasn't expensive and tasted great.

"That's a huge pour. You trying to get me drunk so you can take advantage of me in bed?"

"You said you had a tough day."

I sat down at the table. "Damn, I thought I was going to get lucky tonight."

Placing a bowl of pasta in front of me, Mary Ann rested her breasts on my shoulder for a couple of seconds.

"You never know."

"Don't forget I had a bad day, a really bad one."

I ripped a piece of bread off a loaf and dug in to my dish.

She whispered in my ear, "Tell me about it. Maybe I can do something to help."

"Now we're talking. So, we finally got some help with Dwyer. Some guy gave Dwyer a ride to the Greyhound station. I was certain we had a bead on him, but the Greyhound location is a stop only; they don't sell tickets. You have to get them online."

"Maybe he had someone buy him a ticket on the internet."

"Who?"

"I don't know. Could be anyone. How did he get a ride there?"

"Hitchhiking."

"See, there are people that want to help. Maybe he went to one of those internet cafés and got help."

"I doubt it. Whoever bought it would need a credit card or a PayPal account."

"Maybe it was just someone looking to help, or Dwyer could've paid him something to do it."

"You really think so?"

"Dwyer knows how to manipulate people. You got to keep that in mind."

"Maybe, but what if he arranged the ride to a bus stop to throw us off? Make us think he was leaving."

"But where to? He had to know you'd find out you couldn't buy a ticket there."

"He's fucking with my head. That's what he's doing, or better, thinks that's what he's doing. He thinks he knows me, but he doesn't know Frank Luca."

"Do I even know the real Frank Luca?"

"Aw, come on. You know you do. Better than anybody. And I mean ever."

"I hope so, Frank. You know it hasn't been easy getting you to open up."

"It's getting easier day by day."

"Maybe. You know, I can't believe Internal Affairs wouldn't sign off on me joining the Dwyer case. Why would they disregard Chester's request?"

Couldn't I finish at least half a bowl before we got into that?

"Because Derrick stabbed me in the back."

"What? What are you talking about?"

"Derrick told Chester about Garrison and you."

"Garrison and me?"

"You know, about him harassing you and me going to see him and everything."

"But he knew that a couple of days ago when we talked."

"I know."

"What changed?"

"He found out about a call I made to Garrison."

"You called him? When?"

"With my luck, it turned out to be just a couple of days before he went missing."

"Oh, geez, Frank. You should have said something. It looks like you're hiding something."

"Tell me about it. As soon as Derrick ratted on me, Chester called me in."

"I wouldn't call it ratting, Frank. He has an obligation to report it."

I shrugged.

"What did Chester say?"

"He was concerned about what I said to Garrison."

"What did you tell him you said?"

"I didn't have to. He listened to the voice mail."

"Voice mail? What kind of message did you leave?"

"You know, that I'd kill him. But I was just trying to scare the bastard. That's all."

"You threatened to kill him? Are you crazy? And you left it on his voice mail?"

I nodded.

"Is there anything else you said?"

I mumbled, "That I'd throw his ass into a vat of acid."

"Oh my God. Why would you say something like that?"

I shrugged.

"You know how that looks, with Garrison having been put in acid? It's a wonder you're not in an interview room."

"It's not that bad, Mary Ann. It's just a coincidence."

"Yeah? Isn't it you who always reminds me that there are no coincidences; it's what's called evidence?"

It really annoyed me when she threw my sayings back at me. "All right, already. You going to help me or not?"

"Help you with what?"

"Chester wants me to reconstruct my whereabouts for the time period in question."

"He wants your alibi, Frank."

"You don't think I don't know that? Problem is, it was weeks ago."

"Okay, during the week you're on the job, most of the time with Derrick. Check your calendar and work on filling the gaps and when you were alone."

"Yeah, it's a pain in the ass, but I could probably account for most of it."

Mary Ann had her phone out. "For the weekend and nights, my calendar could help. What days we talking about?"

"I think the sixteenth to the twentieth of February."

"Oh, there's a weekend in there, and President's Day. So, the Friday the sixteenth we went to Joey and Maria's for a barbecue. We didn't get out of there until way after midnight. Saturday night we didn't have anything, but I remember we went to the antique car show at Koreshan Park and picked up takeout from Pincher's on the way back. We were together the entire day. And on Sunday, I had Joanne's baby shower up in Cape Coral. I left at one and got back around eight. Remember?"

"Not the times, but, yeah, I remember you going."

"Then Monday, I don't have anything, but I know I went shopping at the mall for the President Day sales. You stayed home. You said you were going to power wash the deck, but you said you had a bad headache and didn't get to it."

"Yeah, that's right."

"So, all you have to remember is Sunday during the day and Monday, when I was shopping."

"Who the hell could account for all that time?"

"I know you're pissed at having to defend yourself, but you're making a big deal over nothing."

"I was home, alone."

"You sure no one saw you? None of the neighbors?"

"Can't you just say you were with me?"

She lowered her voice. "Frank."

"What?"

"Is there anything you're not telling me?"

Chapter 18

It was good to get to the office. Mary Ann was shadowing me like she was with the CIA. She claimed to accept what I said about my whereabouts, but the atmosphere in the house was drenched in skepticism. I was mad she refused to fill in the holes in what amounted to my alibi, but I understood. She was right. She had been in public places, and if she fabricated being with me and a conflict came to light, I'd really be in trouble.

I stepped out of the conference room after what was now a daily video conference call. The Florida State Police and Highway Patrol updated the status of their patrols in the effort to find Dwyer. The Coast Guard said they increased their presence, but between their drug interdiction responsibilities and Florida's thousands of miles of shoreline, I couldn't expect much.

Florida was a huge state with endless places for Dwyer to hide. But before I could continue searching, I had to formalize the account for my time. Opening a Word document, I began typing. It was slow going. I hadn't gotten to Friday night when my desk phone rang.

A woman claiming to be the girl on the David Lawrence Center video called the hotline. She wanted to talk to the police. This could be the break we had been waiting for.

I parked in front of Jolene Winter's home, which was off Collier Boulevard. The neat ranch was squeezed onto a lot between a gated community and St. Agnes Church. Opening the car door, I realized I'd left my jacket in the office.

A green Ford Focus, with two Save Our Seas bumper stickers, was parked in the driveway. I made a mental note as I rang the bell to recommend that traffic patrol post a unit to slow the speeding on Collier Boulevard. The road noise would keep anything but a hibernating bear up at night. Did Winter have hearing problems?

As soon as the door swung open, I knew it was the girl in the CCTV footage. Jolene Winter was outfitted in Lululemon wear. She knew I was coming and didn't change out of her exercise clothing. She was either unworried or faking it.

I stepped in, realizing she was shoeless. Winter was wearing socks made like gloves, with a space for each toe. How uncomfortable was that? We went to her kitchen, where a cinnamon candle was burning. A bowl of grapefruits anchored the table.

"Thanks for calling the hotline, Ms. Winter."

"I was totally surprised you were looking for me. Mary, from the studio, told me she saw me on TV. I thought she was fooling around at first."

"What were you doing at the David Lawrence Center the morning of April fourth?"

"Applying for a job."

"A job? Are you a mental health professional?"

She smiled. "Not exactly. I'm a meditation yoga instructor. There's plenty of data proving that a combination of meditation and yoga relieves anxiety and—"

"You're telling me that you walked into the Lawrence Center at eight thirty in the morning of April fourth looking for work."

"Absolutely. Why else would I have gone there?"

"Do you know Ethan Dwyer?"

"I do now."

"Did you know him when you entered the Lawrence Center?"

"No. I didn't know anything about him. I didn't even know he was a serial killer."

"Who were you going to see about this trainer job?"

"I'm not a trainer. I am a certified yoga therapist."

"Okay. Who did you go to see?"

"No one in particular."

"You walked in looking for employment out of the clear blue sky?"

"You never know when good things are going to happen. You have to be open to them. You can't live in fear of rejection."

"Why go at eight thirty in the morning?"

"I teach a nine thirty class at the Yoga Loft in Mercato."

"You walked in at eight thirty a.m. and left minutes later. Why?"

"I realized I was in the wrong place."

"There are at least five different entrances you could have chosen. Why that entrance?"

"I asked a landscaper where human resources was, and he pointed to it."

"There's a receptionist right inside the entrance. Why didn't you ask her?"

"As soon as I walked in, I could tell it didn't feel right. I'm good with those things."

"But you didn't turn right around and leave."

"I had to use the bathroom."

"So, now you leave the building. Where did you go?"

"I went to work."

"You went to work? I thought you went to apply for a job."

"I headed over to the administrative entrance, and there was a big no solicitation sign. It didn't feel right to push it. Besides, I didn't like the vibrations of the whole scene there. I couldn't imagine teaching there. It would bring me down."

Was it possible for someone to concoct a story like that as an alibi? I wasn't crossing her off, but if I couldn't find a connection between her and Dwyer I'd have to back away.

***

My phone pinged. Warden Franklin had sent an email. Franklin offered inmates who had contact with Dwyer in the Immokalee jail incentives to reveal what they knew about Dwyer. I had to hand it to the warden, he was resourceful. Providing more time outdoors and a carton of cigarettes was a low-cost incentive. It wouldn't turn a hard-core convict into a singer, but the type of prisoners likely to interact with Dwyer would salivate at the chance to tell what they knew.

Franklin had signed statements from twenty-one inmates who had each paid Dwyer thirty dollars for answers on GED tests. That was six hundred and thirty dollars that Dwyer pocketed. The duality of helping inmates get a degree to make their reentry easier while financing his escape was ingenious. Franklin said the boost in jailbirds getting a high school equivalency degree was attributed to Dwyer's tutoring.

The warden also uncovered a handful of prisoners who said they bought cigarettes from Dwyer. This confirmed my suspicion that Dwyer had conned his visitor friend to raise cash. What other ways could Dwyer have added to his nest egg?

Assuming Dwyer had no outside help, he had a stash that was closing in on nine hundred dollars. And that was just from the test scam and cigarette sales. Who knew what other schemes he'd concocted? There was also the chance that Dwyer might have a lockbox somewhere stuffed with cash.

Did Dwyer use any of the funds to bribe anyone? He could have paid off the prison guards for something. What about paying the guard or someone at the David Lawrence Center?

Chapter 19

Friday the sixteenth was covered. I added a couple of names of people who'd been at the barbecue that night, but worried it amounted to overkill. On to Saturday. After coffee, Mary Ann and I went for a walk. We got back just before ten. We ate breakfast and showered. Around 2 p.m., we drove up to Koreshan Park to check out the antique car show.

We left the park around four, stopped for groceries at the Publix on Bonita Beach Road and picked up dinner from Pincher's. I used my credit card to pay for the takeout. We were home just after six and stayed home the entire night.

Sunday, we followed the same morning routine as Saturday. Mary Ann left for her friend's baby shower at 1 p.m. I put down closer to 2 p.m. She didn't get back until 8 p.m. I had to fill six hours. I looked up what sports were on TV that afternoon. The Pro Bowl was on. It was something I would never, ever watch, but it ate up four hours. Then it was the news and grilling dinner before Mary Ann came home.

Monday was another problem. I used the community gym and came back just before 10 a.m. I showered and had breakfast. I told Mary Ann I had a headache, so I put that down, stating that Mary Ann was home with me all day and night except for two hours when she went shopping.

Reading back what I'd written, I changed a couple of words and added a bit more detail. I hoped it would be good enough to end the suspicion threatening to engulf me. That Derrick would come after me was something I never imagined. I always believed I was entitled to not only the benefit of doubt but special treatment. Was I wrong?

***

I was getting ready to go home when my desk phone rang.

"Detective Luca."

"Hello, Detective Luca, this is Dr. Acorn, from the David Lawrence Center."

"How can I help you?"

"I know you believe we're not cooperative, but something was reported to me, and I felt we had an obligation to pass it on."

"Thank you. What do you have to tell me?"

"It might be nothing, but a young woman, whose name I am unable to share, had a relapse and was readmitted yesterday. During the admissions interview she related an interaction with the individual who left the facility without authorization—"

"Ethan Dwyer?"

"Yes. This woman stated that on her previous stay with us that Mr. Dwyer had paid her twenty dollars to have her come by his room the morning he departed. He asked her to tell the guard she would be waiting for him in the locker room."

"Did Dwyer meet her there?"

"I don't believe so. She said Dwyer didn't want her to go to the locker room, just to tell the guard that she was going there."

"What else did she say?"

"That was all that was reported to me."

"Okay. The sheriff is handling the security breach. He'll want to speak with this woman."

"I'm afraid that's not possible. It would be a violation of her privacy."

"Ethan Dwyer is a serial killer, Dr. Acorn. She may have information to help put him back where he belongs."

"I suggest the he contact our legal department. Would you like their number?"

I wanted to ask that if someone she knew had been killed by Dwyer, would she change her tune, but the scramble in my head had come together. "Not at this time, Doctor."

A picture of Dwyer's plan emerged. Dwyer had complained to the guard about not having sex in over year. He must have solidified the officer's sympathy with a bribe, enlisting a patient to make the ruse real. Dwyer was too religious to have sex with a casual acquaintance. What he wanted was to get out of the guard's sight and into the locker room, stealing the clothes he escaped in.

I called Sheriff Chester with the information and went home.

***

As we looked over the menu, Mary Ann and I enjoyed a glass of Merlot at Citrus. We rarely ate on Fifth Avenue during the high season, but if we did, it was dinner outside at Citrus. The fish was fresh and the owners welcoming. I wanted to mark the day with a memorable dinner. Tonight, I was planning to tell Mary Ann I was ready to have a child. It had taken me time to process what Dr. Bruno had told me, and neither Mary Ann nor I were getting any younger.

A waiter was describing the specials when my phone rang. Mary Ann shifted her eyes, and I ignored the call. I passed on the special, ordering my usual, the tripletail. As soon as the waiter left, my phone rang again. I took a peek but didn't recognize the number and swiped the call away.

A minute later, the phone rang again.

"Let me see who this is."

I headed to the sidewalk. "Detective Luca. This better be good."

"Detective Luca. It's Bob DiBlasi, Ethan Dwyer's brother. I'm sorry to bother you, but I heard from Ethan."

"You did? When? What did he say?"

"He called a few minutes ago. I called you right away, like you said. I mean, after I told my wife."

"Good. You did the right thing. What did he say?"

"He said he was okay and wanted to see me. I told him he should turn himself in, that I was worried for his safety."

"Good. What else?"

"Ethan said he would never turn himself in and that there was no way you were going to catch him."

"He mentioned me by name?"

"Yes. He said Detective Luca can try and find me, but there was no way you would. He said you, and this is him talking, not me, that you didn't have the intelligence, you were no match for him."

"Well, I apprehended him once, and I'll do it again. I just hope he's in one piece when we do."

"You think he's in danger of being shot or killed?"

"That's entirely up to Ethan. We'd prefer not using force, but if he is threatening in any way, all bets are off."

"I hope he comes to his senses."

"Did he give you any idea of where he might be?"

"Not really. He said he wanted to see me, since it might be the last time."

"That sounds like he's still in the area, then."

"I guess so."

"Stay where you are. I'm coming over now."

***

As soon as I turned off Goodlette Frank onto Mangrove Bay, I noticed a couple of new homes had been built over the last year. It was a pretty collection of white clapboard houses in a Key West style. Most homes had docks leading to the Gordon River. That meant Gulf of Mexico access and expensive.

De Blasi had opened the door before I hit his driveway. He stepped outside, looking left and right. Dressed in red shorts and a Rat Pack T-shirt, he came down the driveway to meet me.

"You think Ethan is going to try and come over?"

"Not with my car out here."

"Oh, yeah, right."

"I thought it would be a good idea to discuss how another call should be handled."

"Sure. Come on in."

Seated on a gray couch, his wife shut the TV off as we entered. The home looked totally different. It was decorated beautifully and filled with furniture. I liked the skinny drapes hanging off the double-storied windows.

"This is my wife, Jenny."

She had a foreign look to her, with olive skin, and was wearing tight jeans with a Love Yoga Center T-shirt. Was that the same place the girl in the Lawrence Center video worked?

"Nice to meet you. I have to say, you did an amazing job. The place looks gorgeous."

She smiled, revealing ten thousand dollars' worth of porcelain veneers. "Thank you. It wasn't me, though. We had help."

"It looks great."

The couple sat on the couch, and I took a chair covered in corduroy fabric.

He said, "Detective Luca believes Ethan will call again."

I said, "Nothing is certain, but apparently Ethan feels safe with you."

He said, "Ethan never had anybody. His mother was brutally murdered, and then he went into an orphanage. My parents were good people. They took him in, and since that day I've looked after him. I had to. It wasn't easy at times but . . ."

She said, "What a shame, really. All that intelligence, but he was almost dysfunctional. It's proof madness and genius are just a hair apart."

I agreed, but said, "Above all, both of you have to be careful."

The wife leaned forward. "You think he'd hurt us?"

"No, I don't. However, you mustn't get drawn into anything. Even helping him with something that seems harmless, like money or food, would be construed as help. It would be considered aiding and abetting a felon."

The wife subtly nudged her husband with an elbow before clasping her hands. Had they been planning to assist Dwyer?

He said, "We'd never do that, Detective. We love Ethan, but we'd never break the law."

"Good. Now, if he calls, it would be best to have your lines monitored."

She said, "You want to tap our phones?"

"That would be ideal. The law doesn't permit us to listen in to all your calls, just the calls concerning a person of interest."

"And how does that work?"

"When a call comes in and the party calling is identified, we must drop the call if it isn't the individual we're interested in."

"So, you want to listen in on every one of our calls?"

"Only for a second or two, if it's not Ethan."

He said, "I'm okay with that."

"You are? Well, I certainly am not."

Was that because of the yoga connection I couldn't place? "I understand, ma'am. It's within your rights to decline. Besides, he would probably call your husband."

"Then why did you want to eavesdrop on my conversations?"

"We take a comprehensive approach, ma'am, especially when dealing with someone like Ethan Dwyer."

Her eyes flared.

He said, "That's fine. I don't have a problem. What do I need to do?"

"I'll have an authorization form sent to you. Just complete it, sign it, and send it back. Email is fine."

"Okay."

"I wanted to ask you about the call itself. Was there anything that might be a clue to where he was when he made the call?"

"Nothing comes to mind. I was pretty shocked when I heard his voice."

"Any background noises? Cars passing, horn honking, trains? Anything like that?"

"I'm pretty sure he was outside somewhere."

"What makes you believe that?"

"I don't know. It just felt like he was."

"I really need you to think about this carefully after I leave. Reconstruct the call, try to identify any background clues. Anything you come up with is helpful. If you think of anything, call me immediately."

"I will. It'll probably come to me in the middle of the night."

"That's okay, call me anytime. I mean it."

"Okay."

"One more thing. Do you know if Ethan had another lockbox? Or a place where he'd hide money?"

"I don't know. He was very secretive at times. But I wasn't around him all that much the last couple of years. It's possible he could have stashed something away. Ethan always had a plan."

Chapter 20

It wasn't backbreaking; it was eye blurring and tedious. One of my recommendations after moving down from New Jersey was to create a map identifying the locations of public and private cameras. It took a year for the idea to gain traction, but now we had a tool that saved time. The rate people were adding cameras required that the map be continually updated, but it was a worthwhile effort.

We knew that Dwyer had started out from the David Lawrence Center. He must have known about their surveillance as he appeared on only one camera. A witness dropped him at the Greyhound stop, but Dwyer avoided detection again. The thought that he could have obtained a copy of our map passed through my mind.

Had I elevated him to mythical warrior status and I was the underdog? It felt like trying to hold water in a hand. Dwyer had a sky-high IQ that intimidated me, and he was violent. It was difficult to tamp down the fear that he'd make a public fool of me, or worse.

I couldn't beat him backpedaling. They only way I was going to win the battle was by doing the work. I squared my shoulders and inserted a disc from a 7-Eleven on Collier Boulevard. It was the fifth feed I was reviewing and only a half mile from the Lawrence Center where Dwyer made his escape.

At a time stamp of 2:37 p.m., a man limped into view. He had Dwyer's build and the same jacket he was wearing on the Lawrence video. I stopped the tape and zoomed in. He had a ball cap pulled low and was looking at his feet as he walked. There was something about this guy, but he had a serious limp.

I hit play and watched the man swing his left leg out and around as he headed to the entrance. It was unnatural. Was this Dwyer? I stood and emulated the movement. The knee had to be locked to walk that way.

I'd run into a few guys who tried to throw me off with a fake limp. Most of them could only keep it up for a while. Then they would slip and walk naturally. Dwyer wasn't a regular guy. He'd probably put a brace on to prevent his knee from bending. My cell phone rang.

It was the sheriff, and he wasn't happy. He wanted to see me. Now.

***

The sheriff was wearing a stern look and a striped tie. He peered at me over his reading glasses. There was a file open in the center of his desk. Before my ass hit the seat, he said, "You have some explaining to do, and I want it straight."

"I'm sorry, sir. I don't understand what you're talking about."

He picked up a sheet a paper, hanging it between his thumb and forefinger. It was the accounting of my time in the Garrison case.

"The last thing you should be doing is playing dumb with me, Luca. Your statement, which you signed and attested to, made claims of your whereabouts for Sunday, February nineteenth and Monday, the twentieth. You stated that you were at home Sunday during the hours of two p.m. until Detective Vargas arrived at eight p.m. and Monday one p.m. until three p.m. Are you standing by that?"

"Uh, yeah. I mean yes, sir. I could be off on the times. It was weeks ago and my memory—"

"But you were home."

What did he know? "Yes."

"You are absolutely sure?"

"Yes, sir."

He set his reading glasses on the desk. "How do you explain the fact that two witnesses said they saw you leave your house in your car."

"Witnesses?"

"Your neighbors."

"Was this Derrick? He went behind my back? Talking to my neighbors? Who the hell does he think—"

"Shut it, Luca! Did you think this office wouldn't verify an alibi in a homicide case?"

"I think I'm due a certain respect, a damn presumption of innocence. I think my so-called partner shouldn't be sneaking behind my back. I'm your lead homicide detective, for God's sake."

"Exactly. We need to be sure that no special treatment is given. No one is above the law."

"I know, sir, but I feel like I'm being targeted."

"Why did you lie?"

"It wasn't a lie, I just went out for a ride."

"Where?"

He was quick but so was I. "Nowhere in particular. I was roaming around, hoping I'd run into Dwyer. He's out there somewhere, and sooner or later, I'm going to nail him."

"Why the hell didn't you just say so?"

"My partner seems to be gunning for me, and I thought if I said I was driving around it would give him something to shoot for."

"Now you're talking stupid."

I shrugged.

"It doesn't look good. I don't know if I'm going to be able to prevent this from being referred to Internal Affairs."

"Internal Affairs? Are you kidding me?"

"If I don't refer it, they'll think I'm covering up, showing favoritism."

Covering up? "Do you really have to?"

"I haven't made my mind up, but I'm leaning that way."

If Internal Affairs got ahold of this, it would be a disaster—a colonoscopy a proctologist would be proud of. They'd find out everything, including the fact I didn't change my underwear one day last month.

Should I say something to the sheriff? Could I trust him? Maybe by opening up to him I'd avoid the handoff to IA. I couldn't let this get out; my reputation would be ruined.

I had no one to confide in. Derrick was not only on the shit list, he was at the top of it. Mary Ann was out. It was something I didn't want her to know either. How could I make this go away? Even catching Dwyer wouldn't end the suspicion. What the hell was I going to do?

Chapter 21

We lingered around the lanai table after dinner. It was a beautiful night. The sun was sinking, painting the sky a reddish orange. We finally headed inside.

Mary Ann said, "Shouldn't we shut off the landscape lights?"

"Nah, keep 'em on."

"You were pretty quiet during dinner."

"Sorry. Dwyer is on my mind."

"You have to learn to shut it down when you're off the job."

"I know, but this bastard, he's trying to show me up."

"I don't know about that; you caught him once."

"That's it, though. He wants to outsmart me. Prove he's smarter than me, or anyone, for that matter. I need something to follow. What tactics do you use in the cybercrimes unit?"

"We rely on digital footprints. A person's browsing history, their emails, calendars, photos, that sort of data. It creates leads."

"Dwyer was locked up for more than a year."

"What about any computer or phone he had beforehand?"

"Uhm. We had pulled a bunch of information off it. I'll have to revisit it and see what I can piece together out of it."

"If you need us to check anything out."

"I'm wondering what we can do now to track him down. Even if he had a computer, we would never know—"

"We can set up a trap for him."

"What do you mean?"

"We can create a website about Dwyer, about the fact he broke out, the effort to find him, asking for help, for information about him."

"You think people are going to give information over the internet instead of calling?"

"No. We find that many of the people we're chasing are curious about it."

"Like a killer who goes back to the crime scene?"

"Exactly. But, in this case, he'd think he was invisible but he's not. We'd track every IP address that visits the site and run them down."

"There could be hundreds of thousands."

"We have tools to weed it down."

"I like this idea. A lot. How soon can you get it set up?"

"A day, max. We'll have to do some search engine optimization to make sure that when someone searches, our site comes up first."

"I don't think we can publicize it. Chester doesn't want the press heat."

"This doesn't need it. The less information that's public the more likely a web search would be used for information. Now, we'll need to put a couple of tidbits out there to keep him coming back."

"Oh, I'm gonna love throwing him off."

"We need to keep it real or else he'll get tipped off."

"You think someone like Dwyer would know we could track him through it?"

"Probably, but if we play it right we'll be fine. It almost always works. That's why we never say anything about it."

"If he checks from a café or phone, we won't be able to get a location."

"Frank, don't get too invested in this. You know better than anybody that it's just another tool."

"I know. It's just that I need all the help I can get with this one."

"You'll get him, Frank. I don't care how high his IQ is, you're a helluva lot smarter than him."

Her confidence was miles higher than mine. I was sparring with Rocky and losing.

***

The digital evidence that came off Dwyer's Nokia phone and HP laptop was in an inch-thick binder. The first pages listed all the calls he made and received over the year before we nailed him. There were nine hundred and sixty-three calls in total. It seemed like a lot, but it was less than half the average person. You discount the robocalls and we were down to six hundred and thirty.

Dwyer wasn't a gabber either. Most calls were under two minutes. I remembered going through his calls. My buddy with the FBI was able to lean on the telephone company to identify the nearby cell phone towers the calls used and then to triangulate the location. It was invaluable data that placed Dwyer near various crime scenes.

Who on this list might be harboring Dwyer? If not hiding him, was someone helping him with food or money? The one name connected to the majority of calls was Robert DiBlasi, Dwyer's half brother. It was more proof just how close they were. Dwyer had been house-sitting for DiBlasi, and a lot of the calls were short, of a touch-base duration.

Dwyer had no real friends, just acquaintances, we had discovered. There were just a couple of female names on the list. We had interviewed several women, which led nowhere.

I had an idea: focus on incoming calls from women. Dwyer could have rejected the overtures of one of these women before he got in trouble. Now, in need of help, who better to turn to than someone who was interested in him?

In addition, I couldn't explain it, but there seemed to be no shortage of women attracted to men in jail. There were forty-seven incoming calls from females. Twenty-three of them called twice. I put their contact details into a spreadsheet and moved on.

The sheer number of web searches was staggering. It made me think of how many times a day I popped something into the search bar. Originally, I was looking for connections between Dwyer and any of the bodies. We also searched to see if he visited any sites that gave advice about hiding evidence or evading law enforcement.

What was I looking for now? If Dwyer was the meticulous planner he was looking like, were there any searches on locations to move to? Anything travel related? How to go underground and stay invisible? Survivalist guides?

Dwyer didn't strike me as someone to go off the grid, but chasing killers, I learned never to rule anything out without researching it. In the original investigation, we never uncovered anything pointing to an additional lockbox or bank account.

Dwyer kept as low a digital profile as was possible these days. I scanned the alphabetical list of websites accessed on Dwyer's computer. Though nothing jumped off the page, I made a copy.

Chapter 22

Usually I only put the lanai TV on when there was a tennis match or game I wanted to watch. As I waited for the grill to heat up, I flicked the remote, and ESPN came to life. Watching ex-footballers talk about the game was a turnoff, and I switched it to WINK News.

Flipping a turkey burger over, the newscaster caught my attention with a story about the Collier County Sheriff's Department. The anchor stated that the sheriff's office had confirmed an investigation looking at the possibility that a member of the force was involved in a murder.

There was no mention of the officer or the victim, but I knew what this meant. I glanced through the sliders. Mary Ann was chopping vegetables and the TV was off. I put a soccer game on the lanai TV and continued grilling.

***

I was rinsing the dishes and loading them into the dishwasher as Mary Ann wiped the table. The smell of Windex made me gag; she always used too much of it. The doorbell rang and Mary Ann went to the door.

"Who is it, Mary Ann?" She didn't answer. I put a detergent pod in, selected a light wash, and closed the dishwasher. I heard her talking. There were two male voices. I went to see if it was who I suspected it to be.

As soon as I entered the foyer, I heard her tell them to wait a minute. She closed the door and whispered, "What's going on, Frank?"

"Who is it?"

"Internal Affairs."

"You kidding me?"

"They said it's about the Garrison homicide."

"This is bullshit."

"Really? IA comes to our house, at night, to take you down for questioning about a murder, and it's all bullshit?"

"They're just acting like cowboys. You know how these—"

I felt her hot breath on my face as she hissed, "What have you done?"

I stepped around her. "It's going to be okay. Don't worry. I'll be back in an hour."

***

Internal Affairs was a necessary evil. Most of us distrusted the division that appeared to take aim at officers who were putting their lives on the line. It was easy for IA to criticize someone after an event. An officer has a split second to make a decision. By a large majority, the decision made is the right one. However, from time to time, in the fog of the critical moment, a mistake occurs. It's part of the world we work in.

IA was there to keep the force honest, rooting out corruption and cover-ups. Most of us were all for it. The problem came with the gleeful headhunting that went on when an officer made a mistake. They were a part of the sheriff's department, but in name only. Zero socializing went on between the rank and file and those in IA.

Mckinsey and Troyer, their names sounded like an accounting firm. Neither of them said a word as I followed them from the parking lot into their basement quarters. I couldn't help snickering at the thought that IA was supposed to be all about daylight, yet they operated in a windowless environment.

We silently settled into an uncomfortably small room. Did they know I was claustrophobic and were using a tactic I believed in? It was my first time on this side of the table. I knew how this worked and wasn't going to give them anything. Mckinsey and Troyer were deliberate: make that robotic, as they set up the recording devices and gathered their files.

Mckinsey, who looked like a block of granite topped with a mop of sandy hair, recited the formalities. As his last word faded, Troyer said,

"Things will go easier for you, Detective, if you're up front. A voluntary disclosure is something the department looks favorably upon. Whatever has happened is not going to change. However, the consequences of those actions can be softened by your cooperation. Is there anything you would like to disclose at this time?"

"No."

Mckinsey said, "Are you certain?"

"Yes."

Troyer put on a pair of granny glasses and flipped open a file. "You were the one who first discovered the body of James Garrison. Is that correct?"

"Yes."

"James Garrison was an informant for a case Detective Mary Ann Vargas was working. You cohabitate with Detective Vargas. Is that correct?"

"Yes."

"Detective Vargas filed a complaint that Garrison had harassed her."

Mckinsey looked at me for a response, but it wasn't a question. It was a statement. I stared back and Troyer said, "Witnesses claim you threatened James Garrison at least two times. Is that accurate?"

"Twice."

Mckinsey flashed a smile. "Adding in the menacing voice mail you left Garrison would make three, wouldn't it?"

I nodded.

Troyer chirped. "Witness nods affirmatively. Now, this threatening message, you left it two days before Garrison went missing, correct?"

"There is no way to verify he went missing two days after."

"No one saw James Garrison two days after your call to him. During the call, you stated that you would kill him and throw him into acid. When you reported finding Garrison's body, a rapid decomposition agent, such as the acid you said you would throw him in, was used to disguise his identity, correct?"

"Yes."

"How do you account for the timing of your call and the discovery of his acid-ravaged body?"

"Coincidence."

Mckinsey pulled a sheet from the file. "This is the time line of your whereabouts that you submitted to Sheriff Chester. In this sworn statement, you claimed to be at home alone during periods on Sunday and Monday, which proved false, correct?"

"An oversight. I was out scouting the area looking for Ethan Dwyer, a serial killer who escaped."

"Your subsequent oral revision, made after witnesses reported they saw you leave your neighborhood, claimed that you drove around hoping to sight Ethan Dwyer. Is that correct?"

"That's what I said."

"And that's all? Or would you like to make a further revision?"

"That's all."

Mckinsey and Troyer exchanged glances. Mckinsey said, "That's unfortunate. Video surveillance places you within a half of a mile of where Garrison's body was dumped."

"I said I was driving around."

"On both days you happened to be there?"

"I drove around trying to find Dwyer."

"We have CCTV of you on foot."

How the hell? "I can explain."

Chapter 23

Mary Ann was sitting in the family room. *The Tonight Show* was on, but the TV was muted. I barely set foot into the room when she said, "I don't know what is going on, Frank, but it doesn't feel good."

She shifted away when I touched her shoulder. "Don't worry. I can explain everything."

"I want it straight. If you did something, I want to know. I deserve at least that much from you."

I sat on the couch. "Of course you do. I was doing it for you."

"You didn't . . ."

"No, no."

"Then why was IA here?"

"There was a question about my whereabouts on Sunday and Monday."

"When I wasn't home?"

"Yeah, I went out."

"Where? Why didn't you tell me?"

"I don't want you to get mad, okay?"

The blood drained from her face. "Don't tell me you're having an affair?"

"No. I would never do that. It's just that it's embarrassing."

"Frank, you can tell me anything, you know that. Just say whatever it is. We'll deal with it together."

"I went to a psychologist."

Her eyes widened. If I would have told her I was out killing Garrison, she wouldn't have been as surprised.

"A psychologist? You mean someone to talk with?"

I nodded.

"What is bothering you, Frank? Tell me what's wrong."

"It's not that anything is wrong, it's just that I wanted to be sure . . ."

"You mean us?"

"No, about us having a baby. I know how much it means to you, and I know it would be good, but I was worried and wanted to be sure that if we have a baby that things between us would get better."

Mary Ann took my hands. "Oh, Frank, that's so sweet."

"I guess I was just nervous."

"There's nothing to be nervous about. We'll be fine. Oh my God, I can't believe it. I was so afraid you were going to tell me you had something to do with Garrison's death, and instead you're telling me we can have a baby. I've never been so happy in my entire life."

She jumped in my lap and started crying.

"What are you crying for? We should be celebrating?"

"I'm happy. Trust me. I just can't believe it. I thought it would never happen, and I started to accept that. Boy, did you surprise me. You're the best, Frank."

"You're not too bad either."

"You don't have to say anything if you don't want to, but what was bothering you?"

"Just a bunch of little things. I know things are going to change, but I didn't want us to change, if you know what I mean."

"Never. We have to keep our relationship front and center. Was that it?"

"And the job. You know how important being a homicide detective is to me. I realize I'll have to dial down the hours, but I really love what I do."

"No one is asking you to change, Frank. I don't know what the doctor said, but having a family will give your job new meaning."

"I know. Let's celebrate. I'll open up a bottle of prosecco."

"It's late."

"It's not that late. We have to celebrate."

"Okay."

"Great."

"Oh, maybe I shouldn't. The doctor said I shouldn't be drinking."

"Are you kidding me? You're not pregnant, Mary Ann."

"I know, but I was reading that there are studies that indicate alcohol consumption reduces a woman's fertility, especially in mature women."

My fear that things were going to change came to fruition. In less time than it took to tie my shoes, I was living with a different woman. I'm all for healthy lifestyles, especially when carrying a baby. But this was a clear indication of how obsessed she would be.

"This is exactly what I was worried about."

"What? What did I do? I'm just trying to be careful."

"Careful? I'd call it obsessed."

"That's not true."

"This is supposed to be one of those memorable nights but . . . just forget it."

"No. I'm sorry if I ruined it for you, Frank. I really am."

***

Barry White was crooning, and the aroma of mushrooms and garlic wafted through the air. Mary Ann was singing along as she opened a bottle of wine. Lovemaking music, pasta ai funghi, and wine? Normally, my libido would get an earthquake-sized jolt, but the staging was disappointing and transparent. She was manipulating me.

I caught Mary Ann's eye, and she rushed over, pressing her hips into me as she kissed my cheek.

"You've set some mood here."

"I wanted to make up for last night. You were right; I was overreacting."

"It's okay."

"Let me get you a glass of wine."

"You're drinking?"

"I'll have a little."

"You want to get this over with so we can eat?"

"What?"

"Trying to make a baby. We can do it before dinner, and then you can relax."

"Look who's ruining things now?"

She was right. I was acting like an immature jerk. "Sorry. It's just that I want things to be normal. It's got to happen naturally. We can't force it."

"I'm not forcing it. I just wanted to make up for last night, you know, get you in the mood."

I put my arms around her, grinding against her. "I was born in the mood."

She looped her leg around mine. "And how."

"How hungry are you?"

"Not at all."

I took her hand and headed for the bedroom.

"Hold on. Let me shut off the stove."

Chapter 24

It was weird. I should have gone into Chester's office with my chest out, but I couldn't muster a confident attitude. There was no doubt I was pissed off about the suspicion heaped on me. Derrick was dead to me. There was no way I could work with him. Chester was another matter. I felt he could've been a better advocate for me. But deep down I knew he had to handle it the way he did.

The sheriff had been in a tough spot. If he felt bad, there might be an opportunity to use it to my advantage. As I strolled in, I resolved that if a crack appeared, I was going to push my way in.

Chester rose, extending his hand. "I'm sorry, Frank. I hope you understand the position this office was in."

The office? "It was disappointing, sir."

"I understand completely."

"Thank you."

"I don't know if it's related, and if it was, it's perfectly understandable."

"What's that, sir?"

He cleared his throat. "Your visiting with a psychologist."

"Oh."

"Did the visits have anything to do with the accusations made against you in the Garrison case?"

"What? Of course not. I'm sorry, sir, but this is another attack on my character. There's no doubt it was frustrating to have your partner think you were involved in a homicide, but I'm tough enough to handle it."

"I didn't mean to infer anything, Frank. It was just something I needed to ask about. The mental state of our force is of utmost importance. If any of our men or women are struggling with anything, I want them to have the time needed to—"

"It was a personal matter. If you want to know, I'll tell you."

He remained silent. That was a yes.

"Mary Ann and I are thinking about have a child together. It was something I wanted to be sure about. I felt talking about it would help me be certain I was doing it for the right reasons."

Relief spread across his face. "That's wonderful, Frank. I mean, the part about the two of you going to try and have a family."

I wasn't in the mood to open any more curtains and said, "Is that all, sir?"

"Actually, the reason I wanted to speak with you was about the Garrison case. After the news that there was an internal investigation, the media woke up to it. Since they ended up looking like fools with their coverage, they're suddenly interested in how we're going to solve it."

Much as I wanted to remind him how complicit his department was, it would do me no long-term good.

"How can I help, sir?"

"I would like you to head up the investigation and to bring it to a swift close."

"What about the Dwyer case?"

"You're the best in the business. You can handle both of them, can't you?"

Did he realize how transparent and manipulative he was acting? Yesterday my word meant nothing, and today I was the golden boy. The real question was not my ability to catch crooks but how long Chester's sun would shine on me.

"I know it's not my role to ask, but the fact is, working with Derrick Dickson is nearly impossible for me at this time. Partners need to trust each other implicitly to be effective. And I can tell you that after all of this, I no longer trust Detective Dickson."

"I'm sorry to hear that, Frank. I'm sure if you give it some time, things will—"

"Excuse me, Sheriff. It's not going to get better between us now or ever. I'll take the Garrison case back, but if you expect me to quickly close it, working with Dickson is not going to cut it. I'm sorry, but that's the way I feel."

Chester clasped his hands and studied me. "Since Garrison was a dealer, I'll ask Hanlon to assign someone from Narcotics."

"I'd rather work with Detective Vargas, sir."

"Frank, I'm willing to work with you, but you know the department has rules about that."

"Detective Vargas knew Garrison. She knows the players. It'll speed the case along. Plus, she worked the original Dwyer case."

"This would require an exemption."

"Working with her, we'd hit the ground running. If I have to work with someone new, someone who is not a homicide detective, it's going to take a lot more time. I'd appreciate if you considered my request."

"I'll think it over."

"Thank you, sir. And remember, working with Detective Vargas would be a temporary thing."

Chapter 25

Normally, I would have felt bad pushing Chester like this. But going through what I had, I was feeling barely a tinge of regret as I went for a scheduled leak.

Sitting on the toilet to take a piss had become the new normal for me. Originally, I was embarrassed at peeing like a woman and the time it took to relieve myself, but I'd adapted and used the break to think.

I shuffled into a stall, covered the seat and made myself comfortable. Which way was Chester going to go? Would he really run the interference necessary to get Mary Ann back as a partner? It was doubtful, but at the least, Derrick would be history. The Garrison case wasn't something I was looking forward to running down. He was a dead drug dealer. Why would the department want to waste resources when we had Dwyer to pursue? And Dwyer was a challenge.

A big part of finding him was whether he had help or not. Whether someone helped him get out of David Lawrence was interesting and could be helpful, but what I thought mattered more was whether he had gotten, or was getting, assistance once he hit the street. A trickle of pee finally began as I considered what Dwyer needed.

Anybody on the run needed a place to hide, food, money, and patience. The only thing he didn't need help with was patience. Dwyer had a PhD in that. This guy waited years to exact his revenge. There was no doubt in my mind that he'd be able to stay low for as long as it took. He knew the attention would die down with time. But would Dwyer get the timing right?

The only thing that would keep him in the spotlight was if he went back to killing. Nothing focused the mind or the media like a corpse. It'd be easier if he went back to his murderous ways, and for a second, I found myself hoping he would. Shaking the thought away, I realized just how hard this was going to be. Dwyer was as smart as they come, and he knew how to play the long game.

Unless he made a mistake, and everyone does, it would take all that I had to catch him. I stood and zipped up, wondering if it were possible that Dwyer had prepared in advance for his escape. Without outside help he would have had to store resources. Could he have begun doing that once we started looking at him as a suspect?

Or had Dwyer found a place to hide and had stashed goods there when he started his killing spree? It seemed unthinkable that someone would have the discipline to plan so far in advance. Normally, the idea wouldn't be worth ruminating over, but Dwyer was anything but normal.

He had used a lockbox in the past. The chances he had another filled with money was high. What was risky was gaining access to it. If he had it under his own name, he'd never get close to it. Dwyer would need an alias and a disguise.

False identity documents, like a driver's license, were tougher to get than they used to be but more available than we'd like. He didn't strike me as the type of guy who would have the contacts needed for professional-looking documents. But doing his volunteer work at the church, he was surrounded by the type of people who knew where to get bogus papers.

I had to assume he was using an alias backed by phony documentation. But how would he disguise himself? Whatever he did, he had to do it when he applied for the box and it had to match his papers.

I left the bathroom thinking the level of meticulous planning and foresight necessary probably meant Dwyer had help. Someone with a hole he could hide in. Someone who could food shop and raid the lockbox when needed.

Dwyer was a loner. Most serial killers were. Whom could he trust? The words of his half brother rang in my ears: *I've looked after him. I had to. It wasn't easy at times, but . . .*

He also said he'd never break the law, but so did almost everyone behind bars. We had a tap on his phone, one he agreed to quickly. Was he covering up?

Chapter 26

Driving north on Santa Barbara Boulevard I pounded my palm against the steering wheel. I'd just crossed Golden Gate Boulevard. I was on my way to see the first woman who had called Dwyer, and I'd flubbed a fundamental. It was a reminder I didn't need of how chemotherapy had affected my thinking.

I should have mapped the women I assumed were interested in Dwyer for any overlays there might be. Instead, I decided to see Tammy Branch first because she had called Dwyer three times, not because she lived close to the David Lawrence Center.

Less than a half a mile from Golden Gate, I made a left onto Star Grass Lane. I parked in front of Tammy Branch's home and checked the map on the navigation screen. Dwyer could have walked along the canal that ran alongside Interstate 75 to Branch's street. It wouldn't have taken him more than ten minutes.

A yellow masonry fence encircled the large lot Branch's house was on. This was a perfect place to hide. Was Dwyer inside?

The driveway was gated but open. A pair of garbage pails stood near the curb. Maybe she left the gate open when dragging the cans out. I decided against hitting the call button by the gates; I'd claim to have not seen it if challenged.

A dog began barking as I trudged up the gravel driveway. I reached for my can of pepper spray, even though the dog sounded far away. A brown Subaru was parked under a carport housing five bicycles and a gaggle of hose that looked like it could reach Marco Island.

The door swung open before I could ring the bell. A tall, thin woman with long, gray hair peered at me over her pink glasses and closed the door. She was wearing several necklaces, and both arms were covered in bracelets.

"Can I help you?"

"Are you Tammy Branch?"

She seemed to debate how to answer.

"Yes. Why?"

She wasn't surprised at the sight of my badge. "I'd like to talk to you about Ethan Dwyer."

"There's nothing to talk about."

"I just need a few minutes of your time, ma'am."

"Well, go ahead, then. Make it quick."

"Can we do this inside?"

"No, I'm in the middle of cleaning."

"I don't mind. It's a bit hot out here."

"I'd rather not."

What was she hiding: a dirty house, or a felon?

"Okay. When was the last time you saw Ethan Dwyer?"

"Oh, a long time ago. I really can't remember."

"How did you meet him?"

"At the Spirit of Fellowship Church."

"Did the two of you date?"

"That's really none of your business, is it?"

"If you had a relationship with Mr. Dwyer, it is my business."

"Well, we didn't."

Why was she so hostile?

"Do you work or volunteer at the church?"

"I volunteer, though I'm up there so often they should pay me."

"Tired of volunteering?"

"No. I love working with Minister Booth and his people. They're doing God's work. He always says: We never judge, we help. It says it all."

Did these evangelical churches inoculate their members with something?

"The records indicate that you called Mr. Dwyer on several occasions. What was the nature of those calls?"

"I don't remember. I was probably returning his call."

Was that a female protecting her pride?

"Has Ethan Dwyer asked you for help before or after his escape from custody?"

"No. I told you, it's been a long time since I heard from him."

"Did Dwyer know where you lived?"

Another hesitation. "I'm not sure. But you can find anything out these days."

"Very true, ma'am. I think that's about all the questions I have."

"Good. You have a good day now."

"You too. Say, do you live alone?"

"Why?"

"It's quiet back here. Make sure you keep things locked up, okay?"

"I will."

I walked back to my car wondering why there were two trash cans at the curb. There was no doubt something was off with Ms. Personality. The question was, how far off?

***

Back behind my desk, I reviewed the addresses of the other women who'd called Dwyer. They were scattered around town, none within ten miles of the David Lawrence Center. I was about to check my email when I remembered the Greyhound bus stop.

Marie Vero lived on Monroe Avenue, a short walk from where Dwyer had been dropped off. I jumped in the car.

Vero's pale blue house had a roof that slanted to the right. There seemed to be six apartments in the one-story building. I skirted a large puddle and knocked on the door. Vero had large eyes and a tiny waist. She reminded me of an anxious teenager from the fifties.

I showed her my badge and the color drained from her face. "I have a couple of questions about Ethan Dwyer."

"Ethan? Oh. Come in. I don't know why you want to ask me about him."

It was a small place. There was one door that was closed. It had to be the bedroom. Was Dwyer trying to crawl under the bed? Or was it out a window? She stepped toward the kitchen. I pulled a chair out and sat. Vero grabbed the back of a chair but pushed it back under the table.

She circled the kitchen, touching herself as if she was checking if she was still there. She was making me jumpy.

"You can relax, Ms. Vero. Unless you have something to hide . . ."

"He said he'd kill me. I didn't want to help him. I was scared—"

"Hold on. Take it easy. Tell me what happened."

"Am I going to be in trouble?"

"That'll depend on what you did to help him."

"But I was forced to. He made me."

"Then you have nothing to worry about. If you feared for your safety, you'll be okay."

"I was fearing, I mean, I was scared to death."

"Calm down. What happened?"

"I was watching *Dancing with the Stars*; it's my favorite show. And there was a knock on the door."

"What day was this?"

"Last Thursday."

The same day Dwyer had gotten a ride to the Greyhound stop. "What time was this?"

"Just after the show started at eight. I didn't even get to see one dance."

Where had Dwyer hidden? "Okay. Dwyer knocks on the door and you answer."

"Yeah. I was shocked. I didn't expect to see him standing there."

"What did he look like? Was he wearing a disguise of any kind?"

"He was wearing one of those straw hats, not a floppy one, but like a fedora, but made of straw."

"Facial hair?"

"Yeah, he had a bit of a beard. I was surprised there was so much gray in it."

"What was he wearing?"

"He had on a light jacket, a windbreaker, and jeans. With sneakers."

"Did he threaten you?"

"Not exactly, but I felt scared, you know. He kind of pushed his way in when I opened the door. And he had a phony limp."

"How do you know it was phony?"

"After he came in, he didn't limp anymore."

"Can you show me how he limped? And what leg was it?"

"Uh, it was his left. I'm pretty sure." Vero swung her leg out as she walked. "It was like this."

"Did Dwyer have a weapon?"

"I didn't see one, but he kept patting his side. His jacket was covering something. I'm telling you, I thought it was a gun, and it was scary."

I wanted to tell her to stop embellishing, but the safer she felt, the better the chances were that she would tell me everything. "It must have been frightening. Tell me what happened next."

"He said he was hungry. I asked him what he wanted, and he said anything quick. I opened a can of tuna and made him a sandwich. He had the nerve to take three of my cans with him."

"After he ate, then what?"

"You know, when he was eating, he mentioned your name."

"My name?'

"Yeah, he said he was going to get you."

"Get me? Did he say how?"

"He didn't say, but he was pissed."

He was coming after me. There was no choice—I had to get to him first. "After he made his threats, what happened next?"

"He asked to use my cell phone."

"He made a call?"

"First, he was searching on the internet for a while. I asked him if he needed help, but he said no. Then he made two calls."

"What did he say when he made the calls?"

"I couldn't tell. He was covering the phone and he was by the bathroom when he talked."

No point telling her now that her phone was coming with me. "I understand. After the calls, what did he do next?"

"Well, he sat down for a minute, and then he used the bathroom."

"To relieve himself or to wash up?"

"I'm pretty sure both."

"Was Dwyer carrying a bag with him?"

"No."

"What happened next?"

"I think it was about nine thirty, and he said we had to go. He asked me for my car keys. I thought he was gonna take my car, but he said I was coming with him. I was in a total panic. I thought I was gonna be kidnapped, you know?"

"It must have been frightening."

"It was. And then he asked me for money. I was like, are you kidding me? Here I am struggling to make ends meet, and you want my money?"

"How much did you give him?"

"A hundred and twenty."

It was probably more like fifty. "And then what?"

"He drove up to Bonita, downtown by the band shell. He pulled over and told me that if I said anything about tonight, he'd come back and kill me. I believed him, that's why I never said anything or called the police. I mean, he killed a lot of people, and I figured I'd be next."

"He got out and left you there?"

"Yeah, but he took my keys and said they'd be on the stairs to the band shell."

"Were they?"

"Yeah. He ran off, and I went and got my keys and got away from there as fast as I could. I was shaking, I was so scared."

"You're going to have to come in with me."

"But why? I didn't do anything. I was afraid for my life."

"We'll need you to make a statement under oath, and I'll have to take your phone. It's evidence."

***

Thinking about whether Dwyer had the means to get at me or Mary Ann kept me up. I slipped out of bed and went around the house, making sure the sliders were all closed and locked. Looking out a back window, I thought about how masterful Dwyer was at finding a way to get a message out. But was what he said to Vero about getting me an attempt to scare me or a slipup about his true intentions?

Could Dwyer really count on us finding Vero and her spilling what she knew? If he was trying to threaten me off his trail, there were a lot of other ways to make sure the message reached me. I slid back into bed, hoping the sound of the rain would put me to sleep. It was nearly one thirty, and I needed to rest.

An explosion shook the house. Bolting upright, I grabbed the pistol on my nightstand. It was 3:07 a.m. Had Dwyer made good on his promise?

"Frank! What's going on?"

"Get in the closet! Now. Don't come out until I tell you to."

Hugging the wall, I made my way to a window overlooking the street. Our neighbors were huddled in the street.

I ran to our closet. "It's okay. I think something happened at the McGowan's." I pulled on a pair of sweatpants.

"Are they okay?"

"Looks like it. I'm going over there. Stay inside the house until I get back."

Sirens were closing in. I jammed the gun in my waistband and left the house.

It wasn't Dwyer this time. A bolt of lightning had struck the small propane tank on the McGowan's barbeque on the side of their house. The McGowans were lucky that houses down here are made of cinder block.

Chapter 27

Garrison had a longtime relationship with a woman named Melissa Crandall. The two lived together three different times but had separated ten months before he vanished. Crandall lived in a neat, cinder block home near the intersection of Radio Road and Santa Barbara Boulevard. I pulled in front and looked around before heading up the driveway.

Stepping around a tricycle, I pressed the doorbell. A forty-year-old woman in a red tank top and shorts opened the door.

"Good morning, ma'am. I'm Detective Luca, with the Collier County Sheriff's Department."

"This about Jimmy?"

"Yes, ma'am."

She looked at my badge and stepped back. "Oh my God. Detective Luca? You're the one that the papers said was involved in Jimmy's death."

"I have been completely cleared. I had nothing to do with it."

"There wasn't anything in the papers about that."

"You know how that goes, ma'am, quick to make an accusation, but they forget about making a lot of noise with a retraction."

She studied me a couple of seconds before stepping aside. I entered the main room, which appeared to serve a number of purposes. A contingent of plastic trucks fronted a couch with a pile of laundry sitting on it.

"Sorry, I was folding laundry. Let's go into the kitchen."

A bamboo fan spun lazily as we sat around a white Formica table. Crandall pulled open the refrigerator, sending a crayon drawing to the floor.

"Who is the artist?"

"My son, Jason. He's six."

"Nice. Is he in school?"

"Yeah. My mom watches him afterward. I have to go to work."

"Is Jason James Garrison's son?"

"No. I had him when we were broke up. We had a long breakup, almost two years . . ."

"Got it. I know you weren't together when James was murdered, but I'm looking for information to bring whoever did it to justice."

"He was a good man. I know, he was dealing in drugs. He promised to stop, but that's what really ended things between us. I have Jason, and the older he got, it just wasn't right, you know, to be around that type of stuff."

Love was another form of addiction. "Jimmy Garrison was dealing drugs for a very long time."

"But he used to stop, at least he seemed to. Look, I had nothing to do with what he was doing. Like I said, if it wasn't for the dealing, we'd have stayed together. But instead of him getting out of it, he went in deeper, and I had to leave, not only for Jason but for me. I didn't like it one bit."

"You mentioned him getting in deeper. What did you mean by that?"

"He always said the safest place to be was not on the street dealing but up a step from there. He said the guys on the street were always getting busted, and the cops always went after the top guys, so you needed to be in the middle. Maybe he said that to shut me up, but it made sense."

"And about getting deeper?"

"Oh yeah. It was before we broke up, and it was kinda the spur for me to leave. Jimmy said he was going out on his own, saying he was going to be a supplier. I told him it was crazy, but he said he would make a lot of money and that we'd live really good. When I said I didn't want any part of it, he said he was just doing it to make enough money to retire from it. I knew he wouldn't stop, and that was it for me."

"Do you know if he had permission from the guys he worked for to step out on his own?"

"I don't think so. He was telling Felix about his plans, and I overheard him talking."

"Felix?"

"Hernandez. He worked with Jimmy. He was a pretty good guy. I liked him."

Another dealer who was nice. She claimed not to know where he lived, but it wouldn't be tough to track Hernandez down. I was looking for something: what it was, I didn't know, just something to grab on to.

"Do you know if Jimmy actually went through with his plans?"

"Yeah, he did. He tried to get me back, flashing money around and buying Jason expensive toys."

"Did you know if the people James worked for were upset with him for leaving and going into competition with them?"

"He said something about there being a struggle for control. About some Miami gang coming into the area, and Russians too. He said it was a good time to go on his own."

We knew who Garrison had worked for, and Boy Scouts they weren't. Getting knocked off for challenging the leadership made perfect sense to keep order. And dumping his body into a vat of acid sent a powerful message to anyone with similar aspirations.

"Was Jimmy able to save money?"

She laughed. "You kidding? Jimmy holding on to money was like telling a kid not to eat their Halloween candy."

Either a supplier would front the drugs, or Garrison would need someone to stake him the cash needed to make at least one large buy. "Did he have any well-off friends? Someone who would lend him the money he'd need to go out on his own?"

"I don't know how much he'd need for that. I made sure I stood far away from that type of stuff. I would have left earlier, but I didn't have anywhere to go."

She was pedaling away from Garrison like an Olympian. I wanted to remind her about the mother she mentioned earlier but refrained. She knew more about the dealing than she would ever admit, but I was investigating a homicide, not a narcotics ring.

I left believing it was probably a case of revenge. Jimmy Garrison stepped out of line, and it cost him his life.

Chapter 28

It was all new German cars sitting in front of a bodega a few miles from the Corkscrew Swamp Sanctuary. The back room of Bodega Tequila was the unofficial office of the drug crew that Garrison had worked for. As soon as I walked in the man by the register reached below. I wasn't alarmed; he wasn't reaching for a weapon. The stooge was ringing a bell alerting the rear room a cop was on the premises.

Asking to see Felix Hernandez, the lookout spoke in Spanish to a woman bursting out of an apron. The waitress waddled me to the back door. She knocked, said something in Spanish, and Hernandez opened the door.

Felix Hernandez had dark olive skin and large hands. His black hair was slicked back, attempting to cover a bald spot on the crown of his head. His teeth were good. He wasn't a user of the crap he peddled.

I showed my badge. "Detective Luca, homicide."

"Homicide?" Hernandez had a trace of an accent I placed as Honduran.

"I have questions about Jimmy Garrison."

"What 'bout?"

I looked over his shoulder. Four men holding cards stared back at me. "Your call. We can do this here or somewhere private."

He brushed past me into a front booth. I slid in opposite him.

The waitress toddled over. Hernandez said, "You want anything?"

I said no and he waved her away.

"About Garrison, I understand the two of you were friends."

He nodded, pulling a toothpick out of a dispenser. "Not so close, but yeah, we got along."

"You know who did this to him?"

Gnawing on the toothpick, he shook his head.

"Look, they dumped your buddy in a vat of acid. We had a hard time identifying the body."

"Was he dead before they dumped him in?"

Not knowing that fact meant Hernandez probably wasn't privy to who did it. The coroner said Garrison had been dead before getting eaten by acid, but I needed sympathy.

"I wish he were. Man, I can't even imagine how bad it must have been for him."

Under his breath he said, "Those fuckers."

"Who? Tell me who did this."

"I don't know. I wish I did. I feel bad for Jimmy."

"I understand that Garrison went out on his own."

He nodded.

"Him going solo must have pissed off the guys you work for."

He shrugged.

"You know what I think? I think the crew you work for killed Jimmy, sticking him in acid to keep everyone else in line."

"Look, at the time Jimmy stepped out things were changing, man. They hardly missed him. It's not like he took anything with him. There's plenty of customers, if you didn't know."

"You're trying to tell me he left to sell on his own, and nobody gave a damn about it?"

He tucked the toothpick in the corner of his mouth and said, "That's the way it went down."

"That's hard to believe, given the way the cartels value a life."

"These guys are Chileans. They're nothing like Colombians or Mexicans."

"Drug dealers are all the same to me."

"You're wrong, man. The Chileans are not violent people."

It was a first for me: a sociology lesson from a drug pusher. "You must know something about who might have murdered your friend."

"I don't know anything."

I leaned across the table. "Anything you tell me will be held in strict confidence. You have my word."

He slid out of the booth. "I don't know nothing."

I believed him. He knew more than he was saying, but if it wasn't the gang Garrison had broken away from, who killed him and put him in acid? Someone was sending a supersonic message about stepping out of line. It smelled like a drug killing. Hernandez thought the Chilean dealers were pacifists, but I was far from convinced.

***

When I turned my phone back on there was a message from Chester. He wanted to see me about my "partner requests." I listened to the message twice; there was something in the way he spoke that made me uncomfortable. He couldn't deny me, could he?

I was letting my insecurity get the better of me. Chester had no choice. Dwyer was on the loose, and he wanted him caught more than he wanted to follow any department rules governing lovers from working together. Chester was a politician; he'd find a way to temporarily get around the rules. Mary Ann and I would be hunting Dwyer together in the morning.

Was being around baby-obsessed Mary Ann, twenty-four seven, a good idea? Another case of being careful of what you wished for? I decided that putting up with the hormonal thing was still a good trade for the protection she offered my chemo brain.

In fact, the person I was going to see was someone Mary Ann had asked me about. It was another case where I seemed to miss the obvious. I had interviewed Garrison's longtime girlfriend, figuring she knew him best. However, I never thought to see the woman he was living with after he left her. Maybe I couldn't be trusted to work alone.

***

A For Sale sign was planted in the lawn of the home where Garrison had lived with his girlfriend. It was a massive house for just two people. The Spanish-styled home was listed for almost three million dollars, and there was no mortgage on it—a normal bank loan, anyway. Garrison had come up with three million that quickly? It was more proof why the optionless were drawn to dealing.

Walking up a travertine path, I wondered who would get the three million dollars of equity. It was plenty of motive to get rid of Garrison.

It was a struggle not to be judgmental, but one look at Cynthia Ferris told me all I needed to know about her being a dealer's girlfriend. She had the entire package: fake boobs three sizes too large, puffed lips, a ton of makeup, and clothes that hugged her substantial curves.

Garrison had completed his makeover with Ferris, who was liable to get picked up by the vice crew when she took a walk. Was she the one that triggered Garrison's move from a low-level hood living with an understated woman with a kid to such flamboyance?

Ferris's shoulders sagged when she saw my badge. "Did you catch the guys who did it to Jimmy?"

"Not yet. I have some questions for you."

She looked over my shoulder and said, "You might as well come in."

There was a stack of cardboard boxes in a furnitureless room that could have been a dining room.

"When do you have to get out?"

"We'll see. The agent said, like, it's better if someone's living here. Buyers try to, like, steal it when they know it's empty."

"This is a big place for only two people."

"Jimmy really wanted it as soon as he saw it. He said, like, it was a once in a lifetime thing. It's not like I minded. I can't imagine moving out of here into some tiny apartment."

"This place must have cost a ton of money."

"It was, like, three million."

"Jimmy must have been making a lot of money."

She shrugged. "Guess so."

"You guess so? How else could he afford a place like this?"

"He was a businessman."

"Cut the crap. We all know Jimmy was dealing, okay? At this point, it doesn't matter. All I'm interested in is catching who did it."

"I still can't believe what they did to him."

"Who is 'they'?"

"I don't know."

"You gotta have some idea."

She picked at a cuticle but said nothing.

"Look, I'm looking for information. I don't care what he did or what you did or didn't do or what you know about Jimmy's business. My job is to find the killer. That's all I'm interested in."

"I don't know anything."

"Who was Jimmy working for?"

"He was in business by himself."

She was naive. "Where did he get his supplies from?"

"I don't know."

"We heard he was working with the Morales brothers out of Miami. Does that sound right to you?"

She nodded.

"Who gave Jimmy the money to step out on his own?"

"How would I know? When me and Jimmy started going together, he was, like, in his own business already."

"Who did he hang around with?"

"Nobody special."

"You're going to need to be more specific than that."

"Look, everyone has the wrong image of Jimmy, just because he did what he did. He was a loving guy. I know he ran around some, but you know what? He was turning into, like, a homebody. I think that's why he bought this place. He said he was finally knowing what was important in life. You know, he was even trying to start, like, a relationship with his kid."

Kid? Garrison had a child? "I'd heard about his kid, but it was long ago, right?"

"Oh, I think Jimmy was, like, in his midtwenties when he had him."

That would make the kid around ten. "The mother has custody?"

"No, she was an addict. I think she OD'd a couple of years ago."

"Who's taking care of the kid?"

"The grandma."

"You have a name for me?"

"I think it's Norma, or something like Edith."

"What about a last name?"

"Got no idea."

"Was Jimmy in contact with the kid?"

"He tried, but the old lady wouldn't let Jimmy near him."

"Did Jimmy have any family, siblings, or other children that you knew of?"

"No, I think that's why he was getting the way he was."

"Could it have been because of a death threat or something making him feel he was not going to be here much longer?"

"I don't think so. He was, like, just changing."

She gave me a little more information, but I needed to talk with Garrison's longtime girlfriend again.

Chapter 29

It was past the time for me to take a pee when Chester called me into his office. I had intended to relieve myself after talking with the sheriff, but he had made me so angry I had to flee the office before I lost it.

I slid behind the wheel of the Cherokee and let out a scream as I pulled out of the lot. How could he? I could understand rejecting my request to get Mary Ann back as a partner, but working with Derrick? No fucking way!

This guy expected me to work two cases with a partner I couldn't trust. Asking me to sit down with Derrick to smooth out what he called a misunderstanding bordered on delusional. A misunderstanding was a failure to understand something correctly, like a waitress screwing up an order at a restaurant. Or a guy in a bar misinterpreting a smile from a woman on the other end of the bar. Accusing your partner of murder and going behind his back was something entirely different, more like betrayal.

A walk on the beach always helped me get back in balance. I headed to Vanderbilt Beach, but I was way past the time to take a leak. Public bathrooms didn't work for me any longer. I now knew what women were up against by having to sit or crouch over a bowl. I never gave using a skanky bathroom a thought when I could stand. Now that I had to sit for fifteen to twenty minutes, I was particular as hell. I made a right onto Gulf Shore Drive, pulled into the driveway at La Playa and hustled to the bathroom.

I paused upon entering. It was the bathroom that I'd fainted in—the beginning of my battle with bladder cancer. The night started off with promise. Kayla was in from Chicago and we'd hit it off. She had me believing that I had finally found the one I was looking for. I still didn't know if it was the cancer that made me realize the one for me was there all the time—that the lifetime partner for me was Mary Ann.

Mary Ann had been my partner, and Chester had forced us apart. Why couldn't he have pushed to keep us together rather than caving in to the bureaucrats? The thought of being forced to try to work things out with Derrick halted the trickle of pee. Tickling my gut, I shifted my attention to becoming a father. I was beginning to get excited about it, if not the process.

To me, enjoying the sex we had would eventually result in a pregnancy. Wasn't that the point? To have an expression of our love for each other result in a little one. To be kind, Mary Ann's approach was clinical. We had just begun trying, and already it felt scheduled and passionless. Saying I wasn't enjoying it was an understatement. As my flow increased, I wondered if my sperm felt the same way and were going to refuse to make the necessary swim.

My failure to convince Chester about Derrick made me skeptical I'd find a way for Mary Ann to see the light about the mechanics of having a baby. We had to get past this, but first I had to get through a meeting with Derrick. The more I thought about it, the angrier I got.

I remembered reading that stress reduced a man's sperm count and tried to shift my mind while washing up. I drifted off Chester but landed back on Derrick. How was I supposed to fix the relationship? I was the aggrieved party. It was my reputation that Derrick had stomped on.

Staring in the mirror, I knew I had to focus on all the good in my life. Telling myself that this was just another pothole in life that in five years would be insignificant made me feel better. But as I headed out for a walk on the sand, a voice in my head kept shouting that no number of beach walks would ever lead to a reconciliation with Derrick.

The best option for me was to jump right in and face a problem. Skating around, keeping an issue hidden just below the surface always backfired on me. It was never easy bringing up a touchy subject: in this case, a backstabbing breach of trust. But not confronting it would hinder my ability to focus on catching killers.

In my book, getting this behind me wasn't realistic. What I needed to do was to shove it aside so it wasn't front and center.

Delicacy wasn't my strongest suit when I had a problem with someone. Reminding myself it wasn't the most useful way to navigate a truce, I stepped into my office. Derrick avoided my eyes, pretending to tap at his keyboard. Slinging my jacket over a chair, I said, "We need to talk this out."

"About what?"

I counted to three. "You may feel that you did nothing wrong in suspecting me of killing Garrison, but I can tell you, it felt like my partner had betrayed me."

Did I just say that? Was it too sweet?

"I'm sorry if you feel that way, but I was just trying to do my job."

"I wish you would have just come to me."

"I did. You blew me off. Anytime I tried to get answers, you'd get mad."

"Of course I did. What would you do when someone, especially someone who is supposed to have your back, starts going behind it?"

"First off, I have your back. I wasn't going behind your back. I was trying to get some questions answered. You didn't make it easy stonewalling me."

"It wasn't stonewalling. I was focused on Dwyer. Garrison was a sleazeball, a dead one. Dwyer is an escaped killer. Couldn't you see that?"

"What I saw was that we had a homicide to solve, and the victim was someone you had issues with, okay?"

"Well, you've got to give me the benefit of the doubt. You made a major mistake, and my reputation got trashed because of it."

"I'm sorry."

"And that's it? I had to give an alibi and be dragged out of my house into IA, and you're sorry?"

"You think it was easy for me? I look up to you, man. I was scared out of my mind that you had done something bad. I didn't know what to do. It kept me up at night. I could barely function thinking about it. You're a big part of who I want to be, and I had to find out the truth. I'm telling you, if it was true, I would have left the force for good."

"I'd never let you down, kid. Know that much about me."

He got up and extended a hand. "I'm sorry. I hope you understand."

I took his hand. "What do you say we move on? We got a couple of cases to solve."

Chapter 30

Without Mary Ann to help drink a bottle of wine, I was on my fourth glass of an Italian barbera and feeling it.

"Are you trying to make sure we get a Christmas card from the electric company?"

"You know, keeping lights on is the cheapest security system you can buy."

"What are you worried about, Frank?"

"Nothing, just that after this Garrison thing and with Dwyer out there, it's the least we should do."

"Did a threat surface with Dwyer?"

"Just that he mouthed off to someone. It's nothing to worry about. We'll get him."

When she asked me if I heard from Chester about partnering up, I told her about my talk with Derrick.

"I can't believe it. You're back with Derrick?"

"What's the big deal?"

"The big deal was you ranting that you'd never work with him."

"Well, we worked it out."

"I'm proud of you, Frank."

"Proud? Of what?"

"You worked it out with Derrick. You forgave him for making accusations."

"It was nothing."

"It was a serious rift in your relationship. You had good reason to question things, especially the question about trust."

"I still have my doubts."

"That's natural. He hurt you, and it will take time for the wound to heal."

"The kid was really sorry about everything."

"I'm sure he was. Derrick made a mistake, a big one."

"You know what he told me?"

"What?"

"That he looked up to me. That he was scared that I might have done it and that he would have gotten out of law enforcement if it really was me who did it."

"He said that?"

"Yep. He's a good guy."

"And you're a great one. You're going to make the best father in the world."

"I don't know about that."

Mary Ann picked up a plate, and walking into the kitchen, said, "You will. I know it."

When she came out, she had a thermometer in her mouth.

"What's the matter? You're coming down with something?"

She shook her head and put up a palm. A beep sounded, and she took it out of her mouth. "Normal. That's good."

"And you're just figuring that out?"

"No, wise guy. I'm trying to see if I'm ovulating."

"I thought that was what the calendar on the fridge was for."

"It is, but there's a window we need to catch. If my temperature rises, that means I'm already ovulating. I thought a slight temperature rise meant I was ovulating, but the OB-GYN said it was an old wives' tale and that it meant it already occurred."

"Okay."

"I think we should make sure we try to conceive every night now to be sure."

I'd heard of making love, having sex, getting laid, fucking, even throwing a leg over, but it was the first time I heard anyone call it "trying to conceive." It made little Luca shrink a bit, but what turned me completely cold was her reference to the viscosity of her discharges. Couldn't we just adopt?

***

I pulled the lever on the coffee urn and was reminded of how much help I needed to get little Luca started last night. We got it done, but there wasn't an ounce of pleasure in it. God made it natural for us to reproduce, but we humans complicated that as well.

Back in my office, I shoved the baby thing out of my mind and got back to Dwyer.

Who did Dwyer know in Bonita Springs? Was that where he was holed up? Or was it another ruse? I tried to think of where someone on the run would go. Most people would try to get as far away as they could.

Problem was, Dwyer was unlike most people; in fact, he didn't resemble anyone I'd run into. If the average criminal would take the first rocket out, did that mean Dwyer would stay in close proximity? Was he hiding under my nose? I forced the thought out of my mind that he was staying around to get me, then I pulled up a map of Bonita Springs.

Dwyer was dropped off at Community Park. I scanned the contact list we had developed from his phone records. Nothing within five miles. I knew the area fairly well. There was a pocket where Spanish was the language spoken and money was tight. I remember going into a place on East Terry. It was a one-bedroom apartment, but seven landscapers called it home.

Could Dwyer buy his way in? They needed the money, and hiding among that community would be unconventional, offering him a measure of safety. It didn't make sense though. They may not speak English, but everyone spoke the language of secrets. It would be impossible to keep it quiet.

The feeling that Dwyer was getting help from someone was taking root. Was someone stashing him in their house? Or was he hiding somewhere else and a person was providing food and essentials? If it was the latter, Dwyer would need a way to communicate with his collaborator.

Why did he ask, or as Vero put it, force her to drive him to Bonita Springs? What, or who, was in the area? I stared at the map. Plenty of waterways, and some spilled into the Gulf, but most led nowhere. Why come here? Then I saw it.

The train tracks. They were just yards away from the park. A rush of thoughts swept through my mind. Where did the tracks lead? What kind of trains ran on those tracks? How would Dwyer get on to a train? How many people worked on the trains that ran along there? How long was a train? How many stops did it make?

I didn't know anything about the train system that ran through Southwest Florida. It felt overwhelming. I stood up, took a couple of breaths and picked the obvious place to start. Who operated and owned the tracks? Where did these trains go, and what stops did they make?

Lee County Public Transportation provided me the contact information for the Seminole Gulf Railway. The operator of the system was located in Fort Myers. I didn't need to visit their offices; I needed information and picked up the phone for my education.

The managing partner explained that the Seminole Gulf Railway operated tracks that ran all the way down to Marco Island, though they had abandoned that stop along with ones in East Naples and Naples years ago. Now, the most southern stop was in North Naples, and its northernmost stop was in Arcadia, just east of Sarasota.

He clearly enjoyed telling me that it was his idea to start the Murder Mystery Dinner Train Experience, a gig they currently ran. I couldn't envision Dwyer hopping on a tourist-filled train after being told it only operated from their Fort Myers station, so I asked about the freight end of the business.

When he said they had a stop in walking distance of where Dwyer had been dropped off, I asked, "What other stops does the train make?"

"Well, depending on whether we have a load to drop or pick up, it could be Estero or Fort Myers, where we have two stops each, or Punta Gorda, Fort Ogden, Nocatee, or the end of our line in Arcadia."

"How often does the train run?"

"At least once a day, but we need a minimum of ten runs a week to make a buck."

"When the train is not running, say at night, where is it parked?"

"We run at night if we're busy. But we try to idle her near the first pickup the next day."

"How many trains did you run on April eleventh and twelfth?"

"Let me see. Hold on a sec."

I heard keys tapping.

"We had two both days."

"How many people work these trains?"

"We have a conductor and an engineer aboard at all times."

"Just two?"

"That's it. There's no need for any more. The stops have the cars loaded and staged before we get there."

"How fast does the train travel?"

"Depends what leg we're on."

"Around Bonita?"

"That's one of the slower areas, due to all the crossings—"

"How fast?"

"Ten to fifteen miles an hour. We pick it up when we get—"

"How often you have stowaways?"

"We don't have stowaways. We have teenagers who think it's cool to hitch rides. They don't realize how dangerous hopping onto a moving train can be. I remember years ago a kid lost his leg, got severed right off. The lawyers got a hold of it like it was our fault. How can you police miles of tracks? There's no way, and now we have to pay for sky-high liability insurance."

"Sounds easy to hop on a moving train."

"It's dangerous. I don't care how slow it seems to be going."

I thought about Dwyer and his bad back. Would that prevent him from trying? He had problems with pain, but he was mobile, and at the low end running to catch the train amounted to jogging. Dwyer could do it.

"Kids are kids."

"You said a mouthful. One time these kids hopped on, got stoned on board and fell asleep. They didn't even wake up when we interchanged with CSX, and they ended up in Edison."

"Interchanged?"

"Our tracks end in Arcadia, but we have an agreement with CSX— all the railroads have them with each other, and they take our cars onto to their tracks."

"Wait a minute; say a car is loaded in Bonita, but the cargo in it is going to Jacksonville, you take it as far as Arcadia and hand it off to another railroad?"

"Yeah, it happens all the time. We couldn't pay the bills just moving freight from Naples to Arcadia."

I didn't care about the economics. "Let me see if I understand this correctly. Sticking with the Jacksonville example, a car is loaded in Bonita, going to Jacksonville. You hand it off to CSX in Arcadia, and it gets hooked to a train going to Jacksonville?"

"Yes, that's the way it's done. Interchanges are common."

"And that train going to Jacksonville, are all the cars going there?"

"No. They're heading all over. Some go north from there, others west."

Dwyer could have hitched a ride in a railcar leaving Bonita and moved to another car. Damn it! Dwyer could be anywhere.

Chapter 31

Derrick came into the office with a box of donuts and coffee. I was trying to stop eating donuts. I didn't want my kid to pick up bad eating habits. I bit into a raspberry one; I'd start fasting tomorrow.

I wiped my mouth. "The girl Garrison was living with said Garrison had a kid years ago."

"Let me guess, it was with someone he wasn't married to."

"Yeah. We have to track this kid down."

"He's with the mother?"

"No, she died of an overdose. The kid's with the grandmother."

"In D.C., I swear, more than half the kids are brought up by their grandmothers. What's so important about finding this kid?"

"If he's really Garrison's kid, then he's Garrison's legitimate heir."

"To what, his drug-dealing route?"

"His house. You should have seen this place. It's listed for almost three million, and there's no mortgage on it."

"The money these bastards make poisoning people."

"That's why it's almost impossible to stop. Makes the argument for legalizing it."

"That's bullshit. It'd be a disaster if they legalized it."

"No shit. I'm just telling you what some say about the war on drugs."

Derrick finished a chocolate cream donut. "This kid's going to get three million?"

"He's technically supposed to. But I've got a feeling, we follow the money, and we'll find who killed Garrison."

"You think Garrison was killed over the house?"

"No. It's probably over money or something involving his drug dealing."

"That guy, Hernandez, you talked to, he said it had nothing to do with him going out on his own, but everything we've seen tells me it was."

"That would make sense. Maybe when they saw how successful he was they got jealous."

"What'd he say, the Argentinians aren't violent?"

"Not Argentinians, the Chileans. Hernandez said the culture wasn't violent. Maybe true in a general sense, but there's a subsector of every population that's predisposed to violence; I don't care who they are. Hell, I've seen monks kill."

"If Garrison had a kid, there'd be a birth record, assuming he was listed on the birth certificate."

"Yeah, but birth certificates are considered medical records and are protected under privacy laws."

"Really? I didn't know that."

"I'm going to see Melissa Crandall again. She's got to know something. Meanwhile, why don't you go see the DA and one of Judge Krenshaw's clerks. See what we can do to perform a search of birth records."

"Good idea, Frank."

***

Was it just the time of day or was the area around Santa Barbara Boulevard getting more populated? I remember coming out here a couple of years ago and it was empty. It made me question why there were three lanes in both directions. Traffic flowed freely, but, turning onto Radio Road, I wondered how long that would last.

Crandall was outside, waving to a beat-up Kia backing out of her driveway. Her son was waving back from the car. I wondered if the kid really liked going with his grandmother. When I was his age, I couldn't stand being away from my mother.

Turning to go inside, Crandall saw me approaching and put her hands on her hips. "I've got to go to work."

She wore a red bandanna on her head and a frown on her face.

"It'll just take a minute. I promise."

She walked inside and I followed, spying another pile of laundry on the couch. The smell of baking was in air. On the way into the kitchen, I tried to determine if it was the same pile on the couch as the last time I visited. A plate of chocolate cookies was on the table next to a plate full of crumbs. Was this the bribe needed to get the kid to go with Grandma?

"Smells good."

"You want a cookie?"

"Nah, I'm all right."

"You sure? It's okay. I don't want Jason to eat them all, and I certainly don't like the temptation."

"Well, in that case." I scooped up a cookie and folded a napkin over it. "Thanks."

"I got to get ready for work."

"I'll get right to it. Did Jimmy have a child?"

"How'd you find out about that?"

Why was the public surprised when we ferreted out information? I wanted to put up a billboard on Interstate 75 that read, There Are No Secrets. It would save me a lot of time and the taxpayers a lot of money. "It's my job to get to the truth."

"The truth? There are a couple of versions, aren't there?"

This woman was smarter than I had given her credit for. I'd had my share of cases where I'd caught the killer but never really knew what had happened. It was frustrating. Facts should be facts, but they are seen and processed through personal prisms: shifting and altering them.

"That discussion would take hours. Let's stick with Garrison and his offspring. What do you know?"

"Me and Jimmy were together a long time before I found out. I was surprised, uh, maybe not really surprised, when he said something about it. He was seeing this girl and she got pregnant. He said he didn't know she was pregnant, but I'm not sure about that. I think the girl's name was Carla Nealy."

A woman wouldn't forget a rival, especially one that was impregnated by her man. "I understand she overdosed, and the kid is being cared for by her mother."

"That's right. Evan is with his grandmother."

"How much contact did Jimmy have with his son?"

"Zero. She wouldn't let him see him. She knew what Jimmy did for a living and wanted nothing to do with him."

"What's the grandmother's name?"

"I don't know."

"Where do they live?"

"Carla was from Estero, but I don't know, it was a long time ago."

Learning more than I had hoped for, I headed for my car.

I jumped in the Cherokee and checked my phone. There was a voice mail from the manager at the railroad company. He had the list I had asked for, but it would have to wait. I began dialing Derrick's number to tell him not to waste his time trying to get access to the birth records. Just before it rang, I hung up. It'd be good to let him spin his wheels.

Instead, I called the Lee County School District. If Evan and his grandmother were still in Lee County somewhere, they'd have a record with their address.

Chapter 32

The Seminole Railway manager put me on hold to get the report I'd asked for. I found myself humming to the elevator music that played as I waited.

"Sorry, Detective. We have the report you needed. We had three trains during the period you asked about. A total of a hundred and eighteen cars. Ninety-nine of them were going interlined."

"Interlined?"

"Remember I told you we had an interchange agreement with CSX? Well, those ninety-nine cars went onto their tracks after we got to Arcadia."

"Where were they going?"

"Geez, all over. Some up to Tampa, Jacksonville, Tallahassee, Dallas, Atlanta, and on and on. You name the place, we can get it there for you."

"Was a majority of the cars going to a particular destination?"

"That would depend on the day. On the eleventh we had thirty-two carloads of sand, if you can believe it. Come out of a quarry in Immokalee. Most were going into Charleston, though eight were headed to Pensacola. Beach replenishment stuff. On the twelfth, Long Pine had forty cars of pine needles. The bales were heading to Mobile."

"Thanks. I was really hoping the information would narrow things down."

"Sorry about that. I wish I could help some more."

"You did help. I appreciate it, thanks."

"Say, Detective, I know this is petty, but is it worth reporting that my phone was stolen?"

"What happened?"

"I had it on the passenger seat when I went to dinner. I forgot about it. When I realized I had left it behind, I went to get it. My car's window was smashed in and the phone gone."

"When was this?"

"Last night. Should I report it?"

It wasn't worth his time. "Definitely. I don't know how they handle cellular theft in Lee County, but you might be able to file a report online."

"All right. I'll check into it."

***

Visions of Dwyer hopping from city to city on a train made me sick, but the upside was maybe I didn't have to watch my back so closely. I didn't even know where to start for putting out an alert for someone hitching rides aboard freight trains. Maybe I should just give this chase up and rely on the national network we had for felons on the run. It wouldn't be me reeling in Dwyer, but eventually we'd shove his ass back in jail. This time for good.

Problem was, Dwyer was a serial killer. I couldn't just leave him out there until some cop happened upon him. Lives were at stake. Maybe my buddy Haines with the FBI had a way or an idea. I pulled out my cell, and it reminded me of the railway guy's stolen phone.

Was Dwyer stealing phones and using them to communicate? Not only would it be dangerous for him, but Dwyer wasn't the type to accost someone and take their phone. Taking one out of an unoccupied car was another thing altogether.

I dialed the Lee County Sheriff's Office and was put through to a desk clerk. It was as bad as the train information. In the time that Dwyer had been out on the streets, forty-seven phones had been reported stolen. That seemed high, and questioning it, was told it definitely was. It seemed people filed reports believing their phone was stolen when in fact it was misplaced. They rarely reported the miscue out of embarrassment.

Waiting for the clerk to email over a list of stolen phones, I thought about how the wireless carriers might help identify a call made by Dwyer.

We already had a list of calls made to and from the cell phone he had when he was on his killing spree.

Running a cross-check of those numbers against calls made with a stolen phone seemed like an easy thing to do. However, the phone companies were continually hiding behind privacy concerns and only responded to court orders when we needed help.

But this was different. I wasn't looking for calls made by their customers; I wanted to know about calls made when a customer's phone was stolen. I couldn't imagine their legal departments objecting. Remembering that the first thing lawyers said was no gave me pause, but I was going to frame this in a way they couldn't refuse.

I was going to test my approach with the people at T-Mobile. They were the smallest carrier in the area, and it would involve the lowest number of calls. It would also leave me room to alter my approach if the legal pains in the ass objected.

***

Something was bothering me. Something nagging my erratic memory. It concerned Dwyer. I went outside and circled the building, hoping a walk would bring it to the surface. Nothing. My pee alarm buzzed, and I headed for the toilet like one of Pavlov's dogs.

Settling on the bowl, I concentrated on relaxing my abdomen muscles to get a flow going. The weekend was coming, and we were invited to a friend's beach club. They belonged to La Playa, and it was one of the things I liked to do. I could hang by the pool, walk the beach, and grab a drink. Then we'd shower and grab dinner in front of the Gulf. It never got old.

My stream increased, and it struck me that as much as I knew about Dwyer, I didn't know what he liked to do. What made him tick? Was it only about revenge for him? I remembered a visit we made after he was arrested.

The prison's interview room was painted dishwater gray. Mary Ann and I sat in plastic chairs, waiting for Dwyer to be brought from his cell.

"My ass is killing me, and we didn't even start yet."

"Frank, you've been complaining since we got here."

"What, do you expect me to be happy inside of a jail?"

"I have my doubts he's going to bite on a plea."

"It's all about framing it. Dwyer is a smart guy, and he'll see it's in his best interest to make a deal."

"Put that away."

"What's the matter? We're going to need a record of this."

"If you record it, he's going to be guarded."

I rolled my eyes and shoved the recorder back in my bag as the lock on the door whirled.

Dwyer's zebra-pattern jumpsuit hung, tent-like, off his shoulders. He'd lost a couple of pounds he could ill afford to lose. Dwyer offered his cuffed hands to the guard. I said, "It's okay. Take 'em off."

Dwyer pushed up his glasses before rubbing his wrists. He looked me in the eye, gently lowered himself into the chair opposite Vargas, and said, "I knew you'd be here before my lawyer said you'd be, asking me to cop a plea."

Vargas said, "It's in your best interests, Ethan."

"Oh, come now, Detective. You expect me to believe that? Why would prosecutors present a deal?"

"A trial is a costly and lengthy process."

Dwyer smiled. "The truth is, they fear going up against me in court. They don't have anything concrete, just a series of unconnected strings."

Vargas said, "Don't forget this is a capital punishment case. You lose, and you're facing the death penalty."

I said, "Let's review"—I finger quoted—"the strings, shall we?"

"This chair is hard as a rock. Isn't there anything more comfortable? I've had injuries and they come with rights, even in prison."

We treadmilled it for a while until Vargas said, "You really caught tough breaks in life, and I promise you the circumstances of what happened to you as a child will be considered in a plea arrangement."

Dwyer stiffened. "I didn't do anything. However, purely out of curiosity, what would a hypothetical deal look like?"

"If you tell us everything, helping to close out all the cases, we've got some flexibility."

"Define flexibility."

"You'd save your own life. The DA will drop his insistence on a death sentence."

"What about parole?"

Vargas said, "While it's unlikely, we'd argue the trauma you suffered caused mental instability, and a judge could be inclined to remand you to an institution where release is possible after treatment."

"An institution is a whole lot better place than any jail. Especially one up in Wisconsin, where the winters will make your back problems a lot worse."

Dwyer paused. "All this is interesting, requiring consideration. Can you return tomorrow?"

"Sure," Vargas said, "is there anything we can get for you?"

"A Bible. Make sure it's the New International Version."

"Sure. Anything else?"

"I'm extremely bored. Could you obtain a couple of books to read?"

"Absolutely. What do you like?"

"I prefer autobiographies. However, biographies of almost anyone, excepting politicians or celebrities, will suffice."

Dwyer was a Bible-thumper and a bookworm. I remembered the Bible on his nightstand. It was filled with colored Post-it Notes and highlighted sections. Was that all there was to him?

He was intelligent and loved to read. Was there a clue in that? In the books he read?

Chapter 33

The smell of coffee woke me. Mary Ann's side of the bed was empty. The clock read 6:47. Was she feeling sick? I headed into the bathroom. It was way too early to be up on a Saturday. I sat on the bowl to take a leak. If there was an upside to losing your bladder, it was the end of getting up three times a night to piss.

A fan of sleeping in my birthday suit, I pulled on a pair of shorts and headed for a dose of caffeine. Mary Ann was on her laptop.

"What are you doing up so early?"

She crossed her fingers. "I didn't want to say anything, but my period's late. Today's the fifth day."

The news hit me like a gallon of Red Bull. "You're pregnant?"

"I don't know for sure. Cycles fluctuate, but usually by the seventh day it means something. I'm going to CVS to pick up a pregnancy test."

She looked damn good for not sleeping last night. "You want me to come?"

"No. I'm just buying it. When I get back, I'll take the test."

She came back with two boxes, both a shade of pink. I pawed one named First Response Triple Check Pregnancy Test. It claimed to have three ways to confirm a pregnancy, stating its accuracy was almost 99 percent. It measured a hormone called hCG. I read the fine print. For all kinds of reasons, the percentages dropped to a low of 76 percent.

Mary Ann picked up the other box. It was called McKesson Consult Rapid Diagnosis Pregnancy Test. I wondered how many women were doing the same thing.

She held up the McKesson. "You ready?"

"Me? You're the one taking the test."

"This is about the both of us, Frank."

"Sure, let's do it."

"Get a cup." She headed to the bedroom. "Make sure it's clean."

I grabbed the other box and followed her through the bedroom into the bathroom.

As Mary Ann opened the box, I said, "Use this one instead."

"What difference does it make?"

"I'm feeling lucky."

We exchanged boxes, and after reading the insert, Mary Ann did her business into the glass.

She placed the glass on the counter, and I dipped the tip into the urine and counted, "One, two, three, four, five." I pulled it out, put the cap on, and laid it, window up, on the counter.

"Oh my God, it's turning pink!"

"That just means the test is working. It takes three minutes for the results to show."

Mary Ann grabbed my hand. As we stared at the little window, doubts crept into my mind about my desire for a positive result, and a drag race between dread and joy broke out. I shook the thoughts out and realized that the window we were fixated on was truly a window into the future.

***

Garrison's kid and grandmother lived in a section of Lee County called San Carlos Park. I was alone. Derrick had wanted to come along, but although I had put what he did to the side, I hadn't quite put it completely behind me. I weaved my way from Three Oaks Parkway onto a small street named Aster Road.

Ranch homes were crowded along the sidewalkless street. Their house was shrouded by two giant oaks. The driveway was covered with acorns. A blue bicycle was parked in front of a white Ford Focus.

Sixty-five-year-old Edith Nealy was wearing a tennis skirt and a polo shirt. She was sturdy looking. Her gray roots might have been peeking through, but I had a feeling she could beat a woman half her age. I showed my badge and offered my hand.

Nealy looked in my eyes and took my hand. Her grip was firm but cool. "Pleased to meet you, Detective."

There was a trace of Bostonian in her speech. "I can still hear a bit of an accent. What is it, Boston?"

"No, Providence. It's been over thirty years now."

She didn't offer any commentary on what was left of my New York accent or my resemblance to George Clooney.

"As I explained over the phone, I'm investigating the murder of James Garrison."

"Has nothing to do with us."

She didn't know about the house? "That may be true—"

"It is true. You ask me, he got what he had coming."

"Can you confirm that James Garrison is the father of Evan Nealy."

"Father?" She snorted. "Only on paper."

"Is that a confirmation that Garrison is listed on the birth certificate?"

"Unfortunately, yes."

"I understand that you're Evan's legal guardian."

"That's right. Grandmother, mother, guardian, whatever."

"It's my understanding that Mr. Garrison didn't have a relationship with his son and that you prevented him from seeing his son."

"Is this what this is about? That I kept Evan away from that no-good bastard?"

"Hold on, Ms. Nealy. This has nothing to do with custody. I'm trying to get background on Mr. Garrison."

"Background? You want background? I'll give you all the background you need. Jimmy Garrison was a lowlife drug dealer. That's what he was. He got my daughter pregnant and took off, not that I'd want him around. He never gave a damn about Evan. Not when Carla was alive or after that. When Evan was around five, he'd call and try to see him once a year. It was such bullshit. What did that punk think, that he could just show up whenever he wanted?"

Garrison didn't have a moral right to see his kid, but not privy to the custody documents, I wasn't sure if he had a legal one.

"As far as you're aware, Evan is the only heir of Garrison's?"

"Heir? To what, a trunk full of cocaine?"

"Garrison had a house."

"It's probably got a mortgage larger than what it's worth."

"There's no public record of a mortgage on the property."

"Well, that just means you didn't look hard enough."

"The home is on the market at just under three million dollars."

"What? Where'd he get? Forget it, I know where he got it."

"Unless it can be proven that the asset was used in a crime, Evan is entitled to the proceeds of a sale."

"Well, we don't want it. I don't care how much money it is. It's dirty money, and I wouldn't touch it wearing gloves."

I wondered how long it would take her to rationalize taking the money. "That's something for the courts to decide."

"Is that what you came to tell me? That my grandson inherited a house bought with drug-tainted money?"

"Not exactly. Just calm down for a moment, because this has to do with the possibility someone is going to come looking for that money."

"Is Evan in danger?"

"No, not at all. But there is a possibility that Jimmy Garrison was murdered over a dispute about money. And if that's the case, someone may be coming around."

"Tell me what you know, Detective. If my grandson is in danger, I have a right to know."

"If I knew something concrete, I would tell you. This is a hunch of mine. But there's no reason to panic. They would be looking for the money. They won't harm you or Evan. It wouldn't serve them."

"What should we do?"

"Nothing. Just sit tight. Some lawyer claiming to be working for Jimmy's Garrison's estate put the house on the market. I'm guessing that as soon as it sells, or is in contract, someone is going to contact you. When they do, play along, but call me. You understand?"

I handed her a card, which she held with both hands. "Anything else I should do?"

"No. Act normal and call me as soon as you hear from anyone."

"Do you know who is going to call?"

"If I did, I'd be on his tail already. Just take it easy, act normally, and it will all work out fine. I promise."

Chapter 34

Hanging my jacket on the back of the door, I saw it. There was a white envelope on top of the pile of mail. It was addressed in pencil. To me. The handwriting looked familiar.

Pulling on gloves, I picked the envelope up and held it to the light. It didn't look like anything was in it. I slid an opener along the top and carefully opened it. It was empty. What the hell was Dwyer doing?

I called the lab and told them what I'd received. Maybe there was something they could get off it, but I doubted it. Dwyer was too careful. As soon as the tech took the envelope, I got back to the business of catching Dwyer.

Firing up my computer, I popped open the attachment from Lee County. It had forty-seven cell numbers attached to the stolen phones. What could I do with them? The frigging phone companies wouldn't cooperate, not even when I fed them a line about it involving a kidnapping case. Of a child no less.

"Derrick, take this down to the surveillance unit and compare it to the list of calls the DiBlasis have been getting."

"The DiBlasis? I thought only he agreed to be tapped."

"He did. But when I submitted the voluntary agreement, I asked Judge Whiting if he would extend the coverage to his wife. He thought it was a reasonable request. I amended it and he signed it."

"Wow. You never told me."

And you never told me you were asking my neighbors about my whereabouts when Garrison was found dead. "Must've slipped my mind. Anyway, let's see if anything turns up."

I handed off the list and picked up my ringing phone.

"Homicide, Detective Luca."

"Detective Luca, this is Mattias Goodman returning your call."

I wanted to rip him a new asshole for taking a week to call, despite six calls to his office.

"Thank you for returning my call. I called ten times."

"I do apologize, but it has been extremely busy, frankly bordering on overwhelming. Just for the record, Detective, I believe you attempted to reach me six times."

"You signed the listing to sell James Garrison's home."

"Yes, that's correct."

Even though he was in Miami, I was getting ready to drive down to his office and kick his condescending ass back to Manhattan. "Where did you get the authority to do so?"

"James Garrison executed a will. I am the executor of his estate, and the probate court authorized the sale."

This guy had to be connected. Probate courts are slower than getting the last bit of honey out of a jar.

"And what court was that?"

"Are you inquiring as to who granted the petition? If so, it was Judge Marshall Whitacer of the Dade County Probate Court."

Would I have to stop for gas to make it to Miami? "I'd like to have a copy of the documentation. Whatever James Garrison executed and what you claim the court approved."

"Am I detecting skepticism, Detective? If so, it's entirely unjustified. Even though it's technically a violation of client privacy, I'd be pleased to forward a copy. Mr. Garrison is deceased, after all, and cooperating with my friends in law enforcement is an obligation I take seriously. After all, I am an officer of the court."

I had to get off the phone before my tongue started bleeding. "Thank you, Counselor. I appreciate your assistance."

The cradle of the phone was still vibrating when Derrick walked in with a lottery winner smile.

"We got a hit. DiBlasi's wife's number was one of the numbers. I don't know how you do it, Frank, but you're the man."

"Let me get this straight. A call from one of the stolen cell phones was made to DiBlasi's wife?"

"Yep. Looks like Dwyer called her."

"Why the hell didn't the surveillance team tell us?"

"It was too short of a call. There was nothing to listen to."

"Was there a message?"

"None that they could find. It was a brilliant idea, Frank. I don't know how you come up with these. I thought you were just handing me something to do. I mean, the odds are like, what, one in a zillion?"

"You'll get there."

"I don't know about that. I feel like I'm floundering."

I didn't have the time or interest to play psychologist. There was a lead on Dwyer, and it pointed right at the DiBlasis, my original suspicion.

"I'm heading to see Dwyer's family. Why don't you come along?"

"You sure you want me to come?"

"Take your jacket and let's roll."

***

The sun was casting a yellow hue on Mangrove Bay's white homes. The backdrop of an ominous black cloud rolling in from the east almost made me take a cell phone picture.

Derrick said, "Look at that sky. It's gonna come down."

I was hoping the net was coming down on Dwyer. "Okay, we play this right, and Dwyer will be behind bars before the sun comes up."

"You're sure they know where he is, aren't you?"

"Never sure of anything in this business. But reasonably sure? Probably."

"What do you want me to do?"

I wanted to say, be a goddamn detective. "We have to be careful with them. If they're hiding Dwyer, that would make them complicit. We can't scare them with the threat of going to jail over their actions."

"Got it."

Derrick hit the bell. It was a cascading series of pitches that progressed lower. The final chime hadn't sounded as the door swung open.

"Sorry to bother you, Mr. DiBlasi, but we have a couple of questions."

"Uh, we're just getting ready to go out for dinner."

"This won't take long. This is my colleague, Detective Derrick Dickson."

I elbowed Derrick, who was digging his badge out. "Good afternoon, sir."

"Hi. I'm sorry, but it's not the best time. My wife is in the shower."

"I understand. We'll wait."

"Okay, okay. Come in. I'll let Jenny know you're here. Make yourselves comfortable. I'll be right back."

I couldn't recall how far the master bath was, but there was no sound of running water. We settled onto the gray couch as the faint sound of DiBlasi's voice drifted into the room. Framing the coming storm, the two-story drapery looked even more dramatic.

"I never even knew these houses were back here. This is a nice place."

"And most of them are on the Gordon River, giving them Gulf access."

"Ka-ching."

"You got that right. Two to three million."

"Where'd this guy get that kind of money?"

Before I could say anything, DiBlasi came into to the room. "She'll be out in a minute. Would you like something to drink?"

"No, thank you. We're fine. I know I said it the last time, but I really like the way you put this place together. It's beautiful."

"Thanks. We spent a lot more than I thought we would. I had to look the other way, if you know what I mean."

I did know what he meant. We're all guilty of crossing our boundaries in pursuit of something we want, or as is often the case, think we want. "Well, it turned out amazing."

"We're very happy with it."

Derrick said, "This is my first time back here. Are they still building?"

"I don't pay attention anymore. There may be a spec home or two for sale, but it's pretty much done."

"What's done?" Jenny DiBlasi came into the room wearing the same kind of cover-up that Mary Ann wore putting on her makeup. Her hair was done, but she was makeupless.

"Just the development. The construction in here."

"Oh." She went to the fridge and took a bottle of Pellegrino out. "Anyone want a water?"

"I asked already."

She sat on a white leather stool at the kitchen counter. Jenny was keeping her distance. Did she have something to hide? Or was it a tactic to prevent a close look at her without makeup?

"My partner and I came up here to check on any interactions you may have had with Ethan."

DiBlasi said, "Interactions? We haven't seen Ethan since we visited him in prison. We would've called you—"

"A phone call is an interaction."

"No. We haven't seen Ethan or talked to him on the phone. Right, Jenny?"

"Bob's right. If he would have come to see us, we would have called you as you instructed."

She conveniently failed to mention a phone call. Bill Clinton would be proud of the way she parsed things. Before I could call her out, her husband said, "Ethan's family. We want the best for him, but I'm not about to jeopardize everything I've worked for by helping him now. If he goes to prison again, we'll help him deal with the legal system, but that's the limit."

If he goes to prison again? Did he believe Dwyer would continue to evade capture? Or did he think there was a good possibility his half brother would end up dead?

"I can assure you, Ethan Dwyer will be back where he belongs. This time, with zero opportunity to escape."

"Will he be put in solitary?"

Derrick said, "That's for the prison authorities to decide. Of course, they'll take his escape into consideration, determining the most secure way of housing him."

"He'd have access to books if he were in solitary, wouldn't he?"

"He would, but if he causes any problems, they have the right to punish him and take away privileges, including library access."

I said, "I didn't come to discuss Ethan Dwyer's reading habits." I looked at Jenny DiBlasi. "I want to know why you didn't tell us that Dwyer had called you."

"Me? He never called me."

"Lying about it will only make things worse for the two of you."

"How dare you call my wife a liar!" Bob DiBlasi stood and went to his wife's side.

"What Detective Luca is saying is failing to cooperate will compound things."

"I have no idea what you're talking about. Ethan never called me. He never did before he was arrested, and he hasn't since."

That wasn't true. There was a record of two calls to Jenny DiBlasi from Dwyer's cell phone before he was arrested.

"This could be a misunderstanding, but how do you explain a call made to your phone on April tenth at six forty-five p.m., from a phone we believe was stolen by Ethan Dwyer?"

"What? That's impossible."

The denials were driving me nuts. "Look, a fact is a fact. You can deny it all you want, but we have proof the call was made."

"Wait a minute. How do you know this? Are you tapping my phone?"

Shit. "We, uh, have ways—"

Derrick said, "Surveillance of your phone calls isn't necessary. We had a list of calls made from a stolen phone, and I went through the calls myself, looking for any knowns. Your cell phone number is a matter of public record."

"I don't care what you say. I never spoke to him."

I said, "Look, Mrs. DiBlasi, if you continue to stonewall and deny, you'd be forcing our hand. You leave us no options."

"What Detective Luca means is, if you don't cooperate, we'd have to ask a judge for help in getting access to your calls. But there is another way to handle this. If you'd let me see your phone, I'll check the call log. It may provide some clarity."

"I know I shouldn't be helping you after all these accusations, but I'm really getting tired of all this bullshit. Here, have fun."

Derrick took her iPhone and started navigating. Good thing he was here; I was one of the few not in the Apple universe.

Derrick brought the phone to her. "Okay. You see, here's the call."

"So? I didn't answer it."

"I can see that. Was there a reason?"

"I didn't know the number and figured it was another spam call. I probably blocked it. I always do if they don't leave a message."

"Yes. You blocked it."

The egg was dripping off my face. "You see how easy that was? There was no reason to be hostile to us."

"No reason? You come here unannounced and accuse me of conspiring with Ethan? Who wouldn't be upset?"

Derrick said, "We apologize, ma'am. I hope you can understand it from our perspective. You and your husband are the only family Ethan Dwyer has. With him on the run, unless he's planned better than anyone in history, he's going to need help from someone. A call was made to you. It appears it was Dwyer, making it our duty to follow it. Does that make sense?"

She shrugged, but her husband said, "We understand, but next time don't come here with guns drawn."

We slithered out, and as soon as I hopped into the Cherokee's passenger seat, said, "Thanks for jumping in. For some damn reason, I never thought she'd think the call was just another unsolicited sales call."

"No problem. To be truthful, the idea came to me out of nowhere. We both should have been prepared for the possibility."

"I thought the short duration was just to avoid being tapped. Or just a quick message being sent between the two of them, especially since he knew we were listening in on his phone."

"No doubt."

"Well, I owe you. Thanks."

"No problem, anytime."

"Say, I want to take you to this place we went to. It's called the Cave. They have a bunch of wines by the glass. The good stuff. It's pricey, but you can try different wines and learn what they're like."

Chapter 35

Mary Ann shook her hand loose. "You're hurting my hand."

"Sorry."

She grabbed my hand again. "Oh Frank, here it comes."

A pink line peeked out of the left of the window. There was only one pencil-thin line. One line meant not pregnant. A second line appeared. As the two lines stretched across the window, Mary Ann said, "Oh my God!"

I enveloped my arms around her, and she began to cry.

"I can't believe it, Frank. We're gonna have a baby."

My fear melted away. "We've been blessed."

Mary Ann bent over, staring at the device. "Two lines means you're pregnant, right?"

"Yes, it's really true."

She took her phone out. "I need a photo of this."

I was hoping this wasn't going to be broadcast over social media. "You're not going to post that, are you?"

"Of course not. I just want a picture of it. Maybe one day we can show our kid how it all started."

"You should have taken pictures a couple of nights ago."

She headed out of the bathroom. "I gotta call the doctor; make an appointment. She has to confirm this."

I felt like celebrating. It was too early for champagne, leaving me to settle for a bowl of fiber cereal. I added more blueberries than normal.

***

It wasn't a tectonic shift, but I felt different as I waited outside the garage. The lens I viewed the world through had a different cast. I was going to be a parent. Everything had a longer horizon. It wasn't just my lifespan; I had to think about a longer game. Bottom line was, it wasn't all about me.

Was I finally maturing? What I found surprising was not getting annoyed over Mary Ann's cautiousness. Only a couple of weeks along, she was moving like an old lady. It would have frustrated me a month ago, but she was older than most pregnant women and had to be careful.

I'd made progress, but I thought it was too early to be hounded about turning the spare room into a proper nursery. The other thing that bothered me a bit was her taking too long to get ready to go to work. Morning sickness is what the doctor called it. Maybe I'd take my own car going forward.

Finally, Mary Ann came into the garage. "Sorry."

I hopped in the car. "You feeling nauseous again?"

"No. The phone kept ringing. Every time I answered, no one was there. Maybe I just couldn't hear them."

"How many times did they call?"

"Four times."

Dwyer? Maybe he wanted to hear my voice. "Maybe something's wrong with the line."

"Probably. It happened twice yesterday. What do you have going on today?"

I didn't like the sound of that. "We may have something to work with on the Garrison case. I'm going to see the grandmother of Garrison's kid again."

"I can't believe he had a child and abandoned him. How can people do that to their baby?"

"The kid's lucky he has a good grandmother. I feel bad for her. She had to jump in and become a mother all over again."

"How old is she?"

"About sixty-five. She's very protective of him. I like her. She's good people. When I told her about the money the kid was entitled to, she didn't care. She said she didn't want anything from Garrison, and I believed her. I hope there's a way the money can get to them."

"I bet they could use it."

"No doubt. Raising a kid isn't cheap. Look at the cost of college these days. It's crazy. When I went to John Jay College, it was two thousand a year."

"That was a long time ago, and that's a state college too, isn't it?"

"It's part of New York City's university system. It's probably twenty grand a year now."

"That's still cheap."

"I checked into Florida's program. You know, they have a program where you put the money away today, at what it costs for tuition today. And when your kid is ready and goes to state college, you don't pay any more."

"We should look into that."

"I have the papers for it in the office."

"Look at you."

"What?"

"Nothing. I'm just glad we have each other."

***

There was a black Mercedes parked in front of Edith Nealy's house. Miami-Dade license plates. Blacked-out windows. I drove around it, looking in the windshield. The car was empty. Did whoever was angling for the money from Garrison's house send a thug to intimidate Nealy?

The thought the grandmother was scared had me jogging to the door. I put my ear to the door. Nothing but mumbled voices. I stood on my toes, looking in the door's window. Nothing.

I hit the bell and banged the door with the heel of my hand. The door swung open. Edith Nealy was in sneakers and jeans. There was coffee on her breath.

"I didn't expect you so early."

"Are you okay?"

"Yes. Why?"

I pointed to the hundred-thousand-dollar auto.

"That's Meghan's son-in-law's. Her car's in the shop."

"Can we talk?"

"Sure. We were just having coffee. You want a cup?"

"No, thanks. I'll wait outside until you're done."

"Don't be silly. Come in."

Her friend was another fit sixty-something.

Everyone in Southwest Florida seemed to exercise and watch what they ate. Even though most people liked their cocktails, the area had garnered a Blue Zone designation. I'd seen it posted in a few places but had no idea what it meant and asked Mary Ann.

She said the name came from places around the world where people lived longer than average. A study identified five traits responsible for the phenomenon: putting family first, less smoking, physical activity, social engagement, and plant-based diets. It was something I could get behind, as long as my money didn't run out in retirement.

"Evelyn, this is Detective Luca. He's the one looking into the killing of Evan's biological father."

"Oh. Nice to meet you."

We shook hands and she said, "I'll get going now. See you tomorrow at nine?"

"Rest up, I wanna avenge our loss last week."

Her friend left and she said, "We have a tennis match tomorrow. You play?"

"No. But I've thought about it."

"It's a great game, and you can play your entire life. Evan's just starting to play."

I had to keep that in mind. Tennis was a good way to keep a kid away from bad influences, keep them in shape, and give them something to do as an adult.

"I'll have to give it a try."

"Don't wait too long."

"I won't. Tell me about the call."

"It was from a lawyer. He said his name was Matthias Goodman. He was very formal."

To her, formal; to me, he had a superiority complex. "That's the lawyer who put the house up for sale. What did he say?"

"That they had someone who was interested in buying the house. That it was a cash deal and would close quickly."

"Did he mention a price?"

"No. I guess I forgot to ask."

"That's okay. So, he was just notifying you?"

"That, and something strange. You said there was no mortgage on the house, but he said there was a substantial claim to the proceeds. That's how he put it. I said I thought there was no mortgage on the property. He said something like there was an informal encumbrance on the property."

"Did he give you any details?"

"I asked him, but he said he would send someone to explain it in person."

"When?"

"He didn't say."

"Did he specify a date for the house to close?"

"No, just said it would be fast."

"I want to tell you what I believe is going on here."

"Okay."

"The people that Garrison worked with are trying to get their hands on the money from the sale. Now, whether he owed a debt to them or not is unclear. I believe he did and think he may have been killed over it."

"He was rotten. It's not nice to speak ill of the dead, but he probably got what he deserved. It's interesting, but I don't care what happens with the money."

"That money belongs to Evan. He is lawfully entitled to it. You may not want it, but it would be a life changer for Evan. It's dirty money, but if there are no seizure claims on it, and there aren't, at this point, you should take it. For Evan's sake."

"I don't want to get mixed up with all this."

"We need your help. If you step aside and let these people rob Evan, it would be a shame."

"Look, three million dollars would change everything and ensure that if something happens to me, Evan would be provided for. But these drug dealers are nasty, and it's scary getting mixed up with them."

"If you can find a way to help us, we can put some of these criminals behind bars and keep them away from poisoning more kids with their crap."

"I'm not a crusader, Detective Luca. I'm a grandmother trying to protect her grandson."

"Think of the other grandmothers and the mothers trying to protect their children. We can't fix it all, but if we can put a dent in their operations, we'll save some kids."

"What would I have to do?"

Chapter 36

Driving to see Edith Nealy again, I was feeling good. The sun was shining on more than the Sunshine State. Mary Ann had received confirmation from the OB-GYN doctor that she was five weeks pregnant. Things were coming together.

I had a line to follow on the Garrison case. It was more than a line; it was a commercial fishing boat. Mrs. Nealy needed convincing. She was a tough woman, and though she claimed not to want anything to do with the father of her grandson, I detected a desire for revenge. She disavowed the money but knew rationalization was seeping into her.

Something crept into my head as I pulled onto Nealy's street, and my mood plummeted. It was Dwyer. He was still out there. After setting a trap on the Garrison case, I'd concentrate on Dwyer.

Acorns cracked under my shoes as I headed up the driveway. Was that a kid's voice? I hit the bell and heard running footsteps. The door swung open. It was Evan—sandy hair, freckles, and a gap between his front teeth. His left knee brandished a large scab.

"Hello, young man. You must be Evan."

He took a step back. "Yes, sir. Are you here to see Grandma?"

"Yes. My name is Frank Luca." I extended my hand as Mrs. Nealy came into view.

Evan shook my hand.

"That's a strong shake you have there. Keep that up. You make a good impression on people if you can look them right in the eyes when you shake hands. Okay?"

The kid smiled. "Yes, sir. Like this?"

"Exactly."

"What's in your backpack?"

I lifted the backpack I was holding in my hand. "I wish it was filled with candy, but it's stuff for work."

"Come in, Frank. Evan, Frank and I need to talk about something important. Can you play on the lanai?"

"If it's important, can't I stay?"

"It's important, but it's something private."

"Okay. Can I take my erector set out there?"

"Sure."

I wanted to follow Evan out to the lanai and help the kid build something amazing but followed Nealy into the kitchen.

"He's a nice boy. You did a great job raising him."

"Thank you, but it ain't over yet."

"I've been reading, most doctors agree it's the first six or seven years that really matter."

"I don't know anymore. My daughter Carla, Evan's mother, never gave me trouble until she was around sixteen."

The reminder that parental challenges never end was distracting. Why hadn't I asked the head doctor about dealing with teenagers? "Sorry to bring it up."

"It's okay. I didn't think I'd ever get over losing Carla, and I really haven't, but Evan was a godsend. I was so busy taking care of him that it took my mind off Carla. I didn't know it at the time, but he was a lifesaver."

"He's fortunate to have you, ma'am."

"I don't know. Like they say, the feeling's mutual."

"Thanks for agreeing to help. What you're doing is incredibly important. If it's what I think it is, you're going to have an impact on this drug ring, and there's no telling how many kids that will help."

"But won't they want revenge? I don't want these people coming after Evan or me."

"They won't even know about your involvement. But in the one-in-a-million shot they do, I'll get the both of you into the witness protection program."

"But we'd have to leave Southwest Florida, then. Evan has his friends . . ."

"Don't think of all that now. It's the remotest of possibilities." It wasn't as remote as I made it seem, but I had to play it down or she'd pull out.

"Are you sure?"

"Look, let's see what we get in the first place. Then we can decide on a course of action. Remember, a judge will protect you from having to testify. If it came down to it, you'd do it anonymously."

"Testify? I don't want to be involved in a court case."

I had to open my big mouth. "Let's hold on a second. The express purpose of the surveillance is to find out who is behind all of this—the murder of Jimmy Garrison and what looks like an attempt to steal from Evan the proceeds of the sale of the house. What I want is information that will lead me to them. Once I get insight, we'll come up with a way to disguise the information source."

"I don't want Evan put in harm's way."

"I promise he won't. You have my word."

I unzipped my backpack, taking out three black devices.

"Sonos speakers?"

"We just branded them that way so people would assume they were audio speakers instead of listening devices."

"This is better than wearing a wire."

"Yeah, and since we're not sure when a visit will be made, we're ready all the time. All you have to do is push this button." I handed her a remote with one button and a slide for volume.

"Just push this and that's it?"

"Yes. Leave it by the front door, and when the bell rings just hit the button. If it's just a friend, then shut it off."

"That's a good idea."

"I brought three along. You never know where the conversation is going to take place, and if these guys are on guard they may want to talk outside. Let's put one right here."

Placing the speaker on an end table, I moved into the kitchen. "This is a good spot for one as well." I tucked another speaker into a corner of the counter.

"How far do they pick up voices?"

"The closer the better, but up to twenty feet with normal speaking voices."

"Let's see what Evan's up to."

As soon as I stepped outside, I smelled smoke. It looked like another brush fire had started since it had been so dry the last several weeks.

"Wow! A skyscraper."

"It's not a skyscraper; it's a launching pad for rocket ships."

"Oh yeah, I see it now."

"Grandma took me and Sammy to the Kennedy Space Center. It was so cool. I'm gonna be an astronaut, you know."

"You'd make a fine astronaut. Where's the first place you'd want to go?"

"Sammy wants to go to Mars, but not me. I want to go to Saturn, the place with the rings. It'd be so cool to see that close-up."

"If you have an extra seat on the rocket, I always want to go to Saturn."

"Sure. What's that?"

"Just a speaker. Last time I saw your grandmother I was telling her about these, so I brought some for her to try."

"Can we try it now?"

"I need to get the master controller. Say, when I do, you want to help me set it up?"

"Oh yeah, I love to make things."

"You're on."

Before I left, I made sure each of the devices were recording. I wasn't sure what we'd catch, but I felt good that the bait was on the hook.

Chapter 37

The other trap we'd set finally looked to have snagged something. I took the stairs, two at a time, to the cybercrimes unit. Their work was vastly different than what I did. My world was concrete: interviews and evidence. The cybercrimes unit chased digital trails and sat in chat rooms trying to draw perverts and thieves out.

Mary Ann swiveled her monitor toward me and said, "Read these two comments."

The first was: Ethan Dwyer is in Chicago. I was at the planetarium and went for a walk. I almost bumped into him on the promenade. Hurry, it was definitely him. Ed Nathan

The second one read: I'm pretty certain I saw this guy last night in Times Square around 8 pm. Red Thewyn

"You think it's Dwyer?"

"Pretty certain."

"What makes you think that?"

"Look at the names. They're both forms of an anagram. It's a common, frankly stupid, way people trying to disguise themselves."

"Why would they use a derivative of their own name?"

"I don't know. Maybe to keep an identity consistent, so they don't forget what name they used."

I understood the memory motivation. "But why not John Smith or an actor's name?"

"They're too transparent. If you saw someone use Bradley Cooper, you'd know it wasn't a real name. But the best part is they came from the same IP address."

"Meaning what?"

"They were sent from the same device."

"But can't they disguise them these days?"

"There was no mirroring going on; it was the same device."

"What device and where?"

"Santangelo is working on it right now. He said it wouldn't take long."

"You know Dwyer's too smart for this sort of thing."

"You mean about leaving comments?"

"The entire thing—the comments, the false name thing."

"I know you don't believe in this stuff, but the anagram is a strong predictor, Frank."

"I believe it. I just think Dwyer wants us to know it's him."

"Why?"

"You don't get this guy. He wants to torment me. Why not leave two messages claiming a sighting in the same place, from two different devices? It would be more credible."

"I get that, but even if he used two devices, we'd know if they were in the same location. Here's Santangelo."

"Hey, Frank. How are you?"

"Good, you?"

"All is well. Dwyer's one slippery bastard, huh?"

"Don't remind me. What do you have?"

"Both comments were left using an Apple iPhone 7. Here's the number." He handed me a slip of paper.

I stared at the number. It was the stolen phone used to call Jenny DiBlasi.

"This is a map of a radius of where the messages were sent from. We have stronger pings from this tower. You might want to take that into consideration when you conduct a search."

I took the map. A circle had been drawn encompassing the downtown Bonita Springs area, including the band shell, train station, and Spanish-speaking neighborhood.

"Is there a way to have a message sent on a delay?"

"Not that I know. When someone hits send, it's time stamped. The message could be forwarded, of course, and then sent, but we can trace all that. Or at least we believe we can."

What did that mean? Either you could or couldn't trace it. "Okay. So, it's your belief that both comments originated from the same phone, and the sender was in Lee County?"

"No doubt about it."

"Thanks. Say hello to Marie for me."

"Anytime, Frank."

As soon as Santangelo walked away, I said, "It's definitely him, then. Is there anything else that looks like it might be something?"

"No. The other comments are from legitimate people interested in the case or just gossipers."

"I knew it was a long shot."

"Don't give up. We've been running down the IP addresses of each visitor to the site."

"Even those that don't leave messages?"

"Of course. It's more likely that someone would stalk the site. Come to the web page every now and then to check on any developments or just to make themselves feel good."

"How would you know if something is suspicious?"

"If Dwyer came to the site once, we'd probably never know it was him. People bounce on to sites all the time by mistake. The profile of the person we've established would generally visit the site multiple times, visit each page and spend time on each page. Casual visitors would bounce off a page quickly."

"Don't forget to see if any messages come from Alamo or San Antonio, Texas."

"We're monitoring that, as well as any hits that emanate from cybercafé or public computers."

"All right. I have to get back downstairs."

"Oh Frank, the OB-GYN's office called. They want to schedule a sonogram. We'll get to see a picture of the baby for the first time. I'm so excited."

"Is something wrong?"

"No. What makes you say that?"

"They called you. I don't know much about this, but don't they take sonograms regularly? Why didn't the doctor say something on your last visit?"

"Relax, Frank. She did. Dr. Lupo said they were getting a new machine, and as soon as it came in they'd call."

"Oh. I was just getting a little nervous."

"Everything's going to be fine. Don't be a neurotic, okay?"

"Sorry. I'll check my schedule and let you know what works. I'm not missing this for anything."

On the way back to my office I couldn't help wondering how we'd get anything from the website. It was like looking for one particular grain of sand on Clam Pass Beach.

Chapter 38

It could be another dead end, but in the middle of the night an ambitious idea struck me that might provide a lead on Dwyer. When I told Mary Ann about it, she didn't think it was worth the effort.

The smell of coffee preceded Derrick into the office. He set the Starbucks coffee, he brought me each morning, on my desk. "Good morning. Here you go, Frank."

"Thanks."

"The lab called and said there was nothing on the envelope you got."

"Nothing? No prints?"

"Nope. But you said that."

"What about the handwriting?"

"Sorry, pal, not definitive, was what they said."

"Not definitive? Who the hell else would send an empty envelope?"

"What do you think it means?"

I shook my head. "I don't know, but last night I was thinking about Dwyer."

"Me too."

I took a peek under the coffee lid. It was nice and dark. Maybe I didn't have to check anymore. "I had this idea, but I'm not sure if it's crazy or not."

"Feels like we need crazy; we don't have much."

The kid was growing on me, but it bothered when he would remind me when an investigation of mine was floundering. "We do the work; we'll get the results, right?"

"No doubt."

"So, I was running all the possibilities that Dwyer had help. One of the things we don't know, but seems likely, is that he prepared for this day."

"Even before he went away?"

"Exactly. I told you this guy was a planner like no other on the planet. And a patient bastard too. He had a lockbox at First Florida Integrity Bank on Anchor Rode Avenue. It was instrumental in figuring him out. He had newspaper clippings in there about the car accident and his mother's murder. We learned a ton from it."

"You think he had another one?"

"I'm leaning that way. Maybe a lockbox with cash in it."

"Or a key to a hideaway."

"Nah. Not a safe house, just money. It makes sense. It's that, or someone is helping him."

"Like his brother."

"Could be, but stick with the lockbox for a minute. What if we asked to see the CCTV feeds for every bank in Lee and Collier Counties that had lockboxes?"

"How many would that be?"

"I don't know about Lee, but we have forty-eight branches with lockboxes in Collier."

"That would be a zillion hours of video. That is a crazy idea. Who's gonna look at all that video?"

"We'd focus on branches in Naples, those close to where we know Dwyer has been. Then we narrow down the time periods. Maybe the first three days after he escaped. And we concentrate on the times of the day when a branch is slowest."

"That makes it a lot less crazy. You know what? It's a solid idea, Frank."

"I'm going to need your help with this."

"Of course. What do you need?"

"I can ask Chester to give me some manpower, but they wouldn't know Dwyer."

"I don't either."

"But I trust you to go over it carefully."

"Thanks, Frank. I appreciate the confidence; it means a lot to me."

"You have to be aware Dwyer is going to be disguised somehow. Who knows what he'll look like? He could have facial hair, or no hair at all. Dwyer may have a limp or something. Who knows what he'd think up?"

"You think he'd be able to pass himself off as a girl?"

"Good thinking. We have to approach this as if anything is possible."

"Where do we start?"

"Let's stick with Collier for the time being. We'll focus on branches around the Greyhound bus stop, and that girl, Mary Vero, and any banks around her house."

"How about that woman that lived by the David Lawrence Center?"

"Tammy Branch? I don't know. Something was off with her, but that would mean Dwyer knew he'd escape from David Lawrence."

"But you said he was a master planner."

"You know what; let's look at branches within two miles of her house."

"I'll plot the banks on a map and the time lines."

"Email the list to Zenneti. Tell him we need someone to collect the video from the banks. I don't want you wasting time running around for them. Text me when they start coming in."

***

Did everyone get apprehensive stepping into a doctor's office? It made me think I should appreciate every moment and place in my life. There wasn't a person on the planet that really wanted to go to the doctor, especially anyone who'd gone through what I had. We were justified. Weren't we?

There were at least two times that what the doctor had assured me about required major backtracking. Was it wrong to expect a doctor to get it right more often than a mechanic?

Who came up with the term routine physical? There was nothing routine about it when they found something. It was sheer terror. Bam! You were drawn into their world like ants to sugar.

Dr. Lupo's office was filled with potbellied woman. Mary Ann had the slightest curve to her abdomen. There was no way to tell she was pregnant. It felt a bit silly to be among women about to burst.

All the women had happy glows on their faces. I hadn't noticed it on Mary Ann. Maybe she needed a little more time. It was all stretch pants and tight shirts. What happened to the maternity wear I remembered growing up? I wasn't against it; I liked the way a pregnant woman looked, as long as they didn't gain a hundred pounds.

Would Mary Ann put on weight she couldn't take off? She always watched her weight, so I didn't think so, but I'd have to be ready to help her bounce back.

Mary Ann began chatting with a woman in leopard stretch pants. I wondered if her neon light had burned out. Rifling through a stack of magazines, I couldn't find anything without a smiling baby on the cover.

We held hands as Dr. Lupo spread a gel on Mary Ann's lower belly, explaining the images were going to be blurry.

"Ready?"

"Absolutely, but Doctor, we prefer not to know if it's a boy or a girl. Okay?"

"Sure. Hardly anyone doesn't want to know the sex of the fetus. It's the first thing they ask."

I said, "How does this work?"

"The device transmits high frequency sound waves through the uterus. When the sound waves return, they send signals that the ultrasound converts to images."

"So, it's not a real image, just an interpretation?"

"No, it's real. It just looks like a blurry negative from a photograph. You'll see. Here we go."

Mary Ann squeezed my hand as a black-and-gray image appeared on the monitor.

"Oh my God! Frank, look!"

Our baby was on its back in a black cavity. The head was almost as large as the rest of the body. The legs were flipperlike. There were no arms. I dropped Mary Ann's hand.

"I can't see, any, arms."

"Don't worry, they're there."

"Where?"

"See here? The arm is not fully developed. The fetus is only seven weeks old at this stage, and development is not balanced."

I didn't see anything but a white line that could be anything. I'd have to trust the doctor, but why did she keep using the word fetus instead of baby? Was she keeping things sterile to protect her patients if something went wrong?

Mary Ann said, "I don't see the heart beating."

"The heart is right here. See?"

"Oh, yeah. Wow, this is amazing, isn't it, Frank?"

"Incredible."

"The heart is beating at a rate of a hundred beats a minute."

"Is that good?"

"Perfect. It's right in the middle of the range."

"I read that if you can see the heartbeat at six to seven weeks then it means there won't be a miscarriage. Is that true?"

"It's a good sign, but there's no guarantee."

Walking to the car, my cell phone rang.

"Detective Luca."

No answer.

"This is Detective Luca. Who is this?"

No answer again. I hung up.

"Who was that?"

"Probably a wrong number."

I didn't want to tell her it was the second call I'd received like that.

Chapter 39

I blinked my eyes, closing them as I kneaded the back of my neck. Time to take a break. I'd go to the bathroom, then grab a cup of java after one more video. Next on the pile was a video from the SunTrust Bank at the intersection of Davis Boulevard and Airport Pulling Road.

Grateful that they didn't have much lockbox action, I fast-forwarded through until a man being shepherded by a bank employee appeared. The man was beefy. You could put the appearance of weight on, but this guy was wearing short sleeves. I hit fast-forward until a woman appeared.

She was as thin as Dwyer, but she was wearing a skirt. I fast-forwarded to the end and reflexively pawed the next one from SunTrust Bank. That took less than five minutes. My pee could wait. I hit play then fast-forward.

As soon as a bank employee came on the screen, I backed off the fast-forward button. A second later a wheelchair came into view. It appeared to be a man. He wore a baseball cap. Head down, he was wearing gloves. I hit pause. Then zoom. I got closer to the screen, squinting my eyes.

Could it be him? Toggling between play and pause, I made my own frame by frame. The bank employee inserted a key and swung open a small door. He removed a steel box and set it on the table. He talked to the man in the wheelchair.

He placed the box in the man's lap and walked to the door. The man in the wheelchair swiveled his neck, following the man out of the room. That's when I saw it. The grimace. It was Dwyer.

Alone, Dwyer smiled as he opened the box. He reached in and took three bundles of cash. Dwyer stuffed them into his pocket and closed the box. I couldn't tell if the box was empty or not. Dwyer wheeled over to the door and reached for the buzzer.

Dwyer handed the box to the bank employee and wheeled out of the room. Hitting the back button, I watched it again. Using a wheelchair was a twist I never considered. It was a complicating factor and a testament to his ingenuity. Having the bank employees place the box on his lap was a nice touch. I had to upgrade my opinion of Dwyer. He was good—damn good.

But so was I. It was game on. Feigning a disability by using a wheelchair was a brilliant disguise, but it was a well I'd draw from.

It looked like a stroke of genius, but was it a mistake? How and from where did Dwyer get his hands on a wheelchair? It's not like he'd walk into a place and rent one. How would he get it home? Then it hit me.

How did Dwyer arrive at the bank in the first place? I picked up the phone to call SunTrust Bank. Then I dropped the receiver back. I needed to see this place myself. It was too important.

***

SunTrust Bank was just east of a Walgreens. Pulling into their parking lot, I noticed that the two lots were connected. Dwyer would know every bank had cameras covering their entire property. I'd have to check the surveillance range of anything Walgreens had. If Dwyer arrived by car, he wouldn't have parked in the bank's lot.

A thought hit me, and I pulled out my cell. Googling revealed that Walgreens rented wheelchairs. They also sold them, some for as little as a hundred and ten dollars. Dwyer could have picked up a wheelchair and rolled over to the bank. If that were the case, he wouldn't need an accomplice.

Before going into the bank, I surveyed the area. There was a Home Depot directly across from the bank. I stared at its orange sign. Was I getting a signal, or was it the traffic whizzing by on Airport Pulling?

The branch was dead quiet. None of the five tellers had a customer. Why did they staff it like they were in Miami? I asked for the manager and was given a tour of the lockbox area. It was smaller than the others I'd been in and the one Dwyer had at First Integrity Bank.

Carrying a stack of DVDs containing footage from the cameras covering the perimeter of the building, I headed to Walgreens. Walking through the connected parking lots I noticed that this Walgreens didn't have a drive-through window. That meant less exterior camera coverage.

The pharmacy had a steady flow of people streaming in and out. Maybe a witness or two would be able to add something. I stopped and jotted a note to check on prescription pickups during the time Dwyer was there. If he was there.

Walgreens only had two outside cameras covering their entrance. Leaving the store with their CCTV footage, the possibility that Dwyer had used someone's wheelchair raised its volume. Was it more likely that Dwyer would run the risk of involving someone else in his scheme or go it alone, exposing himself to the chance he'd be noticed in a high-volume store like Walgreens?

***

"I got him, Derrick. Come here." I paused the bank video, freezing Dwyer rolling into SunTrust's parking lot from the left.

Derrick came around my desk. "Where's he coming from?"

"A Walgreens next door; their parking lots are connected."

"It's weird seeing someone wheel across a parking lot like that. I guess it's easier than getting in and out of a car and storing the wheelchair for a quick ride."

"Either he was dropped off at Walgreens, or he bought the chair there."

"Did you get anywhere with obtaining a warrant?"

"I asked Chester to check with the DA. Dusting for prints is useless. Dwyer had gloves on. I'd love to get inside the box, but Chester said he didn't think we had enough."

"Don't have enough? That's crazy."

"I can't believe Dwyer would leave anything behind. There's no reason not to clean it out. He wouldn't risk it."

"So, why would the DA be concerned about privacy?"

"Chester said the video may not be good enough to confirm it's Dwyer."

"If we get the ID he used to open the account, we may be able to tie it back to him."

Derrick was thinking like a pro. "True. Even if we can't open the box, we get the record on what he used to open the account. We'd have the identity he's using."

Chapter 40

The aroma of sautéing garlic made my stomach growl. But what was that music? It sounded like something you'd hear in a spa. Mary Ann was stirring what I hoped would turn into broccoli rabe and penne.

It was the first time I noticed a bump in her belly. I stared at her profile. This was real. Going to the doctor's office and seeing the baby on the scan moved the pregnancy to another level, but this was in our house.

She turned around. "What's the matter?"

"Nothing."

"Frank."

"Just admiring my, my," I almost said wife, "two babies. You and the little one inside you."

Mary Ann put her arms around me. "Sometimes you can be so sweet."

I pressed into her, not from a sexual urge, but to see if I could feel the bulge in her gut. I couldn't. She wrapped a leg around mine.

"Hey, the broccoli rabe is going to burn."

She wriggled free. "What's the matter? I don't get you excited anymore?"

"No, no. It has nothing to do with that. Come here."

"No. Forget it. I wouldn't want to burn dinner."

How did I go from a hero to a goat? I snuggled up behind her. "I just wanted to take a shower. I sweated like crazy today."

She turned around. "You okay?"

"Yeah."

"Your eyes are all bloodshot." She took a step away from me and put a box of penne into a pot of boiling water, "Maybe you're coming down with something."

"It's from looking at all the video today."

"Maybe you need to get glasses."

"Glasses?"

"Yeah, for reading."

"I don't think so."

"When is the last time you had an eye exam?"

"It's been a while. I'll be right back. I'm going to jump in the shower."

It only took me a few minutes to shower. Carrying my clothes to the laundry room, I said, "Anyway, this Dwyer, he's tricky."

"What did you find?"

"He's had another lockbox filled with money."

Mary Ann began setting the table. "How did you find that?"

"Remember the hunch I had about checking video from the banks with lockboxes? Well, it worked."

"That's what makes you good, Frank. I'm surprised you found Dwyer on tape."

"Not only that, but he was in a wheelchair when he went to access the box."

"A wheelchair?"

"Yep. I gotta hand it to him. It was something I'd never considered, but you know what? I think it's going to lead to catching the bastard."

I tested the macaroni. It was ready. I drained the pasta, mixed in the broccoli rabe, and spooned out two dishes. Carrying them to the table, I said, "What's with the spa music?"

"Dr. Lupo said listening to soothing music is good for the baby and helps to keep me relaxed."

I spread cheese over my pasta. "Makes sense. Music has the ability to change your mood in a second."

"She suggested a couple of playlists on Spotify."

Why wasn't it surprising that there were playlists for pregnancies?

Over dinner, I told her how the use of a wheelchair could generate leads with someone helping him and with identifying who that might be.

If Dwyer wasn't getting any assistance, then the chair could help us firm up a time line and close in on his whereabouts.

"You'll get him. I know you will."

"I can't wait to see the look on his face when I slap cuffs on him."

We began clearing off the table. "Don't forget, I have an appointment with Dr. Lupo tomorrow. You going to be able to make it?"

"You know what the name Lupo means?"

"No."

"In Italian it means wolf."

"Really? That's interesting."

I leaned into her. "Don't you think she looks a little like a wolf?"

"Sometimes you're crazy, you know that. Easy, Frank, my breasts are sensitive."

I worked her blouse loose. "Crazy like a fox."

***

Judge Wright signed the order for access to SunTrust Bank's records concerning who opened lockbox 847. The order provided us with the alias Dwyer was using. The bank's files contained a photocopy of a driver's license for a Peter Parker. The address listed was 17 Crayton Boulevard in Naples. There was a Crayton Road and a Crayton Court, but not a Crayton Boulevard.

Dwyer had opened the account just over two years ago. I knew he was a planner, but the depth of it gave me pause. I kept thinking, was another box out there? I ended up assuming there was.

On the plus side, with the photo match an exact, and an address that was bogus, our chances of getting the judge to grant an order to open the box was almost assured. Derrick and I were waiting for the DA's office to give us a green light.

"Is it a bad sign that it's taking so long?"

"Judge Wright is probably in court."

"It'll take all day, then."

"I don't think so. He'll review the request during recess."

"Oh, good. I still can't believe this Dwyer guy. I would have loved to have been on the first case with you."

"He's one of a kind, especially with the amount of planning and patience he shows. Can't help but think he got that way from having to fend for himself."

"I know what you mean. The kid had no parents to teach him. No wonder he ended up like this."

"It lengthens the odds; that's for sure."

"You're going to make a good father, Frank."

"I hope so."

"You will. You're a natural."

I didn't want to spoil his impression of me with my tendencies to critique and being selfish, traits that I'd have to suppress for a shot at a best dad T-shirt.

My cell sounded a text: Judge Wright had signed the order to crack open the box.

Chapter 41

I was staring at the only thing we found in Dwyer's bank lockbox. It was another stick drawing of a man waving. Who the fuck did he think he was? If Dwyer meant to rile me up, he had exceeded his wildest expectations.

I caught myself. Being emotional was no way to catch a killer. I was doing the four, seven, eight breathing technique I had just read about and opened my eyes when Derrick came into the office.

He was carrying a bag from Subway. "Hey, Frank, did you ever ask Muchado about Garrison?"

"Hector Muchado? The guy we talked with on the Boyle murder?"

"Yeah, the guy in the halfway house."

"No. Why?"

He unwrapped his sandwich. "I was poking around, talking to one of my informants, Louie the Loser."

The smell of vinegar hit me. "The drunk?"

"Yep. He brought up Muchado's name. Said he used to work with Garrison before he went away."

"Was he sober or making shit up, like the last time?"

"No, I believed him. He didn't say much, but I thought if you hadn't talked to him, it might be worth it."

"I don't know, sounds like a long shot."

"Your call."

Derrick popped open a can of Coke and dug into his lunch as I debated whether to take the ride to see Muchado. It was unlikely that he'd provide anything I could use, but Derrick was a noisy eater, and the office smelled like cheap salad dressing.

"I'll see you later."

"Oh. Antonio called, said he'd see you soon."

"Antonio? Antonio who?"

"I don't know. He sounded like you knew who he was."

Could it be? "I think it's Dwyer."

"What makes you think that?"

"The Alamo is in San Antonio."

"If it's him, this guy's got melon-sized balls."

"I assume it was a two-second call?"

"Yeah. Frank, you got to be careful, man. This guy might be going off the rails."

"Tell me about it."

***

Cigarette smoke hung in the air like it'd been nailed there. Hector Muchado was one of five hardened men smoking on the porch. He was sitting in the corner. The men scattered like rats as I walked toward them.

I held up my ID. "Just want to have a few words."

He looked at my badge with dead eyes.

"You have nothing to worry about. I wanted to ask a couple of questions about someone you knew."

He took a long drag and said, "Who?"

"Jimmy Garrison."

"Don't know no Jimmy Garrison."

"Come on, Hector. I know you know Garrison. Like I said, it has nothing to do with you."

"Don't know him."

"I'll put in a good word with your parole officer. I don't have to tell you, they can break your balls if they don't like you."

He crushed out his cigarette. "What do you want to know?"

"Garrison was murdered."

"I don't know nothing about that."

"I know that. You were in the same ring as Garrison."

"What about it? I've been out of that for years, man."

"What can you tell me about him? Who would want him dead?"

"I don't know. I was in the joint when he stepped out."

"What did you hear when he did? I'm sure people got pissed."

"When Jimmy broke away, they let him go. Didn't do nothing about it."

"That's unusual, isn't it?"

He shrugged and tapped a cigarette out of a Marlboro box.

"You know, stepping out of line brings consequences, and it's always fast, isn't it? What made them wait so long to send a message?"

"Jimmy had some kinda protection. They couldn't touch him."

"What sort of protection? From another gang? A cartel?"

"I don't know for sure, but I heard somebody connected had fronted Jimmy."

"Someone from the mob? The Russians? Turks? Chinese?"

"I don't know, man."

"Come on, Hector. You know. Just tell me, and I promise it will be worth it."

"I was inside. We don't get everything, you know."

That wasn't true. Inside a prison, word spread like the flu. "Just give me a name, and I'm out of here, and things will get easy for you."

"I don't know. All's I can say is it was just somebody they didn't want to cross."

Pressing Muchado for more was like squeezing a coconut for its milk. He probably knew more, but I couldn't blame him. He'd be out on the street in five months. He had to be cautious. I thought Muchado was a beaten man; years inside took a heavy toll. He wasn't a threat. I'd put in a word to his parole officer to cut him a break every so often.

The traffic on Immokalee gave me more time than I wanted to think over the Garrison case. If the gang Garrison left was afraid to take revenge, who was behind Garrison's venture? That there was big money involved was no surprise. All our attempts to find out what network Garrison worked for ended with multiconnected Miami players who were midtier at best.

The speed with which Garrison accumulated enough money to buy a three-million-dollar home was stunning. It was wealth created at Silicon Valley speed. The only asset we could nail down was the house. It had to be key.

I couldn't ignore that a turf war had broken out or that another crime organization wanted to muscle onto the gravy train Garrison was piloting. But my instincts were telling me Garrison had crossed someone, and it involved money. Unless they were in South America, drug dealers lived in unassuming quarters. They projected through their Lamborghinis and Ferraris. Could someone have felt Garrison was attracting too much attention?

It came back to the house again.

***

I swung open the door, scanning the women seated around the room. Mary Ann was still waiting. I strolled over, and she broke into a smile.

"I didn't think you'd make it."

I pecked her cheek. "I got a little hung up."

"Oh, your friend Antonio called."

"Antonio? You sure?"

"Yes, he said something about sending you fireworks. You're not getting fireworks, are you? You know how much I hate them."

I didn't want to scare her before seeing the doctor. "No, it was just a bad idea of mine. You know, to celebrate the baby and all. Forget about it."

Before she could say anything, they called her name.

We were shown into an exam room. The nurse weighed Mary Ann. She had gained two pounds. They took her blood pressure twice.

I said, "Is something wrong?"

"It's high, but let's see what Dr. Lupo says."

"Did you get the blood work from Quest?"

"Yes. It's in her file."

"How does it look?"

"You'll have to wait for Dr. Lupo. She'll be right in."

"Why wouldn't she tell us about the blood test?"

"Take it easy, Frank. She probably isn't allowed to discuss things like that."

"I hope there's nothing wrong."

"All along, I thought I'd be the one who was nervous. Boy, was I wrong."

There was a quick knock on the door, and Dr. Lupo stepped in.

"How are you feeling, Mary Ann?"

"Good. Surprisingly well."

"Lie back. Let's have a look."

Lupo examined Mary Ann in a way that made me turn my head. When she was finished, she peeled off her gloves.

"You and the fetus are doing fine, but I'm concerned with your blood sugar and hypertension."

Not one but two issues?

Mary Ann said, "What's the matter?"

"There's nothing to be concerned with at this point. It's something to keep our eyes on. Your blood pressure is on the high side. Gestational hypertension is not unusual in a pregnancy, but it generally occurs in the second half. Let's see what happens with your next visit. If we move it up a week, does that work for you?"

"Yes."

"You mentioned something about her blood sugar."

"That's also a bit high. Gestational diabetes is fairly common, and like elevated blood pressure will disappear after delivery."

"So, nothing to worry about?"

"At this point, no. Also, pick up some iron pills. Your levels are on the low side, and I don't want you becoming anemic."

Mary Ann put on a mask, but I knew she was disturbed at what Dr. Lupo had told her. I was rocked. I tried to find a way to pull the doctor aside and grill her about it, but I knew if Mary Ann found out, I'd not only be in the doghouse, but it would have a lock on it.

How much more crap would be dropped on my doorstep? The adage you get what you can handle is bullshit.

***

We went straight home. There wasn't an opening to say anything to Mary Ann about who I thought Antonio was. I grilled a couple of hamburgers, insisting we eat inside. After cleaning up, we put the TV on. An hour later Mary Ann said, "This movie is terrible. I'm going to get changed and read for a while."

"Okay. I'll watch a little sports."

Guys were chasing a puck on a sheet of ice, but who was winning wasn't something that registered. The game was chewing gum for my eyeballs as I wondered what the meaning of Dwyer's calls were.

I couldn't think of anyone I knew with the name Antonio. It had to be him. He called Mary Ann and Derrick under the same name. Who else could it be?

I went around the house, making sure the doors were locked. It was only a little after nine, but I decided to head into the bedroom and read as well.

"You're not watching TV?"

"Nah. I'm going to lie in bed next to you and read that John Adams biography I bought last year."

"You left the light on in the family room."

I wanted it on. "I'll shut it later."

Reading about John Adams was the perfect antidote for my worrying. He was an amazing man. In the middle of reading about the week-long horseback journey he took to Philadelphia, Mary Ann dropped her book. She had fallen asleep.

I picked the book up and she woke up.

"Go to sleep."

"I am." She shut her light, kissed me, and went to sleep. She was out in a minute.

I kept reading about Adams. How come everybody knew George Washington but not John Adams? He sounded more important.

Reading about an early meeting where they discussed breaking away from England, I heard it:

A gunshot. It hit our house. I shoved Mary Ann. "Get on the ground. Away from the window."

"What?"

"Somebody shot at our house."

"Oh my God. I'm calling for help."

I reached up and grabbed my gun off the nightstand. "I think it might be Dwyer."

She started crawling to the closet. "I'm coming with you. Let me get a shotgun."

"No, you're not! You stay here and wait."

"Frank, I can help."

"No. You're pregnant."

I crawled into the family room, got on my knees and looked out a window. Nothing. I pulled a chair over for cover, reached up and threw a switch. The lanai lit up. Nothing. I checked windows on each side of the house but found nothing.

Cracking open the front door, I heard several sirens approaching. I relaxed. When a brother or sister officer was in trouble, you'd get enough support to fill a stadium.

As a contingent of officers searched the grounds of our community, my cell phone rang. It was the sheriff.

"I heard there were shots fired on your home. Is everyone safe?"

"Yes, nobody is hurt."

"What happened?"

"We were in bed reading, and I heard a single shot go off. It was about nine fifty. It hit the front of our house, by one of the windows."

"Did they find the bullet?"

"Still looking, sir. It ricocheted. Looks like the shooter was aiming for the window from behind a stand of magnolias across the street."

"I told you I'd post a car. Now you have no choice."

"I should have taken you up on it."

"You think this is Dwyer?"

"I have to, sir. Nothing else makes sense."

Chapter 42

Derrick and I were hunched in front of monitors, going through hours of video of the Walgreens entrance. We bantered back and forth about football to keep from falling asleep. I wasn't a fan, but he was. It was something I would have to wean him off. He mentioned the Dallas Cowboys.

"Mary Ann doesn't know a thing about football, but she says she's a Cowboys fan. She even has a Tony Romo jersey."

"How's she doing?"

"She's tough. Having a patrol car out front helps."

"I spoke to her yesterday about it. She seemed fine. I was talking about the pregnancy. You said there were some issues."

"She's doing good. I'm the one who is nervous."

"It'll be fine, Frank."

"I hope so. The doctor scared us. You know, it's a lot riskier having a kid when you're over thirty-five."

"Yeah, but with the improvements in medicine the last twenty years, it's not that big of a deal."

He was right, to a degree. It minimized, not eliminated, risk. "She always took care of herself and tries to get me to do the same. It's one of the things I love about her."

"You make a great couple. You going to get married before the baby is born?"

"Uhm, we're thinking of it." We weren't. Or at least I wasn't.

"I don't want to butt in or anything, but you should. It's the right thing to do."

He was right again. But was he out of line? The phone rang. As luck would have it, it was Mary Ann. I listened. I hung up.

Jumping out of my chair, I said, "Let's go. Mary Ann got a hit on the website. She thinks it might be Dwyer."

We raced up the stairs into the cybercrimes unit. Mary Ann was on the phone and standing behind her desk. She hung up.

"Sit down, Mary Ann. You shouldn't be standing."

"It's okay, Frank. Sitting all day is not good either. Hiya doing, Derrick?"

"Real good, Mary Ann."

"What do you have for us?"

She turned her monitor toward us. A mumbo jumbo of numbers and letters filled the screen.

"See this here?"

She pointed to a series of numbers interspersed with periods highlighted in red.

"This is the third day in a row this address appeared. And four times each day. Each time, about two hours in between visits."

"That's what makes you think it's Dwyer?"

"That and the fact that whoever it is visits each page every time, not bouncing off a page but staying long enough to see what, if anything, has been updated."

Derrick said, "Does the IP address belong to a phone or a PC?"

"It's a computer hooked to the internet through Comcast."

"Is the location stagnant?"

"Yes. Here's the location we pinned down from the hits."

I said, "Are you sure this is where it's coming from?"

"As sure as we can be without a court order."

The location was in an area known as Quail West, an exclusive, gated community featuring expensive homes on oversized lots. It was an unlikely place for a man on the run to hide. But this was Dwyer. He was unconventional and dangerous

What was he doing in Quail West? Was a wealthy friend giving him a safe harbor? Was the friend even home? Dwyer had house-sat for his brother in the past. Maybe the brother recommended him to a friend?

Can't be. People knew Dwyer had escaped. Did Dwyer know the home was empty and had broken into it?

"Frank? You okay?"

"Yeah, yeah, just processing all this. Let's get rolling."

"Do we need backup?"

I shrugged for Mary Ann but knew we did.

Mary Ann said, "Are you sure, Frank? Dwyer is dangerous."

"I was testing you. So, you really think this is him, then?"

"Nothing is definite, but whoever it is left an interesting pattern."

"Derrick, call downstairs and get two cars to accompany us. Make sure they're unmarked."

Mary Ann said, "Tell them you want two officers in each car."

Derrick looked at me and I nodded. "We'll meet them in the parking lot."

Mary Ann handed me a piece of paper. "Take this with you. It's the IP address. If Dwyer's not there, you can verify if it's the same computer or not."

Chapter 43

I tossed the keys to Derrick, who said, "You sure you want me to drive?"

"Yeah, why not?" I climbed into the passenger seat.

He started the Cherokee. "You'll never guess what I did last night."

"What?"

"Me and Lynn were going to dinner down at Molto, and I couldn't find a parking spot. It was raining, so I figured I'd valet it. There was a car ahead of me, and the valet came over with a ticket. He said to leave it. So, like a moron, I jump out of the car without putting it in park. It goes right into the car ahead of me."

I laughed. "Oh geez."

"It was so embarrassing. I felt like an idiot. Now I gotta deal with paying for the repairs."

"Was there a lot of damage?"

"Not too bad, but I'm sure it's going to be expensive. To tell you the truth, the embarrassment is worse than the cost."

"I won't tell anyone if you won't tell anyone about what I did last night."

Pulling away, Derrick said, "What happened?"

"It was about two in the morning, and I go to take my leak. I'm sitting on the bowl and I smell something. It smells like smoke. I'm trying to figure out what the hell it is when I think, holy shit, Dwyer set the house on fire. I run into the bedroom, wake up Mary Ann, and tell her to wait on the lanai."

"Are you kidding me?"

"I wish I were."

"What was it?"

"Ended up being the AC blower. It burned out."

"My story is worse than yours."

I didn't know about that. He simply forgot to do something. Me? I had a serious case of the Dwyer jitters.

***

The home at 901 Williston Way meandered over the wide lot it sat on. There was a breezeway separating a four-car garage area from the main portion of the house. It had a unique feel to it, straddling contemporary and coastal styles. I was looking at several million dollars' worth of elegance.

As agreed, the two officers spread out to cover the back of the home, where there were sure to be scores of sliders and the garage area. The other two stood guard on each side of the mansion. Derrick and I walked up the drive, around a fountain, to ten-foot doors. We could see clear through the house, past the pool to a large lake.

I gave the signal and rang the bell. An organ sound, worthy of a cathedral, bounced around the home. A slim woman with a sleeping child attached to her hip came to the door.

"Can I help you?"

We held our badges up. "Police, ma'am. Are you the owner of the home?"

"Yes. Why? What's the matter?"

"You're Angela Leary?"

"Yes. That's me."

"Would you mind if we came inside?"

She looked at our badges, then our faces. "Okay, but I need to know the purpose of this visit."

We stepped into a white marble foyer. To the left was a black grand piano and a wall full of modern art. To the right was one of the longest dining tables I had ever seen. King Arthur wouldn't need more seating.

"Do you know an Ethan Dwyer?"

"No, I don't think so. It's vaguely familiar though."

She seemed genuine. "Are you home alone?"

"Yes, except for her." She smiled at her daughter.

"We believe an escaped felon is in the area."

She held the baby closer. "Oh my God. Are we in danger?"

Derrick pointed through the back windows at one of our officers. "We don't believe so, ma'am."

I said, "To be absolutely sure, we'd like to search the house. With your permission, of course."

Derrick handed her a card. "If you'd like, you can call the sheriff's office to confirm our presence here."

"No. It's okay. Should we wait outside, just in case?"

"It's not necessary. You can stay in the foyer, but if you're more comfortable outside, go ahead."

She took a step toward the door. "We'll be right here."

"How many bedrooms, ma'am?"

"Four. The master's down here, and the children's rooms are upstairs."

We quickly searched the first level. There was a laptop in the center of a desk in the office. Derrick tapped on its keyboard. It wasn't the one used to visit the trap Mary Ann had set.

Doubt was seeping in as we trudged up the stairs. Clearing a room with a crib, I spotted the attic access. No one normal would hide in an attic. The heat would kill them. Had Dwyer found a way to survive up there? I wasn't going into that oven.

We entered the last room. It had a rocket ship painted on one wall and a ceiling covered with stars. The lucky kid had a bed whose frame was a sports car. This boy had it all. I tucked the decorating ideas into a mental file and cleared the walk-in closet.

Derrick was going through the desk and pulled open a drawer.

"Frank, we got an iPad."

"Check the IP address."

He tapped on it. "It's locked. We need a password. You want to forget about it?"

"No way. Let's take it to the mother."

The mother was on the phone as we came down the stairs. The kid was still asleep in her arms. What I would give to sleep like that.

"It's all clear, ma'am."

She finished her call, and I asked, "How old is your son?"

"He'll be twelve in July. Why?"

Derrick held the iPad up. "Is this his?"

"Yes. Why? Don't tell me he's been—"

"It's password protected. Would you happen to know the password? Otherwise, we'll have to take it with us."

"Oh, try Saturn."

"No good."

"Then it has to be Mercury."

"That's it."

Derrick tapped on the tablet and checked the slip of paper. "It's a match."

"You sure?"

"Yep."

"What's going on?"

"Ma'am, have you had any visitors the last three days?"

"No."

"Have you left the house unattended?"

"No. Billy was sick and we stayed home, except when we went to the doctor's."

"Can you tell me why your son would visit a website about the investigation into an escaped prisoner?"

She smiled. "Billy's fascinated with people on the run. His favorite movie is *The Fugitive*. He's watched it a hundred times, made me watch it so many times I can recite lines in it. And *The Shawshank Redemption* and *Escape from Alcatraz* are two other ones he loves."

"I see. We're going to have to take this with us, just to be sure someone hasn't been using it."

"But that's crazy. No one else used it. I'm telling you my son is obsessed with escapes."

"I'm sure he is. However, we have to follow certain protocols. Once we clear it, we'll have it dropped off to you."

***

The only thing that was going right on the Dwyer case was that he hadn't killed anyone. How long would my luck hold out?

My alarm to urinate had rung three times. I couldn't put off taking a leak any longer, or I'd risk ending up in surgery again.

"Derrick, pull into Publix. I have to take a piss really bad."

I tottered in hoping like hell the stall wasn't being used. I pushed the door open. The stall was empty. It was the only luck I'd had. I grabbed a handful of towels and covered the seat.

Sitting there, I thought of what step to take next to find Dwyer. I felt like we had nothing, but the more I thought about it, I softened my feelings. We knew a lot about Dwyer overall and quite a bit about what he'd been up to since he escaped from David Lawrence.

Dwyer had been more active than most people on the run. He'd been to see a woman he knew before going in, forcing her to drop him off by the train tracks in Bonita Springs. Did he take a train? That question was wide open. He'd left a pair of drawings: one a taunt, the other a picture of what we believed was the Alamo.

Did he leave them for us to find? They were ripped to shreds. I automatically thought it was all orchestrated to make it seem like we weren't supposed to find it. Was I giving him too much credit? He took a shot at us and was harassing us but from a safe distance. So far. He was smart, but not a super-action figure.

Then again, he had baited us on Mary Ann's web trap. Dwyer had used an acronym of his name, a thinly veiled attempt to disguise himself when leaving conflicting comments from a stolen phone. Was it classic misdirection, or was something else going on?

I also knew he had planned for this day years ago, stockpiling money in a lockbox. What I was unsure of was if he really was gunning for me and whether he had help. It was time to dig in on that aspect.

Dwyer's half brother was my number one. We were monitoring his phone, and he knew we suspected him and his wife. I didn't know as much as I should about DiBlasi's wife. An in-law, especially in this half-brother relationship, wouldn't feel an obligation to help.

I had to know if there was some history that would compel her to break the law. As I washed up, I worried I was grasping at straws. I assured my reflection that it was a valid line of inquiry. If there was nothing there, I could eliminate the possibility, moving the case forward.

I hopped in the Cherokee.

"You okay?"

"Yeah, sorry to keep you waiting so long. Half the time I forget how long it takes me to pee."

"No problem. What next on Dwyer?"

"It's a helluva lot harder to reel him in if we don't know if he's getting help. He can stay hidden a lot longer with help than he could on his own."

"Makes sense. Where we going with this?"

"I'm going to go see the brother again. I want you to go back over the women Dwyer was in contact with before going into prison. Also take a look at his phone call logs, and make sure we didn't miss anything, male or female."

Chapter 44

Cruising east on Golden Gate, I felt good. I was in motion, pursuing the assistance-to-Dwyer question. It wasn't the most urgent, but it was something. I was just about to turn onto Goodlette Frank when my cell rang.

It was a brief call. I hung a U-turn. Putting my foot to the floor, I headed for Estero to see Edith Nealy. A visitor had just left the grandmother and legal guardian of Jimmy Garrison's kid.

Arms crossed, the grandmother was waiting outside. We met in the driveway. She was wearing tennis whites and a thin smile. Nealy began talking as I walked up the driveway. I put a finger to my lips. She held the door open, and we went into her kitchen.

"Who came?"

"He said his name was Edgar Ramirez. But I think he was giving me a phony name. He didn't look Hispanic at all. I'll show you."

"What are you going to show me?"

She pulled out her phone. "I have video of him."

"You took a picture of him?"

"Damn right I did. He didn't know. When he rang the bell, I put the speaker on and went to see who it was from the den window. When I didn't recognize who it was, I hit record."

The visitor was in a dark-colored suit and a red tie—not your average drug dealer outfit. His face didn't ring any bells.

"Did he say who he was representing?"

"He was nervous. Said he was from the lawyer's office."

"Matthias Goodman's office?"

"He never said. I should have asked. I'm sorry, but it had to be. It was about the house. He was—"

"Hold on. Let me get the recording, then we'll talk it over. What room were you in?"

"The kitchen."

Opening the speaker, I clicked the digital recorder into playback mode. Twenty seconds passed. I heard distant voices. The voices cleared up.

"Thank you for seeing me, Ms. Nealy. You have a nice home here for you and Evan."

"What do you want?"

"As Evan's legal guardian, we need your cooperation in resolving an issue concerning his biological father."

"Go on."

"Mr. Garrison is listed on the deed of a property as the sole owner. That property is scheduled to close within twenty days."

"That was fast."

"It was. Now, there's a technicality that needs to be addressed, and we need your cooperation with it."

"And what would that be?"

"Your daughter's son, Evan, is the sole, legal heir to James Garrison's estate. Therefore, any proceeds from the impending sale would technically accrue to his benefit."

"That's right. Evan's entitled to it."

"That's where the conflict arises."

"Conflict?"

"The property in question is not encumbered by any recorded liens. However, the funds that were used to purchase the property were lent to Mr. Garrison by one of our firm's clients."

"And who might that be?"

The guy calling himself Ramirez was a lawyer, not a thug, but I still found Nealy's toughness surprising.

"I'm sorry. I'm not at liberty to disclose that. It's confidential."

"And what does all this mean?"

"The proceeds belong to our client, not your daughter's son."

"Really?"

"Yes. It might be helpful to keep in mind that James Garrison was not really a father to your grandson. The custody proceedings are evidence they had no relationship whatsoever."

"And you came here because?"

"The firm would appreciate your signing over the rights to the proceeds. In return, the firm will acknowledge your assistance in keeping this from going to court and make a payment in the sum of fifty thousand dollars to a college fund for your daughter's son."

"You expect Evan to settle for fifty thousand dollars when he's entitled to three million?"

"The firm's clients would strenuously object to the characterization of Evan's rights as entitled."

"Let them object."

"That would be unfortunate, Ms. Nealy. The clients are, um, can be, shall we say, volatile."

"What does that mean?"

"It's the firm's recommendation that you accept the generous offer made. Strictly between the two of us, I'm authorized to go as high as seventy-five thousand dollars as compensation."

"I'll have to think this over."

"Time is of the essence, Ms. Nealy."

"I understand, but you couldn't possibly expect me to give you an answer today."

"The clients are anxious to resolve this matter in an expedient manner."

"Okay."

"The documents are drawn up, ready for signature. Naturally, the cooperative sum, now seventy-five thousand dollars, stands ready for transfer. It should be noted that we can arrange for the transfer before the sale is consummated, if that would be helpful."

"Like I said, I'll think about it."

"I was hoping we could come to an agreement today, but I understand your need to contemplate. That said, I'd urge you to come to a decision quickly."

"I understand."

"Thank you, Ms. Nealy. It was a pleasure meeting you."

"I'll show you out."

The recording ended. I disconnected and removed the digital device from the speaker. This woman did as well as any undercover agent I'd worked with. I had to be conscious about not getting her involved any deeper than she was.

"I have to commend you on the way you handled yourself, Ms. Nealy. You are one special lady."

"It was nothing. We're talking about Evan here. Nobody messes with my grandson."

"Well, call it courageous or not, you're not only protecting him, but many other kids as well."

"I don't know of anybody but Evan."

"Did he say anything that might not have been caught on tape?"

"Nothing other than a greeting when he first came in."

"Where's the card he gave you?"

She opened the kitchen junk drawer. "Here it—"

"Don't touch it."

"Why?"

"We may need to get his fingerprints off it to support that it was him today and I don't want to add any more to it."

"Okay."

I used a napkin to insert the business card into an evidence bag.

"What's the next step?"

"We need to identify who came here today."

"You want me to come down and look at photos?"

"That's not necessary. You sit tight, and if this guy or anyone else comes by or calls, let me know. Also, if they do happen to come around, and I don't think they will yet, don't talk in the kitchen. I took the recorder out."

Chapter 45

Jacket over arm, Derrick came into the office.

"Man, it's hot out there."

"You'll get used to it. How long you been here now?"

"About a year, if you can believe it."

"Time stops for no one. Father Time is undefeated."

"That's a good segue. Tammy Branch, the woman you said was hostile."

"Yeah, what about her?"

"She just lost her mother. Could be why she was like that to you."

"You talked with her?"

"No, she wasn't home, so I knocked on a neighbor's door. Guy named Phillips. Said her mother lived with her for the last ten years or so. She was pretty sick apparently."

"What was wrong with her?"

"I don't know. Why?"

"Was she in a wheelchair?"

"Uh, I didn't think to ask. Sorry."

"It's all right, you'll get there. Call Phillips and find out."

"I'm on it."

"I'll see you later. I want to revisit the half brother. You should probably come along after saving my ass the last time, but I'm meeting Mary Ann. She wants me to look at cribs, if you can believe it."

"It won't be long now, Daddy."

I hoped he was right on that. I couldn't wait for the pregnancy to be over. Becoming a father was something I was looking forward to, but that wasn't it. Mary Ann just wasn't herself. I knew it was hard to be yourself with a baby growing inside, but that wasn't it either. She had pregnancy-related health issues, and with her age, I just wanted it over—her and the baby safe.

Also, an end to running around for the million things parents had to have these days would be nice. Anytime I tried to rationalize with her about some needless device, I was either cheap or old-fashioned. I couldn't win one debate when it came to baby stuff. Wasn't parenting supposed to be a partnership, like marriage?

The thought of marriage reminded me of the feeling that we ought to do it. I knew it was strictly a formalization and maybe old-fashioned, but having a kid is a huge responsibility, and being married felt like that is the way it should be.

A wedding. I couldn't go through a big ordeal. Mary Ann was levelheaded and didn't seem interested in something like a big affair. Then I remembered what my dad had said: from the moment a baby girl is born, they are inundated with bridal images.

***

DiBlasi was hunched over a box in the garage when I pulled up. No longer empty, there were boxes and shelving holding things he'd probably never use. I closed the Cherokee's door and DiBlasi stood up.

He was surprised to see me.

"Is everything all right?"

Was that a way of asking if Ethan was okay? Or did he know Ethan was okay and didn't know what else to say?

"Yeah, I was in the neighborhood and thought I'd stop by."

"Oh, okay. How are things going?"

"Pretty good. Have you heard from Ethan?"

"No, not at all."

As he replied, I scanned the garage. Hanging next to a pair of umbrellas was an aluminum cane with a neoprene handle. It was the type they gave you in rehab.

"If he tries, remember to get ahold of me immediately."

"Will do."

"Your wife as well."

"She knows what to do."

"How is she feeling? I remember she was sick."

"She's recovered fully."

"That's great. I can't remember what happened to her."

"Jenny had an appendix that burst. Then she became septic, and they couldn't control the infection."

"Oh boy, that's sounds nasty."

"It got worse. She was in bed so long her muscles weakened, and she basically had to learn to walk all over again."

"I feel terrible for you guys. She was in a wheelchair?"

"She had one but didn't really use it. She went into rehab for a month and was able to get around. She mostly relied on a walker, then a cane, until she regained her strength."

"What a mess. You never know what life is going to throw your way."

"Nothing truer than that. We had our plans to move down here, bought the house, and then, bang, out of nowhere, Jenny was in intensive care and it was touch and go. I swear, I thought I was going to lose her."

"That's why they say live for today."

"You got that right."

"Well, I'm glad she's doing well."

"Thanks."

"I always wondered, all the equipment people get when they go into rehab."

"What do you mean?"

"Things like a cane, a wheelchair, what do you do with them when you're done? Do you donate them?"

"Yeah, that's what we did, we donated them. We didn't need them, you know, so, why keep them?"

Didn't he realize the cane was hanging twenty feet away?

"Might as well give it to somebody who needs it."

"Absolutely."

"Plus, you probably get a tax break for donating, right?"

"I don't bother with stuff like that anymore. It's not worth it."

Saving a few bucks on taxes is not worth it? "What kind of places take those types of things?"

"Um, you know, I remember Jenny mentioned it, but I don't remember. She handled it."

"So, you didn't have to bring it to them. They came and picked them up. That's good."

"I'm not sure, but we were glad someone could use it. And it not only cluttered up the garage, it was a reminder of what happened."

"Might be good to keep around, then. Helps you appreciate things, you know?"

"I guess. Look, I've got to get moving."

"Is your wife home?"

He froze. "No, she's out. I don't know when she'll be back. Why?"

"No worries, just wanted to say hello. I'll stop by another time. Enjoy the rest of your day."

After two steps I heard the garage door begin to close. I turned around. DiBlasi was walking into the house and tapping on his phone.

Chapter 46

After a round of mental ping-pong, I went with my instincts. It was something to mark, to commemorate, even at the risk it might feed into the idea of a larger celebratory affair.

I'd booked a table at Bleu Provence, and Mary Ann almost ruined the plan, saying she wasn't sure she was up to going out. She didn't know my motivation. I had no intention of revealing it, so I told her we were double dating with Derrick.

We were shown to a corner table, and as the server removed two of the settings, Mary Ann said, "No, there's going to be four of us."

I told the server it was okay and ordered a bottle of Pinot Noir that I had looked up yesterday.

"When did he back out?"

"He was never coming." I leaned in. "I wanted to have a night alone with you. We need it."

"What's going on, Frank?"

"Nothing."

"Don't tell me nothing. I didn't want to go out, and you gave me a line about Derrick."

The server set down two glasses. They were nice glasses, shaped like tulips. I wondered if restaurants had a rule: if you buy a bottle over seventy-five dollars you get the fancy glasses.

Mary Ann said, "We only need one glass."

"Pour her a tiny amount, just for a toast."

Mary Ann eyed me while I took a sniff of the wine the server had poured. I sipped it and gave my approval. The server poured a splash into Mary Ann's glass and filled mine.

I held my glass up. She looked at me and picked up her glass. I clinked her glass and said, "With a baby on the way, I'd say it's time we get married."

"Did you say 'married'?"

"Yep. Married."

She put down her glass and wiped a tear from her eye. Then she grabbed my hand, giving me a long kiss.

"Thank you, Frank. I'm so happy. I really wanted us to get married but didn't want to say anything."

I took a sip. The wine was tasting better. "It's the right thing to do. We're right for each other."

"When do you think we should do it?"

"Soon. But I don't want to make a big deal of it. I mean, it is a big deal, but no big party or nothing."

"I don't care about all that."

"Me neither. But we should go away for the weekend. Maybe stay on the beach somewhere close, like Marco or Sanibel Island. Something like that."

"I don't want to be in a bathing suit looking like this."

"Are you kidding? I think you look as sexy as you ever have." It was true; I liked the way she looked with the growing bump in her midsection.

"You're just saying that to make me feel good."

"No. Really. It may sound weird, but it turns me on."

"You're nuts, Frank."

Feeling good, I capped the dinner off with a glass of cabernet, and Mary Ann had to drive home. We settled on a couple of dates next month to tie the knot, agreeing to do a small lunch at the Turtle Club followed by a quiet weekend at the Marriot on Marco Island.

***

Jacket over shoulder, I was about to leave when Mary Ann waddled into the office.

"There was a hit on the website. It came out of Alamo, Texas. Verizon was the ISP."

"Are you shitting me?"

"It was late last night, just after eleven our time, ten in Texas."

"Could it be Dwyer?"

"Whoever it was hit all the pages but one, the one with pictures of Dwyer on it."

"What about the bouncing thing?"

"Not a lot of time on each page. Varied from three to ten seconds."

"Do you think it could be him?"

"Tough to say, but you asked us to watch for anything out of Alamo."

"How would he have gotten to Texas?"

"Train, plane, car, you name it. It's fifteen hundred miles, a two-, three-day drive."

"That would mean the drawing he left, he didn't want me to find."

"I guess not."

"Or, better yet, he wanted me to think he was trying to throw me off his trail. Dwyer's been dropping bullshit signs all over the place. He's building an impression they're all misdirections. Then he goes to a place he thinks we'd never look for him."

"Really? You think he'd go to that extent rather than just melt away?"

"Absolutely. Dwyer really believes he is smarter than everyone."

"How you going to handle this?"

"Get a location for me and keep watching it. I want to know if he comes back to the site."

"Right now, this is what we have. A Chrome notebook was used. Best we can estimate, it was on Rene Street."

I was just about to go see Tammy Branch. Was it now a waste of time? It needed following up. Dwyer could have used her as a stepping-stone to Texas, if that was where he was.

But this was new, hot information. I pulled up a map of Alamo, Texas. Rene Street was just off the intersection of South Tower Circle and Moore Road. What the hell was I looking at? I was lost; nothing meant anything.

I zoomed in. There was a place called Arturo's Tavern that backed up to Rene Street. Was that relevant? I looked up the place. They served food. Maybe Dwyer could slip in and out of there to get his food. Who knew, maybe he was working there as a dishwasher.

And the name of the street, Rene, wasn't that French? Texas was a helluva lot more Hispanic than French. Did that have any meaning? Was Dwyer challenging me with some kind of mental Rubik's Cube?

As far as I knew, we had zero contacts in Texas except Dallas and Houston. I needed on-the-ground intelligence, someone who could discreetly scout around. Dwyer would pick up on a cowboy cop poking around.

We needed a court order to get Verizon to give us the exact details on an address and a name. After the last episode with the kid's iPad in Quail West, I didn't want to try for it yet.

Chapter 47

It was easy identifying Edith Nealy's visitor. Lawyers, as officers of the court, are fingerprinted. The lab dusted the card and ran it against the database, and bingo, we had a match with George Aviles.

Aviles had passed his bar exam three years earlier and had joined Goodman and Sokol upon graduating. How did this kid get himself mixed up in something like this? The district attorney didn't believe Aviles had broken the law during his visit with Nealy. However, the DA made it clear it was unethical and could result in a disbarment. But the DA also said Aviles was a member of the Miami Bar Association, and like a lot of things in Miami, there was substantial wiggle room.

Nobody outside law enforcement understood how corrupting the mounds of money drugs generate were. It seeped much further than people assumed, all the way to electing officials and making laws. It was tough to speculate on what Aviles would turn into in ten years. But whatever that was, it was certain to be controlled by a cartel boss.

Picking up the phone, I called Goodman and Sokol. I left a message for Aviles to call me, saying I was a friend of Nealy's and wanted to be sure the bonus would be seventy-five and not fifty thousand dollars.

It only took ten minutes for my phone to ring. I answered, taking a page from Dwyer's book, "Hello, this is Lou Frank."

"Mr. Frank, this is George Aviles. You left a message?"

"Thanks for calling back. Edith is concerned about the offer you made."

"What about it?"

"Could we meet and talk about this?"

"I'm rather busy."

"Edith said this was urgent and wanted to be sure that she could get the higher amount, not the original offer you made. And, well, if it's seventy-five thousand, she'll be able to sign whatever paperwork is needed, but she wanted me. We've been neighbors for years, and after her husband passed, she kinda relies on me. I don't mind, but sometimes it can get old, if you know what I mean."

"Ms. Nealy is prepared to execute the documents?"

"If you mean sign, yes, she's ready. She wants me there to be sure about the money."

"I can be by Ms. Nealy's home in an hour. Does that work?"

"That would be great."

***

Aviles was dressed in a beautiful blue suit, not quite the hand-tailored duds of high-profile defense attorneys, but expensive nonetheless. I watched him walk up the driveway. He was carrying a briefcase and a confident attitude.

I opened the door before he rang the bell.

"Mr. Aviles, come on in."

I didn't know what he expected, but whatever it was, I wasn't it. "Mr. Frank?"

"That's me. Let's get this going. Edith could really use the money."

"Is she home?"

"On her way back now. Let's go in the kitchen. I just made a cup of coffee. You want one?"

"No, thank you."

I stepped aside. When he passed me, I stood, back to the door, and pulled out my badge. "I'm with the police."

He turned around, whiter than a coloring book image. "I—I don't understand."

"I'm going to give it to you straight, George. You see this." I pulled out the recording device. "The entire conversation you had with Edith Nealy was recorded."

"There wasn't anything illegal in that conversation. I was simply conveying an offer a client asked us to present."

"It's called coercion. And the way you used it to steal millions of dollars from a rightful heir, a minor, no less, is certainly illegal. You're participating in a conspiracy to defraud a minor and his senior guardian."

"No. It can't be. Uncle Matthias said it was completely legal."

"Matthias Goodman is your uncle?"

"Yes."

"Let me tell you something, kid, and you'll sleep a lot better if you listen and learn. People like your uncle make a lot of money weaving their way around the law. It's all technical bullshit. They're making arguments on the letter of the law, not the spirit of the law. You start down that road, young man, and you'll never come back. You get paid big money from the dirtiest of clients, but they're the ones who own you. You hear what I'm saying? You want to sleep at night? Get out now."

Aviles looked like he was about to cry. He set his bag down, then picked it back up. "I'm leaving."

"No, you're not."

"You have no grounds to detain me."

"I'm going to throw you a lifeline. I suggest you take it before it's too late."

"What do you what with me?"

"Who is behind the effort to get the money from Garrison's house sale?"

"That's privileged information. If I revealed it, I'd be violating attorney-client confidentiality."

"Come off it. It's not your respect for the law but the fear of your clients that's keeping your mouth shut, and your eyes as well. Now, who is it?"

"I can't say. Everything will be ruined. I . . ."

"I know I'm asking you to stick your neck out, but is this what you went to law school for? To work for a bunch of scumbag dealers? To help steal money from a kid?"

"I knew I shouldn't have taken Uncle Matthias's offer."

"It's okay. Good money is hard to turn away from."

"I can't leave now."

"It's now or never. You're young enough to start over. You provide us with the information we need, and we'll get you out of here, to somewhere you like, with a new identity if you feel threatened."

"I can't. I just can't."

"You walk out of here, I promise you'll regret it. The DA has more than enough to get you disbarred. You'll never practice law again. Then how good are you to them?"

"Disbarred? You can't do that."

"No? Try us. Your actions were borderline illegal, but even a fifth grader knows how unethical it was. I don't give a damn how powerful your uncle thinks he is; he'll never get the Dade County Bar Association to let this go. And if by some miracle he did, we'll go to the press with it."

"I could be disbarred?"

"It's not could be, it's will be, if you don't cooperate."

Chapter 48

Distracted, I drove to see Tammy Branch. Mary Ann's latest blood tests had deteriorated in regard to her sugar levels, and her blood pressure readings were also slightly more elevated.

She seemed to be tiring more quickly than usual, especially over the last three weeks. It was now routine for her to take a nap when she came home. Most nights she would be in bed by nine thirty.

I wanted her to stop working. She'd get the rest she needed and be safe with a cop sitting outside the house. Dr. Lupo said it wasn't necessary and recommended she cut her hours back or go to three days a week. Mary Ann was mulling over what to do.

Heading west on Golden Gate, I passed the David Lawrence Center, and a Dwyer flood carried concerns about Mary Ann out of my head. This is where the nightmare began. Minutes later, I was back on Star Grass Lane.

Slowing down in front of the yellow fence bordering Branch's home, I was convinced the location couldn't be a coincidence. The gate was shut, blocking the driveway. A neighbor pulled out of a driveway a couple of houses down and slowed as he approached. I waved and the driver smiled, returning the wave.

Hitting the entrance call button, I surveyed the area. A voice cackled over the speaker, "Who is it?"

"Detective Frank Luca."

After a pause she said, "What do you want?"

"I have a few questions for you."

"It's not a good time."

"It won't take long."

"I'm sorry, but I'm busy."

"I wouldn't want to have to drag you in, ma'am. But I will if I have to."

A second later the gate creaked open.

Tammy Branch was standing on her tiny porch, the front door behind her closed. She had rings on almost every finger.

"I told you everything I know about Ethan."

"There's just a couple more questions that I have. Shall we go inside?"

"No."

What was she hiding? "I understand your mother passed away recently. I'm sorry about that."

"Thank you. Mother was sick for a long time. She suffered, especially at the end. I know I'm supposed to say she's in a better place now, but I miss her terribly."

Branch was a weird bird, but she had feelings like the rest of us. "It's never easy, I'm afraid. You'll get through it, even though you don't think you will."

She blinked her eyes twice. "I guess."

"If you don't mind me asking, what did she die from?"

"Mother had a couple of issues, but mainly it was complications from diabetes."

Just what I needed to hear. "Oh, my wife is prediabetes right now. What kind of complications?" Mary Ann and I weren't married yet, but I found myself referring to her as my wife when talking to strangers.

"Her kidneys weren't functioning properly, and she had a foot amputated. Plus, she was going blind. Your wife better watch it."

"That's terrible. It's mainly because she's pregnant, but we're keeping an eye on it."

"You have to take care of yourself. Mother wasn't the best at that."

"With an amputation, she must have been in a wheelchair."

"Yeah, and this house wasn't designed for that."

"How long ago did she die?"

"February fourth."

"This is going to sound a little crazy, but I volunteer with a charity, and we take all kinds of used furniture and things. If you have anything of your mother's that you'd like to go to good use, let me know."

"I'm not ready to part with anything of mother's. I haven't even gone through her things."

"I understand, but maybe something like the wheelchair. There are a lot of people who could use it."

"Like I said, I'm not ready."

"You live alone?"

"Yes."

"Have you heard from Ethan Dwyer?"

"No."

"You still working with the Spirit of Fellowship Church?"

"Of course. I enjoy being a part of their ministry. We bring hope to people who society has cast aside. We'd be a much better place if we accepted that everyone is a sinner. We all make mistakes, and with support, we can redirect ourselves, focusing on the prize of salvation."

This woman had the fire. "Well, I get the message, but in my line of work I see too many repeat offenders not to be skeptical of giving people more than a second chance."

"That's where you're wrong. Take children as an example. How many times do they make the same mistake over and over?"

It was an interesting point. I would have to be mindful as a parent to know the difference.

"Killing someone is a lot different than not doing your homework."

"If you have a true yearning for forgiveness, God will grant it. It's never too late, and it doesn't matter what you did. All that matters is making God the center of your existence."

"So even someone like Ethan Dwyer, who took the lives of at least five men. He should be forgiven for what he did?"

"Of course, as long as he is sorry, truly sorry, for what he did."

"We happen to disagree, but I understand your position. It makes a lot of sense, and I'm going to think about what you said."

Damn right I'd be thinking about it. My first thought was to get a warrant to search her place.

Derrick asked, "When do you think we're going to hear?"

"I wish I knew. Some of these judges, like Whitehead, are quick, and others ask the DA to give them precedent."

"Which one do you think we have a better chance of getting?"

"I want the Verizon one. That way we can see if it's Dwyer in Alamo or not."

"I don't know if it's him, Frank. He never went back to the site."

"Remember, he's a smart bastard. He has to know IP addresses are traceable."

"I know it's circumstantial, but getting a peek inside Tammy Branch's house is high on my list after what she said to you the last time."

"She lives right by the David Lawrence Center. Dwyer could have walked by the canal unnoticed. Then, two times she wouldn't let me in the house. Nobody does that. Plus, the mother used a wheelchair."

"It's a perfect place for Dwyer to hide. The neighborhood is quiet; the houses are on big lots—"

The phone rang. I answered. We had the Verizon warrant.

Chapter 49

The telecom companies fought law enforcement whenever we requested data. No matter the circumstances, even a kidnapping involving a child, they would respond like a dumbbell to an information request. That said, once we were armed with a court order, they were lightning fast. It pissed me off. They had the data we needed at their fingertips.

Verizon said the account used to get on the internet was registered to Arnold Diaz. The address on the account was listed as 412 Rene Street. I had to hand it to the DA, when he crafted the request, he was inclusive, asking Verizon for information on any and all accounts, including cell and landlines.

Diaz had a cell phone with Verizon and a landline. I grabbed the call log we had compiled on Dwyer. It was organized by area code. I flipped through the pages looking for 956, the area code on both of Diaz's lines. Nothing. When were we going to catch a break?

Opening the records portal, I ran Diaz through the system. No touches in the national database. I reached out to the Texas State Police. They had nothing on him but provided his DMV records.

Diaz was thirty-eight years old, five foot ten, and two hundred and twenty pounds. I studied his chubby face. Come on, buddy; talk to me. Tell me you know Ethan Dwyer. It was possible he could know him and not realize he had broken out of prison. A breakout in Southwest Florida would have a hard time getting air time in Texas if a killing wasn't connected to the escape. I could see Dwyer concocting a convincing story concerning his release if an out-of-state contact asked about it.

Should I fly down to Texas? I was torn. I didn't trust anyone with Dwyer. They didn't know how cunning he was. I could go and be back in a day and a half while Derrick pursued the other lines on Dwyer. However, the Garrison case was a wild card. We had to be ready to move. The house closing was approaching.

It didn't matter. Dwyer was at the top of my list. I put my jacket on and climbed the stairs to see Chester. Waiting for an audience, a text came in from Mary Ann. She was tired and wanted to go straight home, asking me to pick up bread and yogurt. She wouldn't want me to go to Alamo, and I'd be worried about her if I did. It wasn't a good idea.

Standing to leave, the sheriff's door swung open. Chester said goodbye to the union representative and looked at me.

"I only have five, Detective."

"Thanks, sir, but if you're busy I'll come back."

Over his shoulder, he said, "Let's get this out of the way."

I settled into a chair. "This is about the hit on the site we set up to lure Dwyer into visiting. Verizon turned over the account holder."

"Is it him?"

"It's registered to an Arnold Diaz. We're not sure."

"The location was in Alamo, wasn't it?"

"Yes, sir. And that's why I'm here. I'd like to fly down and check this Diaz out myself."

"Why not have the Texas State Police check it out?"

"I'm afraid Dwyer would outsmart them. They don't know anything about him, how smart he—"

"Do you have anything else to corroborate Diaz with Dwyer?"

"We have the drawing found in Dwyer's cell."

"That's not only nothing, it's less than that. The sketch was what made you look at the hit in the first place, isn't it?"

He was right, and I was embarrassed. Chester was great at assessing a situation, but not much help at offering solutions.

"It's an unusual place to get a hit from."

"Ask the Texas State boys to check it out. I've got to get moving."

It didn't feel right to push Chester, so I kept my mouth shut. I took my time going back down to my office. On one hand, I'd be around for

Mary Ann; on the other, if Dwyer slipped through because I failed to fight to go, I'd need sleeping pills for the rest of my life.

***

Back behind my desk, I called George Aviles, leaving a message for the Garrison lawyer. Where the heck was Derrick? I went to the cafeteria to get a cup of coffee, thinking over what to say to the cops down in Texas. Back behind my desk, I sipped java, settling on a plan.

I called Aviles again. Was he dodging me? Maybe he skipped town, like Dwyer seemed to have done. Checking my emails again, I picked up the phone and called the Texas State Police.

After getting an assurance from a Captain Dell, I was in the middle of sending a text to Mary Ann when my phone rang. It was Aviles.

"I apologize for not answering your calls. It wasn't to avoid you. I needed to get somewhere where I could talk freely."

"No problem. I understand. Confidentiality is key to making this work. I'm glad you made the right choice to work with me on this."

"There doesn't seem to be any choice. If I refuse, you'll report me to the bar association, and chances are, I'll be disbarred. That would ruin my life. But before I agree to anything, I'm going to need certain assurances. We're dealing with an unstable group of people. They don't hesitate when exacting revenge, many times abhorrently so. They're capable of anything."

I didn't want to bring up a bath in acid. "We understand the nature of the threat. What assurances do you need?"

"To begin with, entry into the witness protection program."

That was a federal decision. I hoped Haines, my FBI contact, would be able to help, and said, "Not a problem."

"My relocation must be in a warm climate, but not somewhere like Arizona. I want to be near the sea."

"Southern California or Texas maybe?"

"My preference would be Texas."

"I think that can be arranged."

"Another nonnegotiable point is that I want to practice law. My new identity must come with a license to practice law in Texas, for example.

Florida has specific Florida state laws in their exam. I'm pretty sure Texas and California have similar requirements. I'm not looking for a pass here. I'll learn the state-specific statutes, but I want to practice law from day one."

I had no clue about how that worked, but I'd leave that to the legal eagles to sort out. "I can't see that being an issue."

"It's not that I don't trust your verbal agreement, but a decision of this magnitude must be codified, and the federal government must be in agreement vis-à-vis witness protection."

My job was to bring him in, and that's what I was going to do. "Absolutely. How soon can you come in?"

Chapter 50

Heading into the stairwell, my phone rang. It was Mary Ann.

"Hey, how you doing?"

"Not good."

"What's the matter?"

"I feel like crap. I can hardly get out of my chair. Can you take me home?"

"Uh, sure. I'm about to go into a meeting with the DA. The FBI is, hopefully, going to cut a deal with Aviles on the Garrison case."

"Oh, that's good. How long you think it's going to be?"

"You know what? Let me call Derrick."

"No. Go to your meeting. I'll wait."

"No, he'll drive you home."

"I can wait."

"I don't want you to. Derrick is going to take you home and that's that. I'll see you as soon as I'm done here."

Derrick was happy to help. I told him to help her get inside the house. It relieved me of some my guilt as I stepped into a crowded conference room. The windowless room was eerily quiet, smelling of apprehension. I glad-handed Haines and sat next to Aviles.

**

Boy, was I glad I had developed a relationship with the FBI's Tommy Haines. I didn't have much experience with G-men, but Haines seemed to have hooks everywhere. Was it Haines, or did every agent have the kind of pull he did? Haines had done advance work to fast-forward the process, getting Aviles what he wanted. They hammered out the language in the proffer, and Aviles signed it.

He was on board and began unloading. The information he gave on the Miami gang involved in the Garrison case was shocking. He claimed the gang was a cooperative effort, possibly involving a city commissioner. He identified the individual as Malcolm Medina but couldn't provide anything but anecdotal evidence. Aviles agreed to work with the feds and see what could be developed.

Aviles also said he had no direct knowledge of who killed Garrison but knew who was directing the effort to get the proceeds from the sale of Garrison's home.

The name, Luis Redondo, was a familiar one, even to those on Florida's West Coast. Redondo was the Columbian version of John Gotti. He was a careful man who distanced himself from his crew with layers of management. Aviles said Redondo reported directly to a Columbian cartel known as the Baja Brigade. What Aviles disclosed made perfect sense.

Garrison had been fronted drugs worth millions to start his operation. He got off to a fast start, exceeding his master's expectations. At one point, Garrison used the money he was supposed to funnel to Redondo on a big house.

Garrison tried covering the scheme, claiming he was expanding, but was found out and became disposable. With Garrison out of the way, Redondo instructed Goodman to get his money out of the house. Goodman turned the task over to Aviles, and here we were.

My primary concern was not catching Garrison's killer but making sure Edith Nealy and her grandson were safe. I trusted Haines. He understood the danger Evan and his grandmother were in. He would offer them participation in the witness program as well.

This was now an operation the feds were running. We'd provide support, but it was their case now. It didn't bother me that much. I skipped down the stairs to my office, and my phone rang again. I froze, hoping it wasn't Mary Ann. It wasn't. It was Chester, and he wanted to see me, now. I sent Mary Ann a text and headed back up the stairs.

***

There was a tall bag in the center of his desk and the smell of Indian food in the air.

Chester's feet were on the corner of his desk.

"Come on in, Frank."

"Hello, sir."

Chester swung his feet off the desk. "I heard you put something big together on the Garrison case."

He heard? I was out of the conference room less than three minutes. Had one of the lawyers, who shuttled the proffer agreement in and out of the room, tipped Chester off?

"I don't know how far they're going to be able to take it, but it looks good."

"You took a difficult situation with the Garrison case and turned it into a major win for the department."

Difficult? Was that what this was? Being accused of murder by your own partner was called difficult?

"I'm glad it worked out."

"It's good to turn this one over to the FBI."

"I'd like to stay on this, sir."

"You did more than enough already."

"I'd really like to see it to the end."

"Can't allow that, Frank."

"I don't understand, sir."

"I want you to concentrate on getting Dwyer. The Alamo, Texas lead was a dead end."

"What? What happened?"

"When you were in with the feds, the captain with the Texas State Police, you were in touch with, called. Detective Dickson wasn't in, and they patched the call through to my office. They went to see, I can't remember the man's name, anyway, but it turns out he's living there alone and he's clean. They're confident he's not mixed up in anything."

"But why would he visit the Dwyer site?"

"Said he always wanted to be a police officer but couldn't pass the test. They said he hangs out with a couple of local officers and is well known to the department down there. They said he applied to the fire academy but has to lose some weight to get accepted into the program."

"Did they sound like they were diligent about it?"

"Yes, it's not Dwyer. You need to pursue the other lines you're developing. I don't want you distracted by the Garrison case."

"I can do both, sir."

Chester leaned forward. "Frank, you can use the break. I hear Mary Ann is not feeling well. Do everybody a favor and make sure she's all right."

Was he conducting surveillance on his detectives?

"She's going to be fine, sir."

"I'm sure of that, but my mind is made up. Let the feds get it to the finish line. You make sure Detective Vargas stays healthy."

Healthy? Did he know something?

"Thank you for your concern, sir. I'll get going now."

"Let me ask you: how did you turn Redondo's lawyer around."

"Just doing my job, sir."

"You're a credit to this department, Frank. We're fortunate to have you here."

"I enjoy working here. Naples is a special place, and I'm going to do my best to keep it that way."

Chapter 51

"How is Mary Ann feeling?"

"She had a pretty good night, thank God. I told her to take the day off, but she felt good and came in. Thanks for taking her home yesterday."

"Anytime, man. You don't want to take chances."

"Trust me, I'm not. Oh, last night we changed the date to tie the knot. We're moving it up a week to be sure she feels good."

"You still going to Marco?"

"Yeah, everything is the same—lunch at the Turtle Club and then Marco, just a week sooner."

"I'm happy for the both of you."

"Thanks. I really have to nail Dwyer beforehand."

"You're only gone for the weekend. Don't sweat it. If he's still out there, I'll be watching."

"I'd rest easier knowing he was back where he belongs. You know, I've been starting to worry that he's going to start killing again."

"What makes you think that?"

"I can't nail it down, but I keep thinking he's planning something big."

"Like what?"

"I don't know exactly, but he could be lining up a couple of victims he wants revenge on. Maybe get them all together in one place, like the Spirit of Fellowship Church, and mow them all down."

"You really think so?"

"Anything is possible with Dwyer. The bastard took a shot at my house. Who knows, maybe he'll bait us and take one of us out before we get to him."

"Frank, if you know something, go to Chester, get us some help. Maybe get the feds involved."

"I know this bastard better than anyone, and I'm going to drag his ass back to jail if it's the last thing I ever do."

"Don't take any risks, man. This guy is a nutjob, and you have a baby on the way."

He was right. "Don't worry. Let's get back to work."

I stared at the map we made with Dwyer's known locations. A whisper in my head kept rising in volume—Dwyer was still around here.

I called the DA to ask about the warrant on Tammy Branch's house and was told the judge hadn't responded yet. I needed something to pursue, because the alternative was that Dwyer had fled the state, maybe even stowing away on a Seminole freight train. That would mean it could take years before something triggered Dwyer's arrest. During that time, Dwyer could be piling up bodies.

My desk phone rang. It was Mary Ann.

"How you feeling?"

"Good. Look, it could be nothing, but we had two interesting hits this morning on the Dwyer site. They came out of Spain."

"Spain? What's so interesting about them?"

"They came from a city called Alamo."

I wanted to tell her if Dwyer was in Spain, we were safe, but asked, "There's an Alamo in Spain?"

"Yep. I didn't know either."

"What else you have on it?"

"The two hits came from the same device, a Nokia phone."

"What about the bounces and duration spent?"

"The first one went through each of the pages, averaging eight seconds in duration. The second visit was quick, just the home page and comment page. It was like whoever it was came back to check something."

"What the hell would Dwyer be doing in Spain?"

"Don't know, but I figured you'd want to know about it."

"Yeah, thanks. I gotta think this through. I'll talk to you later."

Typing Alamo, Spain into the search bar, I said, "Derrick, you're not going to believe it, but they got a hit on the Dwyer site from a place called Alamo but in Spain."

"Spain?"

"Yeah, it says here that Fuente Alamo de Murcia is a town about twenty kilometers from Cartagena, which is on the sea. Cartagena? There's a Cartagena in Columbia too."

"How would Dwyer get there without a passport?"

"It would be tough. But there's doc forgers who've been known to make good ones."

"He wouldn't know those types of guys."

"Under normal circumstances I'd agree, but he got papers to open the lockbox, didn't he?"

"But with passports we're talking a whole other level."

"Exactly. Dwyer is on a different plane than other crooks."

"Do you think he's screwing with our heads, Frank?"

"You mean with the Spain angle?"

"Yeah. Would he go to that extreme to get someone to hit the site from there?"

"He didn't have any contacts in Spain or anywhere overseas that I recall. He'd need somebody to help him."

"Oh, that's easy, man. He could post something in a group or chat room, and I bet you he'd have twenty volunteers."

"In Spain?"

I looked at the map. This place was only fifteen minutes from the ocean. With Dwyer's back problems, he needed a warm climate. I was about to check the average temperatures when I realized that if Dwyer was there, he was less than a hundred miles from Algeria. If he got into Algeria, we'd lose him forever. I stared at the African continent, and my eyes drifted to Morocco, Algeria's neighbor. You could swim to Morocco from a place in Spain that was just south of Alamo.

I leapt out of my seat. "Derrick! Was Jenny DiBlasi Moroccan?"

"Moroccan? She didn't say, did she?"

"No. But does she look Moroccan?"

"I don't know. What's that supposed to look like? That's in Africa, isn't it? Aren't they real dark over there?"

"No. It's North Africa, kind of more like the Mideast. I went to school with a couple of North African kids. They were lighter skinned, just like Mediterraneans. People thought they were Sicilians."

"Oh, I guess she could be. She looked a little bit like a foreigner, second or third generation maybe."

"Let's look up their marriage license and see what her maiden name was."

"Where were they married?"

"Probably Jersey or New York."

Derrick made a call to New Jersey and found out Jenny DiBlasi's maiden name was Matoub. I checked the internet for Moroccan surnames and came up empty. Searching through Algerian surnames I got a hit. Matoub was Algerian.

If Dwyer was leaving Spain, we had to move fast. We had to grab him before he slipped into Algeria. I was going to notify Interpol first—give them Dwyer's pictures and the alias he was using. I would almost bet he had at least one other alias. Interpol would have to rely on photos to stop him from traveling.

While pondering whether to call the State Department, an assistant district attorney stepped into our office with the warrant to search Tammy Branch's house.

Chapter 52

Even though I was fixated on the Algerian possibility, I organized a small caravan to search Tammy Branch's home. Derrick pulled up to the gate, and two unmarked cars parked on the street. The sounds of kids playing in a pool floated in the air. The six of us hopped the yellow wall surrounding the home. A pair of officers ran to cover the rear of the house.

Derrick jogged out front and was pounding on the door as the officers fanned out. The door opened and Tammy stepped out, pulling the door shut. She surveyed the officers. She had three butterfly hair barrettes dotting her gray hair and was wearing more necklaces and bracelets than an aboriginal.

"What's going on here?"

Derrick stuck the warrant in her face. "We have a warrant to conduct a search of the premises. Step aside."

She adjusted her glasses and peered at the document. Derrick said, "Step aside, ma'am. You'll have to wait outside. Is anyone inside the home?"

She shook her head as an officer guided her off the porch.

We drew our guns. Derrick swung open the door, and his hands fell to his side. "What the hell?"

I shoved Derrick aside. The room was filled waist high with stuff. Branch was a hoarder. No wonder she didn't want us inside the house. How the hell did she live like this? There were plastic bins crammed with clothing and bags, of who knew what, piled on each other.

A curved entryway was blocked by cardboard boxes stacked chest high. I stood on my toes, verifying that the clutter continued into whatever room was behind the boxes. The claustrophobic feeling was made worse by the eight-foot ceilings. This place had to be built in the sixties.

I said, "Can you believe this shit?"

Derrick said, "I don't know what to say. This is frigging insane. I saw that hoarder show on TV once, but seeing it in person is a whole other thing. What to do you want to do?"

"You mean, besides throw up? We're here now. We might as well go through this place, you never know."

"Dwyer can't be here."

"Get the officers to help. All this shit creates places to hide. It has to be probed."

"Tell them to start in here and the room behind this. I'm going to find the kitchen."

I followed a two-foot-wide path that meandered to the kitchen. Just outside the kitchen entrance were two back-to-back dressers. Covering their tops were enough paper bags to supply a Publix grocery store for a couple of years.

The kitchen floor wasn't covered, but the countertops were. I couldn't tell what the tops were made of. Even the tops of the cabinets were stacked with pots, pans, and Tupperware containers. On top of the refrigerator were three toasters. One of them looked like something the Flintstones would have used.

I hesitated before opening the refrigerator, pulling on gloves. There was a box of pizza. I held my breath and lifted the cover. Four pieces of pizza, two plain and two with pepperoni. There wasn't any hair growing on it, so it hadn't been there too long. In back of the pizza were two cartons of milk. One regular, the other skim.

I reached in and grabbed the whole-milk carton. The expiration date was a week away. I checked the skim-milk bottle. It expired in three days.

The other shelves had containers of leftovers and scores of canned fruit. Six bottles of ketchup and three different jars of mustard lined the door shelf.

"Derrick!"

"What's up, Frank?"

"Make sure you're on your toes. I don't want you getting distracted by all the shit lying around here."

"Don't worry about me."

"Be on the lookout for anything male: clothes, shaving cream, razors, men's deodorant, even condoms."

"I got it, but don't forget, it could be any male friend of Branch's."

"Please, keep your eyes open."

I snaked through a hallway lined with stacks of cassette tapes, TVs, and piles of newspapers. A nightstand, with two shadeless lamps, obstructed the doorway to the master bedroom. The room had two twin beds and two personalities. The near side had clutter mirroring the rest of the house. The far side, while not neat, was at least livable. It had to be where the mother had slept.

I made my way to the end of the room. A pile of medical paraphernalia, including a wheelchair, confirmed it was the mother's side. A leather recliner, too big for the space, overflowed with clothes. I examined the wheelchair, hoping to define it as the one used by Dwyer to get at his lockbox, but couldn't.

I opened dresser drawers, all impossibly stuffed with clothes, before moving back into the hallway. A pair of barstools piled on each other partially blocked the entrance to a room. I squeezed past and froze.

There was a mattress on the floor. Three stacks of books were near the head of it. I bent to check the titles: *The History of the Roman Empire, Stellar Exploration, The Case for Christ, The King James Bible.* I stood. Was Dwyer bunking here?

Scanning the room, I headed to the adjoining bathroom. I circled around a cluster of lamps, stepping into the yellow tiled room and stopped short. The window was wide open.

Sticking my head out, I yelled, "Did anybody see anything?"

The two officers guarding the rear both shook their heads. I surveyed the backyard. About twenty yards away was a preserve. Was Dwyer hiding in there? Pulling my head back into the bathroom, I called out, "Derrick! Derrick! Get in here!"

He came into the bedroom, and I pointed at the mattress.

"Holy shit! You think Dwyer's been here?"

I hiked a thumb to the bathroom. "If he has, he probably went out the window."

"I can't believe it."

"Out back there's a preserve. Take the officers there and comb it. Look for anything. I'm gonna talk to Branch. See what she says now."

Chapter 53

It felt liberating to be outside. Tammy Branch was sitting on a step, chewing on a nail. I looked down at her.

"Get on your feet."

Branch rose, shaking her arms to force the throng of bracelets down her wrists.

"Who's living here with you?"

"Nobody."

"Come on, Tammy. Don't lie to me."

"I'm not. Since Mother died, I've been living alone."

"What kind of milk you drink?"

"Milk? What's that got to do with anything?"

"What type of milk you drink? Almond, low fat, regular?"

"Regular milk."

"Don't like skim?"

Her shoulders sagged. "I—I drink it sometimes. Have to watch my weight, just like everybody else."

"Watching your weight but eating pizza?"

She toyed with her necklaces.

"Who's sleeping in the third bedroom?"

"Nobody."

"Really? It looks used to me."

"No one is using it."

"Bring her inside."

I took two deep breaths and went back in. It was still shocking to snake my way through the heaps of crap to the back bedroom.

"Now, look at this, and tell me there's no one living here."

"I don't know what you're talking about. No one is using this room."

"Whose books are those?"

"Probably Mother's."

"Where is Ethan Dwyer?"

"I already told you. I don't know."

"We're going to take DNA samples from here and the bathroom. If it turns out to match Dwyer's, you're going to be up to your ass in alligators. Trust me, you don't want to add obstructing justice on top of harboring a fugitive. The judge is not going to be happy with you. I can easily see him putting you away for twenty years."

"The only judgment I care about is God's."

"Get her out of here."

***

Stepping outside, I called for a forensics team to come out and see if they could find proof of Dwyer having been here. I circled to the back of the house. Walking toward the preserve, I spotted Derrick and two officers making their way out.

"Anything?"

Derrick held up a sneaker. "It was stuck in the brush."

I put on gloves and held it. It was an Adidas. Size nine. The shoelaces were untied.

"How far in was it?"

"Thirty yards or so. I left a marker."

"Dwyer may have heard we were coming. He puts on these before going out the window. He heads for the woods and one falls off. How deep is the preserve?"

"A hundred yards. Then it runs into the backyards of the houses along Sea Grass."

"We need to get some manpower over there, see if any neighbors—"

"I called already. They're on the way."

"Good."

"If he went through the preserve, chances are he went toward Santa Barbara Boulevard. It's tough to say where the hell he could be now."

I handed the sneaker back. "Well, he isn't going to get too far with one shoe on. People are bound to notice a guy with one, or no shoes, if he ditches the other one."

"I'll get a couple of cars to canvas along Santa Barbara."

"Make sure they check the closest shoe stores or something like a Walmart. We're gonna get this bastard."

"Well, at least it doesn't look like Dwyer took off to Spain."

"I'm not counting anything out. I want to go back inside and take a closer look. Maybe we can make it easier for forensics with all the crap in there."

It was my third time entering the house, and I still couldn't believe anyone could live like this. Anyone who didn't think it was a disease or a mental illness needed to walk into one of these places.

Essentially, hoarders couldn't throw anything out. I understood some people's reluctance to throw an item away that still worked, but keeping newspapers that were amber colored and a chair with three legs?

I went into the kitchen, rummaging through a bank of cabinets. Nothing but crammed dinnerware and glasses interspersed with empty bottles. The hinge to the door on the pantry was broken. I lifted the door up and out and couldn't believe my eyes.

Receipts and coupons covered whatever canned and boxed food was stored. You'd need a shovel to find a can of peas. I opened the wall oven; it was filled with plastic bags. I closed it quickly and headed back to what could have been Dwyer's sleeping quarters.

Dwyer was a reader, but though there were lamps blocking the entrance to the bedroom, there wasn't any light to read by at night. I bent down and lifted the mattress. Nothing. I pulled the sheets off, revealing only a brown stain.

I moved heaps of junk around looking for an article of men's clothing, any clue Dwyer was here, but came up empty. The bathroom didn't have a razor, deodorant, or toothbrush. Maybe no one had been using it. There was a hair by the drain and it looked black. I'd let forensics grab it.

Going back into the bedroom, my phone sounded a text. It was from Derrick. He forwarded me an email he received from the State Department. Jenny DiBlasi had traveled to Algeria five months ago.

Did she go there to set up Dwyer's safe passage into Algeria from Spain? It had to be easier to get into Algeria from Spain. What should have been difficult was getting into Spain. You didn't need a visa, but getting there from the United States would be risky. Did Dwyer slip into Mexico or Canada and leave from there?

Mexico obtained its independence from Spain in 1821, and the two nations had an intertwined history. It had to be easier for visitors from Mexico to get into Spain. I moved under an air-conditioning vent and leaned against the closet door as a wave of nausea hit me. A picture of Dwyer's bookshelf bore into my mind: Dwyer had studied Spanish in prison.

Chapter 54

I was certain Dwyer had just been here. Everything I knew pointed to it. Was I wrong? Was he in Spain waiting to move into Algeria? If so, he'd melt into Algeria, especially if Jenny DiBlasi's family had any kind of money to spread around.

Dwyer should be building rockets or solving world hunger. He knew not only how to plan, but it was clear he could execute. How was I going to let Chester know he'd slipped through my hands into Algeria? I leaned against the wall to steady myself before going into the bathroom.

Sticking my head out the window, I sucked in fresh air. I thought about the DiBlasis. My self-anger quickly shifted on to Dwyer's half brother. I was going to drive straight there as soon as forensics arrived. Locking the both of them up was small consolation, but I'd get a measure of pleasure when I hauled their asses in.

Even though it felt useless, I had to get an alert out to Interpol and the Algerian authorities about Dwyer. The air-conditioning shut off as I entered the bedroom. Squeezing into the hallway, an idea hit me.

I stretched my arm up. The ceiling was eight or ten inches above my fingertips. I looked at the barstool, trying to recall the seat height of the ones we bought for our lanai counter. If I remembered correctly, it was about thirty inches.

Slowly lifting one barstool off the other, I carried it into the bedroom, placing two legs inside the closet. A pile of chest-high magazines was directly below the attic's access panel. I patted my pistol, snapping open the holster's retention band.

Stepping onto the barstool, I waited for the air-conditioning to cycle back on. The crunch of gravel announcing forensics arrival made me lower a leg back to the ground. The air-conditioning cranked on, and I stepped back up and onto the magazine pile.

Palms on the wooden panel, I popped it up and over. Grabbing the attic edges with both hands, I hoisted myself up. Elbows onto the attic floor, the heat hit me. A channel of light from below bounced off the eaves.

I lifted my ass onto the floor. A stream of cool air coming off the AC unit diluted the mustiness. Pistol in hand I rose, hitting the light switch. Blinking twice, my head swiveled owl-like.

Black mold covered the boxes of junk outlining the access perimeter. A pile of tile was stacked next to a leak pan. There was a bright green sticker on the AC unit. I took two steps toward it. Something was behind the unit. I raised my gun.

"Hands up, Dwyer."

No response. I took another step forward. The air-conditioning shut off. The fan's rotation slowed to a stop. I crouched down. Voices wafted up from the house. I sprung to the left. There was something tent-like next to the unit.

Gun out front, both hands on the grip, I stepped forward. A sheet hung off the unit. I crouched behind it, propping my pistol on its aluminum ductwork.

"Hands where I can see them."

No reply. Was anyone under there? Or had Dwyer planned to use it but bolted out the window instead?

Reaching to my left, I grabbed an eight-by-eight-inch tile. I flung it at the sheet.

"Ow! That was completely unnecessary."

It was him.

"Come out slowly, Ethan. Hands up."

As Dwyer emerged from under the sheet, I yelled down for help.

"Put that backpack down and get your hands on your head."

Dwyer was feather thin. His sweat-soaked T-shirt clung to his rib cage. Several days' worth of stubble filled his sunken cheeks. We stared at each other. Dwyer's arms were dirty. A line of blood meandered from his knee, disappearing into a sneaker.

His invincibility had disintegrated into vulnerability. He was so pitiful looking it almost evoked a touch of sympathy for him. How could I have doubted who would prevail in this battle?

I insisted on cuffing him in the attic. With his hands and ankles shackled, we lowered him through the opening. I needed five minutes alone with Dwyer and asked the others to wait outside.

In the daylight, Dwyer seemed to recover. His shoulders were square, defiant. He had a look, not quite smug, but nowhere like defeat. My pistol was holstered, but I opened the retention strap.

"Have you been here the entire time?"

"Predominately."

"Were you in contact with Tammy while in prison?"

"Tammy was oblivious to my plans. She is a woman with extraordinary empathy. She had no prior knowledge, and frankly, was stunned when I appeared at her door. Originally cautious, it was her faith in a just God that afforded me safe refuge."

She'd need God's intervention to save her from the harboring and obstruction she'd committed.

"How much help did your brother and sister-in-law give you?"

"Neither of them offered a scintilla of assistance."

"You faked a serious case of depression to get into the David Lawrence Center. How did you know it would work?"

"It's simply the law of unintended consequences. Legislators make laws intending to create solutions. However, invariably, especially when dealing with discriminatory issues, avenues of abuse are opened. I simply exploited the Baker Act."

The sheriff had already been in touch with the county's representative in the state legislature on closing the loophole he'd used.

"I'm curious. Did you have anyone helping you at the David Lawrence Center?"

"I prefer not to besmirch the reputations of people who assist those with particular needs. However, they're so wrapped up in privacy protection you could walk around with a firearm and go unchallenged."

"Did you use your freedom to even any scores?"

"That would be your particular area of expertise, wouldn't it?"

"Did you?"

He smiled. "The only response fitting to offer is a resounding maybe."

No corpses had surfaced in the county since Dwyer had broken out, a sign that he hadn't, but it was no assurance. I'd have Derrick scrub the missing persons list weekly.

"Was that you who shot at my house?"

Another smile. "I'll refer you to my prior response."

Man, did I want to put a bullet in that big brain of his. "What made you believe you could get away with breaking out?"

"Is that a serious question, Detective? Certainly, you're aware of the statistics evidencing the ease at which thousands evade law enforcement. Even residents of the FBI's ten most wanted list, who arguably garner the highest focus from the authorities, half of them are on the list for ten years. And those are the known fugitives."

"Getting caught, that would make you not as smart as you thought, wouldn't it?"

Dwyer's eyes narrowed.

I jabbed a finger into the center of his chest. "Easy, tiger. Let's get you back where you belong."

After Dwyer was loaded into a squad car, I went back into the attic. Throwing back the sheet he had hung off the AC unit revealed the yoga mat he had lain on. There was a series of small holes along the length of the main output duck, providing enough cool air to keep it tolerable. There was nothing else. It was an emergency hiding place that had failed him.

Lowering myself into the house, I sorted through his backpack. Tucked into an outside pocket was a revolver and a box of bullets. I put my nose to the barrel. It didn't appear to have been fired recently.

Everyone could learn a lesson in efficient packing from Dwyer. It was no bigger than a pack carried by a high schooler, yet it had two pairs of pants, three shirts, two pairs of shorts, a baseball cap, sandals, a Bible, six cans of tuna, a bar of soap, two liters of water, toothpaste, a knife, a bottle of aspirin, and a dozen power bars.

I wondered if Dwyer had another stash or two somewhere. It was probably loaded with supplies.

Chapter 55

The nursery was coming along. I was putting up a border filled with bunny rabbits while Mary Ann was swapping out the bedding. It was the third set she'd bought. I wisely kept my mouth shut climbing down the ladder.

"What do you think?"

"Oh, I love it. It's so cute."

Originally, I thought a border was totally unnecessary.

"It kind of finishes the room, don't you think?"

"It matches perfectly with the new bedding."

The bell rang. It was Derrick. I had asked for help in moving a dresser in our master bedroom to make room for a bassinet.

"Wow, Mary Ann, you're getting big."

I'd learned that was the wrong thing to say to a woman. "She looks great, doesn't she?"

"Absolutely. My mom used to say that pregnant women glow. There's no doubt. How you feeling?"

"Pretty good. Cutting back to three days a week was hard, but it was the right thing to do."

"Next month she's going to two days, and then a month before her due date she's going to take her leave."

"They give you the time, you might as well take it."

"Oh, wait till you see the nursery."

After a quick tour, Derrick and I shifted the dresser to another wall.

"Thanks, pal. I appreciate the help."

"Anytime. You guys ready for the wedding next week?"

"Yeah. It's really no big deal. But I'm looking forward to sitting on the beach for a couple of days."

"That does sound good."

"Got time for a glass of wine?"

"Sure."

We retreated to the lanai. I read about New Zealand wine in the paper and wanted to see if he also thought it was good. It was inexpensive, and if he liked it I was buying some more.

"I'll be right back."

I grabbed the wine. It had a screw top, so I opened it inside and poured two glasses.

"Here you go."

Derrick took the glass of Pinot Noir and said, "Oh, I heard corrections rated Dwyer an HO5. He'll be in solitary for a stretch and then to max. Let's see how he likes only an hour a day of sunshine."

"He's going to die behind bars if they don't screw up again."

"You think he'll try to get out again?"

"No doubt. It'll take years before they give him any freedom inside. But we know he can play the long game."

"This is pretty good. What is it?"

"Pinot Noir from New Zealand. Most people think of Sauvignon Blanc when they think of New Zealand and wine, but they make excellent Pinot too. It's a lot cheaper than the ones from California."

"How much does it cost?"

"This one was only twenty-six bucks."

"Wow, I really like it."

"Haines liked it too."

"You saw Haines?"

"He came over yesterday. I invited him to lunch. He was such a help on the Garrison case."

"I never got the full story on what happened. Nobody is talking since Chester put the zipper on it."

"Edith Nealy signed off on the document Goodman's office prepared in exchange for seventy-five K. Haines said they alerted the banks involved, putting tracers on the money. When the sale closed, the title company followed Goodman's wire instructions. The money was sent to a trust account under the Goodman firm's name, bouncing out ten minutes later to an account in the Cayman Islands. Then the funds went to the Bahamas before landing in Miami in an account under Carmen Redondo, Luis Redondo's sister."

"A game of pinball."

"Except they're playing with three million dollars."

"They got enough to nail Redondo?"

"For fraud. They tried to find out who killed Garrison, but nothing yet. It had to be Redondo who gave the orders because they offered him a deal, but he refused."

"What'll he get?"

"Nine years, but he'll probably be out in four."

"What about that councilman?"

"They're putting together an undercover operation to see if they can get Medina to bite."

"And the kid and his grandmother?"

"They're in protective custody. When the dust settles, Haines said they'd be relocated."

"What about the money?"

"It'll go into a trust account for the kid."

Derrick held out his empty glass. "Wow. You really started something, didn't you?"

"You mean turning you into a wine fan?"

"That too. One more glass and I'm out of here."

Mary Ann and I said goodbye to Derrick.

"I didn't realize he was staying so long. I wanted to take a ride to Bed Bath & Beyond."

"We were talking shop. He never heard the total story about the Garrison case, so I filled him in on what Haines told me. Oh, and he told me he heard that Dwyer was going to get ten years tacked on to his sentence."

"Oh, that's good. What happened with the woman who helped him?"

"I can't believe I forgot to tell you."

She looked at me knowingly. "So, tell me now."

"Tammy Branch's lawyer came up with a defense claiming her mental state was compromised by the depression she suffered by losing her mother. Said her loneliness amplified her depression."

"I heard of loneliness depression. It's fairly prevalent in the elderly population."

"Makes sense. Anyway, Whitaker had recently lost his mother and was sympathetic, but what sealed it was the pictures of all the crap crowding her house. The lawyer produced pictures claiming the hoarding was triggered by depression."

"What did she get?"

"Two years, suspended. Branch completes a year of outpatient treatment at the David Lawrence Center, of all places, and she's free."

"That's outrageous. Dwyer is a killer!"

"I can only bring them in, Mary Ann. That's all I can do."

"Some of these judges need to spend some time on the street; see what we deal with close up."

"Amen. I'm starving. You want to grab an early dinner at Nemo?"

"I don't know if I feel up to it."

"We should go, because in three months, when the baby comes, we're not going anywhere."

"All right, as long as we stop at Bed Bath & Beyond first."

The End

Thank you for taking the time to read *Cop or Killer?*. If you enjoyed it, please consider telling a friend or posting a short review where you obtained the book. Word of mouth is an author's best friend and is appreciated. Thank you, Dan

Dan has a monthly newsletter that features his writing, articles on Self Esteem & Confidence building, as well as educational pieces on wine. He also spotlights other author's books that are on sale.

Sign up—www.danpetrosini.com

Other Books by Dan

Luca Mystery Series

Am I the Killer—Book 1

Vanished—Book 2

The Serenity Murder—Book 3

Third Chances—Book 4

A Cold, Hard Case—Book 5

Cop or Killer?—Book 6

Silencing Salter—Book 7

A Killer Missteps—Book 8

Uncertain Stakes—Book 9

The Grandpa Killer—Book 10

Dangerous Revenge—Book 11

Where Are They—Book 12

Buried at the Lake—Book 13

The Preserve Killer—Book 14

Suspenseful Secrets

Cory's Dilemma—Book 1

Cory's Flight—Book 2

Cory's Shift—Book 3

Other works by Dan Petrosini

The Final Enemy

Complicit Witness

Push Back

Ambition Cliff

Made in United States
Orlando, FL
11 December 2022